Secondhand Heart

Hearts of Three Rivers #3

AMITY LASSITER

This one's for you, Mr. Lassiter.

<u>Hearts of Three Rivers</u>

Runaway Heart
Homecoming Heart
Secondhand Heart

ACKNOWLEDGMENTS

This book challenged me in ways that seemed absolutely impossible, and just when I thought I had a handle on it, life threw wrench after wrench into my carefully laid plans. There is no way I could have finished this book without the encouragement of Mr. Lassiter. He helped me keep my head above water while finishing this book and simultaneously trying to plan our wedding. His encouragement and steadfast faith in my abilities (that sometimes exceeds my own) is absolutely necessary for my career as an author to succeed.

Thank you to Keriann McKenna, my editor, who is possibly my biggest cheerleader. You consistently go above and beyond in your work for me and I can say with absolute certainty I could not have done this—*all* of this—without you.

Thank you to my beta readers, who don't believe any deadline is 'too tight', and stay up all night to read for me. Nicole, Mallory, Shannon, Tiffany, Shay—I appreciate what you do for me (and my ego) more than you can imagine!

And of course, thanks to my parents. Without their encouragement through my childhood to believe in any dream that could cross my brain, I would never have been able to step off this ledge into this crazy world of publishing.

-ONE-

"YOU'RE not going to get rid of me that easily, brother." Finn Baylor chuckled as he felt his mount hump up underneath him, driving his head down to let out one epic buck. Finn rode it out with quiet hands and a steady seat while his sister-in-law, Emma, doubled over with laughter from the outside of the ring.

The horse, Thor, was a stout bay paint that looked like he'd been bred just for the bucking stock, but was supposed to be a child's mount. That's how he'd been sold to the Turners, anyway. Two rides and one little boy's broken leg later, they'd discovered he just wasn't suitable. They'd brought him to Finn with hopes he could turn him around to be a suitable ride for someone. *Someone who likes a challenge, maybe*, Finn thought, as he urged the horse into a jog. The gait was smooth as silk, and the horse was responsive, just a little—*ah, there it is*, Finn thought as the horse bounced exuberantly into a lope and let out another buck—spoiled. He shook his head and pushed the horse around the outside of the pen until he made two laps without a buck, then Finn let him break to a walk, and patted his neck lightly.

"He's not a bad horse," he told Emma as they walked past her. He gave the horse the bridle, to give him the benefit of the doubt, and Thor relaxed a little. "He just objects strongly to *work*."

1

"Right, I think they were just using him for pony rides before Steph got him."

"Probably for good reason." Finn laughed, stopped the horse, and asked him to back a few steps, before guiding him to the middle of the ring. "When's Nate pulling in again?"

Emma slipped her phone out of her pocket and glanced at its face. "Anytime."

"Alright, I know you've got work to do. I appreciate your help," he said to Emma, swinging one leg over the horse's back and stepping down. He took one rein down off the horn of the saddle and patted the gelding's shoulder. "You and I are gonna get *real* personal, buddy."

"I don't mind. It was amusing, to say the least." She shrugged, sliding her phone back into her back pocket. "I do have a couple client horses to ride today, but I wanted to be out here when Nate shows."

As if on cue, the deep rumble of a diesel rig could be heard coming up the drive. Emma opened the gate as Finn led Thor toward her.

"Good timing, now we can get on with the rest of our day. I'm interested to see this wildebeest you signed me up for."

Between regular ranch work, the problem horses like Thor he took on, and the six colts they had in on a training contract for Grant Reicher, Finn's hands were beyond full. He would have said no, and did at first, but Emma and Nate had tag-teamed him until he relented. The horse had been a client of Emma's when she was at the big racing outfit in Denver, and the owner was friendly with Nate, so they called it a personal favor. Finn didn't understand why *he* was the one doing the work on said 'favor', but figured he'd be able to cash in on the return eventually.

Regardless, he was passionate about rehabilitating horses other trainers had deemed 'useless,' so he was a little intrigued. Emma told him the horse, named Encore, had been struck by a car, and lived to tell the tale, which was rare in itself. By her report, after extensive physical rehabilitation at Renegade Racing, he was physically sound, but needed confidence in the saddle. And that was all he knew. A lot of the horses he brought in had even less recorded history, so while he had to juggle his schedule, Finn figured this horse's sessions should be by the book.

Nate Montgomery's big, flashy rig pulled into the yard, making a wide arc. Emma waved and started toward the truck as it pulled to a stop. Lifting a hand in greeting, Finn headed toward the barn, where he made quick work of stripping the gelding of his gear and sending him out into the back paddock for a roll. He always enjoyed a visit with Nate, who had grown up with the Baylors right here in Three Rivers, but moved on to a successful rodeo career in Denver the minute he'd been able to.

Emma's dog, Tucker, was wiggling excitedly around the group of people standing beside Nate's truck as Finn emerged from the barn. He hadn't seen her in the passenger seat, but a curvy little slip of a blonde was standing tucked up under Emma's arm, the difference in their heights almost comical. They'd probably met sometime during the years Emma had been in Denver working.

"And the star of the hour," Nate said, turning as Finn approached. "Finn Baylor, horse trainer extraordinaire."

The girl turned, flashing him a smile that produced a pair of perfectly matched dimples, and a little pinch in the middle of his chest he didn't

3

expect. He had six inches or more on her but she met his gaze confidently, with warm cocoa colored eyes a man could get lost in. A thick curtain of shoulder-length blond hair framed her heart-shaped face and little bow of a mouth.

He chuckled and tipped his hat, then held out his hand. Her firm, confident grip produced a pleasant little shock of energy when their palms touched. "Lily Jacobs."

She was cute as hell, and he could tell she was a spitfire to boot—Nate's standard type, and when he'd had a type that wasn't his wife, she'd have been his own, too. He supposed he shouldn't have been surprised his friend was bringing home a girl to meet his Nan. It was about time.

"Good to meet you, Lily. So how'd Nate coax you out of the creature comforts of Denver and into tumbleweed territory?" Finn asked.

Lily raised a brow, glanced up at Emma, then across to Nate, clearly a little confused. "... my horse?"

Of course. Nate's girl, a horse in trouble; that's what made it so personal for his friend.

As if he'd heard himself being discussed, the trailer moved as the horse inside shifted.

"Why don't you go grab him? I'll get your bags." Emma suggested, giving Lily a squeeze before she released her.

The girl grabbed a lead rope from the bed of Nate's truck and headed for the small, man-sized door on the front of the trailer, while Nate positioned himself at the rear door to assist. Emma opened the back of the crew cab and emerged with a huge duffle bag, a laptop bag, and a bulky one-strapped backpack. He raised his brow again.

"Who's moving in?" Though he had a sinking suspicion where this was going, Finn was utterly confused.

"Lily," Emma replied, as if he ought to know better than to ask a question like that. It was not an uncommon tone between the two of them.

"Whoa, whoa, hold the phone. This isn't a guest ranch. Where are you going to put her?"

"My place?" Emma responded, shaking her head. "What does it matter?"

It didn't, not really, but it wasn't his general practice to have owners hovering over him while he worked with their horses. Especially not one cute enough to make him stand up and take notice for the first time in a long time.

Cuteness aside, nine times out of ten, a problem horse's biggest problem was the handler, and Finn's policy was not to borrow trouble.

"And what about Nate?"

"What? He'll stay at Nan's."

"I know she can be old fashioned, but surely she's not worried they'll close the distance between couch and bedroom?"

Emma's brow knit together. "What are you talking about?"

"What are *you* talking about?"

Just as they squared off, a commotion came from their left and a big, glossy, black draft cross with a rope hanging from his halter exploded backwards out of the trailer.

"Shit!" Emma swore, swinging the bags she'd shouldered into the bed of the truck before she booted it to the fray.

Finn cussed under his breath and followed her.

Nate had spread his arms and Emma followed suit, trying to box the gelding in. Agile, the horse rocked back on his haunches, dodging first Nate, then Emma. He was wily for a horse with a road map of scarring on his hind quarters and back legs.

Finn shook his head, and then looked up to see Lily standing white-faced in the door of the trailer, her fingers curled around the aluminum door frame like she was drowning. He frowned, then stepped forward, snagging the end of the rope out of sheer luck. The horse fought like his life depended on it, but Finn reeled him in a little at a time, speaking quietly under his breath. The words were gibberish, but the tone communicated perfectly the message he wanted to convey, the message he conveyed to all his clients: *I'm not here to hurt you. We can work this out. Let's be partners.*

It took a minute, but the horse finally stilled, though his eyes remained wide and he released short, loud breaths through flared nostrils. Bit by bit, Finn moved up the rope until he got to the horse's head, and touched his jaw lightly. The horse flinched and stepped sideways, but then dropped his head, settling.

"There you go, brother," Finn murmured.

Nate stood back, holding his hands up. "I cede to the horse whisperer."

Finn shook his head and shot a glare at Nate; he hated that moniker, and his friend knew it. It belonged to Robert Redford and Hollywood, and all the showmen who wanted to capitalize on it. 'Miracles' produced fame. Finn didn't perform miracles, and he didn't want fame, he just wanted to help horses; and he used nothing but common sense to do it. *People* were often a side effect that came with fame and horses, a side effect he wasn't interested in... except maybe until now.

He looked up and saw Lily uncurling her fingers from the aluminum door frame, some color returning to her face. She was terrified of her own horse. Dangerous horse plus scared handler was the worst combination.

"You alright?" he asked her.

Her wide eyes were glued to the gelding at the end of his lead rope. He pressed his lips together and slid his hand down the horse's neck. The gelding had settled like nothing had happened at all. "He's alright. Come on down."

*

Lily drew in a breath and all of the emotion she'd been feeling in one shot. Her palms throbbed hot from the harsh bite of the rope Encore had pulled through her hands, and the adrenaline dump left her feeling like she wanted to cry, but she wouldn't. Lord knew she'd shed enough tears in front of Nate and Emma, but she'd be damned if she cried in front of a stranger, especially a stranger so sexy cowboy cool, with that easy smile and low voice that made her belly simmer. Oh, by association, he was practically family, but the man staring up at her incredulously probably already thought she was an idiot who couldn't even handle her own horse. She'd hold the tears until later. She'd become an expert at it, only slipping when she had these little panic attacks, usually triggered by something Encore had done.

"I-I'm fine." She hoped her words sounded more convincing than they felt.

On legs she hoped wouldn't show the tremors running through them, she stepped down out of the trailer, the same step had scared the bejesus out of her horse, like most things did these days. After the accident, she'd worked damn hard for him to physically be the horse he'd been before, but when it came to all the other parts of him—the parts that counted—Encore was a different horse altogether. If she'd known—begging Nate not to let them put him down while they loaded her into the ambulance—things would turn out this way, she might not have been so insistent. But now, here she was, with a horse she'd never been unable to control in the ten years she'd known him, and an inconvenient batch of panic attacks, ready to be set off at a moment's notice.

"Thank you for catching him." She frowned when her voice still trembled. *Best not to speak at all.*

She crossed the space between the trailer and Finn, sliding her fingers under Encore's mane, and let the hot rope burn on her palm rest against his silky neck. It was easy to forget he was like this now. Most of the time he was completely normal. Then, something in his rear blind spot would startle him and he'd lose his mind, climb the walls of his stall, regardless of who was in there with him, or bolt off completely unreasonable.

He was dangerous, now. A dozen Denver cowboys had told her so. Not worth the time and money to try and fix him. They wanted to lay him down, beat him into submission. He wasn't malicious, he was just scared, scarred beyond the physical wounds he'd endured—just like she was.

She'd called Emma in tears a week ago, after she'd been trapped in his stall when a barn worker dropped their feed cart outside his door. Then Nate had called her yesterday, showed up with the trailer this morning promising her if anyone could help Encore, it would be Finn Baylor, and here she was. She didn't know what the hell she was doing; she just knew it was the excuse she needed to get out of Denver; away from her prying mother and the bad memories. And if it helped restore her equine partner to even a shadow of his former self, it was worth it.

"He wouldn't have gone far. The horses up here in the paddock would have drawn him in, eventually." Finn met her eyes and shook his head. He might not have meant it, but he'd adapted a soothing tone that made her settle and narrowed her vision to exclude just about everything, including Emma and Nate standing grouped at the end of the trailer—except him. If his methods with horses were half what they seemed to be with a spooked woman, she understood why Nate called him the horse whisperer. "Now, why don't we get him settled in?"

He offered her the lead rope. Maybe he hadn't completely written off her competence, even if she didn't have much confidence in it anymore. When she took the soft, coiled up loop from him, their fingers brushed together and another little shock jolted through her. Not the same as the adrenaline of her panic attack. Softer. Warmer. Better.

She nodded, steeling herself with another breath, and followed Finn toward the round pen. He kicked a couple flakes of hay from a loose bale beside the pen under the panel and pulled the gate open for her.

"Emma told me he stocks up if he's stalled, right? Side effect of the injuries?"

"Yeah." And he was ten times more dangerous in a stall, with his vision blocked in three directions, than he was in an open space like an outdoor pen or pasture. At least here, he had somewhere to go when he decided to flee his demons.

"So he can stay here, for now." He glanced at Nate, who had followed, along with Emma. The two of them stood against the panels of the round pen, watching as Lily led her horse in and unclipped his lead rope. The gelding dropped his head immediately, snuffling at the tracks of horses past, completely oblivious to the heart attack he'd just given her. "I'll start working with him in the morning, and we'll see what we've got."

Lily looped up the rope and slipped out of the gate he'd held open for her. "Great, what time?"

She might have been imagining it, but she caught the tail end of a sour expression when she turned back to Finn.

"Look, I'm not sure what Emma might have told you..." He shot a look at his sister-in-law that could freeze fire. Like night and day compared to the soft, gentle man he'd been just minutes before. "But I just work with horses."

"Oh... I'm not looking for riding lessons. I'm just interested in the process."

"Right." He rubbed the back of his neck and she knew he was going to say something she didn't like next, just by the way his brows knit together when he looked back up at her. He was a handsome man, and his natural instinct with Encore made him that much sexier. He dressed like the dictionary definition of cowboy, with a black felt Stetson sitting low on his brow, a blue plaid shirt rolled up his forearms and tucked into a pair of jeans that fit just right. A pair of dusty boots with spurs, and a silver oval belt buckle completed the look. None of it looked even close to new. His strong jaw was accented by at least a day's worth of stubble, and his slate eyes were reminiscent of his brother, Noah's, but deeper, more luscious, like a swimming hole she wanted to sink to the bottom of. His dark hair was cropped short, most of it hidden under the brim of his hat. "I don't normally let clients watch sessions. I'm sorry if you've come here looking for something besides a normal hands-off training experience—"

"Oh, no, I just figured since I was here..."

"You 'figured' wrong." If it was possible for his voice to get harder then, it did, and just as Lily started to try to retrace her steps and figure out where she'd gone wrong, Emma slid in between the pair of them, linking her arm in Lily's.

"Hey, Noah just got back from town and he brought lunch. You wanna head back to our place? Encore's fine. We can come up later on and check on him; I have a couple horses to ride. And Finn'll be up here working anyways."

Breathing a sigh of relief, Lily nodded. Emma had been an anchor for her since she'd first moved Encore to Renegade Racing's state of the art facility. It was primarily a training business, but they had one of the only hyperbaric chambers for horses in the area, and a pool for rehabilitative swims. While she wasn't formally schooled, Emma had an impressive eye for lameness and body soreness in horses, and knew which professionals to call in when she couldn't do the work necessary.

Lily had been in a wheelchair when she first showed up at Renegade to watch Encore's sessions; told she'd be lucky to walk again; but watching the way her horse progressed was motivating and now, a year after the accident, she only limped when she slept wrong or the weather was nasty. The drive here, while only two hours, had been exhausting, but she'd been so relieved to see Emma's face at the truck window, she'd all but forgotten about it.

She glanced at Finn for affirmation of Emma's promise, and he nodded.

"I'll be right here."

-TWO-

"YOU got a bee in your bonnet?"

Feeling like he'd fallen for the old bait and switch, Finn retreated to the barn, hoping to brood alone. Nate followed, close on his heels.

He picked up the discarded saddle and bridle he'd stripped off Thor in his haste to see the new arrival and hung them up on the only available pegs in the disorganized tack room. He kept meaning to look after the tangle of leather goods and thick layer of dust in the room, but with as many horses as he had in right now, and another new one to boot, he hardly had time to get everyone rode, never mind spend half a day organizing the room. Fall was his busiest time with training horses. The weather wasn't too hot, and most of the ranch work, like all but the last cut of hay, and calving season was over—but everyone else was busy, too. He picked up a woven Navajo patterned saddle pad and shook it out, coughing when the cloud of dust erupted from it. It only further fueled his irritation.

"I know she's your girl, Nate, but you know I don't like an audience." While his methods were humane and gentle, sometimes an emotionally invested owner would misinterpret a bit of tough love as something worse, and he preferred to steer clear of those sorts of interruptions. That was his line, anyways. The truth of his agitation today went a bit deeper than he cared to admit, even to himself.

"Wait, *my* girl?" Nate laughed out loud.

"She's not your girl?" Finn emerged from the tack room with a frown. His friend was leaning against a stall door with his arms crossed, wearing a smirk.

"Oh *hell*, no. That girl has turned me down a half a dozen times. My ego finally demanded I quit while I was still standing." Shifting, Nate tucked his hands into the pockets of his jeans.

Interesting, Finn thought. He pulled a square bale of hay off a nearby stack and a folding knife from a sheath on his belt. Snapping it open, he sliced through the strings on the bale, separating flakes to put in each stall. The horses were out most of the day, barring a couple of tough catches that needed to be ridden, and any in hard work were brought in for feed at night and in the morning.

"Really?" He regretted asking almost as soon as he did. He had been out of the game for a long damn time, and even a flicker of interest exposed to any of his family or friends would instigate questions he didn't want to answer. More than once, they'd tried to talk him into town, into Danny's bar, into a passing fling. Cutter Anderson was the worst; working the bar, he always knew who was single and looking to mingle. Finn most definitely wasn't. He'd tried. He'd taken a couple of girls out for dinner, but there wasn't a single place in the tiny town that didn't make him think of Sunny, so he'd given up on that endeavor at least a year ago. His mother pressed on hopefully, but he just wasn't ready, and wasn't sure if he'd ever be. "I can't imagine a girl like that turning you down."

*And if she turned **you** down, I wouldn't stand a chance.* The errant thought took him completely by surprise. There hadn't been a time in the last year when he'd truly considered his chances with a woman, never mind worried about competition.

"She's a different kind of girl than you expect, Finn. Tough as hell. Stubborn streak a mile wide. I *told* Emma it wasn't a good idea to bring her, but... well, you know Emma."

His sister-in-law's stubbornness would have been funny if it was directed at anyone else. Nonetheless, Finn chuckled, shaking his head. "Yeah, I know Emma."

She'd practically grown up a Baylor, so it had only been right when his younger brother, Noah, had made it official this summer in a small civil ceremony. But she rarely gave him an ounce of slack when it came to much of anything. And if she'd told him this new horse's owner would be staying to observe the process, he would have drawn the line. Sparks would have flown. She'd played this one smart; giving him only the information he *needed*, until they showed up and he didn't have a choice but to go along with it or be an asshole. *Asshole for the win.*

"And Lily's not a lot different. See what I was up against?" Nate held his hands out, palms up, innocent.

"Fair enough," Finn asked, taking up a spot and an identical pose next to his friend. "So what's the deal on this horse, Nate?"

"He's got some major amped-up flight instinct. You know they were in a wreck..."

"No, Emma just said the horse got hit."

"They called me to figure out what to do with the horse. She wouldn't get in the ambulance until I got there." Nate shook his head, his eyes fixed ahead as he remembered. Judging by the scars Finn had noticed on the gelding's hindquarters, it wouldn't have been pretty. "But they were both just as hurt, one as the other—"

Nate zipped up, then, his face telling. He'd said too much. Somebody—probably Emma or Lily—had told him to keep his trap shut, but the ease of their long friendship made it too simple to say more than he was supposed to.

One thing was for certain—this woman's tenacity was impressive as hell. Not just refusing to head to the hospital until her horse was taken care of, but coming through the hell of the aftermath of a wreck and *still* being determined to see it through with her horse. She was either admirable or absolutely nuts.

And she wasn't going to give him a break, either.

Deciding not to press his friend any further, Finn picked up one last stray lead rope, and then straightened. "How long you staying?"

"I'll stay the weekend, I guess. Visit Nan and Banks while I've got the chance, and leave Monday or Tuesday. The fall circuit is starting soon and then I'll be busier than a two-peckered billy goat."

Finn nodded. Despite high tailing it for Denver the minute he could, Nate was still close to what family he had. His brother, Banks, had been voted into the Sheriff's office as one of the youngest the county had seen, five years before, and his grandmother, Aida—called Nan by everyone and their uncle— kept three quarters of the volunteer organizations in the town afloat. The family was well liked and respected, and he couldn't think of a single person who wasn't happy to see Nate roll into town, almost like a celebrity.

"Besides, I wanna make sure Lily has a ride home if she changes her mind about working with an asshole like you." When Finn looked up, Nate had a great, toothy grin on his face. If he'd been anybody else, he might have gotten a poke in the face for it, but Finn was well accustomed to his friend's teasing. And besides, he *had* kind of been an asshole to Lily.

"Well, before you get out there schmoozing, why don't you come in for a beer?"

-THREE-

"'EVENING." Finn's voice sounded close at Lily's back, startling her spine just a little straighter. She was halfway up the steps of the big house, and she took hold of the rail before turning to offer a smile to him. She didn't know where he'd come from, but it clearly wasn't the barn, because his dark hair was damp and clinging to his forehead and he wore a pair of dark-wash denim jeans, marginally less dusty cowboy boots than before and a blue plaid long sleeved button down shirt, untucked. She could smell the faint freshness of soap when he got closer. And she cursed herself for thinking about how damn good he looked when he'd been so prickly with her earlier.

"Hey. Did you end up getting Kit rode this afternoon?" Noah asked as Finn joined them on the porch.

"I did. Couple more rides and I'd like to expand her horizon a little. Maybe you and 'Jack can come ride fences with us this weekend."

"Sure." Noah nodded, then pushed the door open. "Honey, we're home!"

The spicy scent of something delicious wafted through the house, greeting them at the door, and they followed a feminine voice welcoming them in around a corner and into a huge eat-in kitchen with a butcher block table big enough for everyone and then some.

A curvy woman with long auburn hair swept into a messy bun worked in front of the stove alongside a shorter, teenage version of herself. Though she'd never met them, Lily knew from Emma and Noah's stories this would be the oldest Baylor brother, Dane's wife and her sister. A man, presumably the oldest brother himself, sat at the table with a red haired toddler on his lap, scribbling with wax crayons on a big piece of butcher paper with a little boy. Wordlessly, Finn shuffled around the edge of the group and slipped into a chair next to the little boy, taking up his own crayon. He curled his other arm around the back of the boy's chair, and the youngster started to point out the things he'd already drawn.

"Right, so... introductions." Emma strode into the kitchen and when the little girl lifted her arms, she swept her up and onto her hip like a natural, much to the child's delight. "This is Gracie, that's Gage," she pointed to the little boy at the table. "Dane, the big brother." Nodding to the women at the stove, now, "Ren and her sister, Kerri. Everybody, this is our friend from Denver, Lily Jacobs."

When Ren turned from the stove, Lily could see the telltale bump of pregnancy at her midsection. A warm smile crossed the other woman's face and she crossed the floor, ushering them in. "Come in, welcome, Lily. Emma's told us so much about you."

Lily found herself swept up in the family's easy rhythm over the next thirty minutes while everybody but Ren and the kids cracked open a beer and worked at setting the table. It became evident quickly, from the way Noah and Ren teased each other, Dane's gentle touch on his wife's arm as he moved past her, and the way Gracie and Gage changed laps a half a dozen times, that the glue holding this family together was their love for one another, and it was easy for Lily to feel included, even if she'd only just arrived. Even if Finn remained silent, not affording her so much as a passing glance.

It was Kerri who started the conversation about riding; Emma had warned her the teenager, though she had just started her junior year, was still horse crazy. Boys barely hit her radar. Soon enough, they'd be a distraction, and Lily envied Kerri the ability to focus on the horses. When her boyfriend, Jon, had dumped her two months after the accident because she 'cared more about Encore than this relationship', when she still had trouble getting out of bed unassisted, she'd regretted getting distracted by men in the first place. Then again, she couldn't deny the weak fluttering in her stomach every time Finn's dark slate gaze crossed the table, even though it looked a bit more like a glower every time it passed over her.

"So that big black draft cross is yours, then?" Kerri asked, sliding forks and knives onto the table with an ease that told Lily she'd done it a million times.

"That's Encore, he's my main squeeze."

"He's beautiful. Emma said you guys go fifty miles in a day?"

"We used to. Not every time," Lily smiled, thinking of the first short competitive ride she'd gone on. It had taken five hours and her behind had been so sore after the fact she could hardly walk, but she'd been hooked ever since.

"So it's like a race?"

An enormous pan of lasagna was placed on the table, along with garlic bread and Caesar salad, and everybody found a chair. Lily sat between Emma and Dane, across from Kerri, who was flanked by

Noah and Finn, with Gage on one end of the table and Ren at the other end with Grace.

"Yeah, but just finishing is a win in itself. Being the first across the line is incredible, but it's just as rewarding to finish, you know? There are vet checks to pass, and your horse has to be in decent condition beforehand, so crossing the line at all is like a reward for your hard work outside of the race."

Kerri seemed to consider her words and then nodded.

"It sounds like a lot of work." Lily lifted her head when she heard Finn's words, surprised he was interested at all. He hadn't moved his focus from his plate of food.

"Yeah... it's a big time investment to get a horse fit for that kind of distance." She hardly knew what to do with herself now that she wasn't riding three times a week to prepare for the competitive season. These days, she would have been happy to ride for five minutes, never mind five hours. "I really miss it. But if all I can ever do with Encore again is take him for a leisurely stroll down a smooth forest path, that'll be good enough."

"You'll totally do that." From where she sat beside her, Emma squeezed her arm. "I know you will."

The vote of confidence meant more to her than Emma could realize. For so long, it had just been Lily inside her own head telling herself she would make her body, and her brain, and Encore all cooperate again one day so she could ride. Her mother, while she was just trying to be helpful, was actively discouraging when it came to Lily's hopes to ride again, and had strained their relationship.

"We'll see what we can do about the horse." Again, Finn spoke without lifting his head, or bothering to make eye contact. Lily gave him a long look, and he must have felt it, because he finally looked up, his eyes flickering to hers for just a second, like he could barely afford her the time of day. What the hell was his deal? Was he really just that bad at interpersonal relationships? So far, everyone else on the Baylor ranch had been welcoming and warm and interested, but Finn had given her the cold shoulder, and this was just day one. As first impressions went, they weren't off to a good start, and she hoped his dislike for her wouldn't rub off on his work with her horse.

The truth was, she needed some time away from Denver, and she was lucky her line of work allowed it. Emma had been the one to suggest it in the first place, insisting they needed some time to catch up, and she'd been happy to oblige. Of course, it meant twice weekly calls to her mother instead of the visits, but it was an acceptable sacrifice for the potential to get out of the place she associated with not only the accident, but the painful recovery, and all of the doubt, too.

"So what are you planning to do while you're here, Lily?" Ren leaned ahead around her husband and offered a warm smile.

"Well, I'm a photographer by trade, so I can keep working and do my own thing, even if I'm not in my hometown. I'm under contract for the National Western Stock Show in January, but until then, I can take a little bit of a break. I don't often get to take photos just for the fun of taking photos, but the ranch is really inspiring..." She shrugged, pushing a crouton around her plate. Everyone at the table was focusing on her and her words, except Finn, of course, who was particularly interested in his piece of lasagna, and she was suddenly self-conscious.

"Oh yeah?" That was Dane, now, his tone kind.

"Yeah. I've spent a lot of time in the last few years taking photos of livestock and action shots of cowboys." She resisted the urge to lament about how long it had been since she'd had a chance to take photos for art's sake, rather than for a contract, but the truth was it had been a long time. She didn't regret a second of the work she'd been doing in Denver for the last few years; it had given her the opportunity to meet some incredible people, and animals, but there was something about finding the lines and shapes and shadows in a scene that spoke to her. Capturing that image for others to appreciate thrilled her more than the adrenaline rush of bull riders and barrel racers. "I think it would be interesting to work on a project about ranch life. I mean, I'm pretty well versed in rodeo stuff, but I don't actually know a lot about how it works on this end of things. And I think it'd be interesting."

"A project, like an exhibit in an art gallery?" Kerri asked, her voice keen and her attention rapt.

"Well, maybe. If I can find somewhere for it to go. If not, I think it'd still be fun, and then I'd have the photos to share with you guys, of course." She shifted back in her seat, cutting off a piece of the lasagna. "Enough about me, though. This is silly. What about you, Kerri? Emma tells me you were her first barrel racing client."

The teenager puffed with pride, and launched into her history. Happy to have the focus off herself, Lily dug into her food and listened to the whole family discuss Kerri's initial lack of experience when she and her sister had first come to the ranch, right down to this summer's high point win with Emma's horse, Alamo.

Later, Lily tried to help with the cleanup while

Ren put Grace and Gage to bed, but Dane, Noah, and Emma wouldn't allow it. Finn had disappeared into the house shortly after Ren and the kids had, and Lily sat at the table while Emma and her brother-in-law worked around one another, teasing and familiar. Finally, she rose.

"Washroom?"

Dane craned his neck and pointed to a door off the kitchen. "Down that little hall and to your right."

When she emerged from the bathroom, she noticed the hall she'd come through was lined with hanging photos. Ever the photographer, she couldn't resist the urge to stop and take a look.

There were a few older ones of the four Baylor brothers. Though they all looked different, those slate eyes were similar in all of them. She knew from Emma that the youngest, Gavin, had died in an accident with his wife, June, leaving Gage under the care of Dane. As she moved along the line, the boys got older. There were pictures of the boys on ponies, chasing calves, scrambling to fill their mother's lap. A picture of Noah and Emma as high schoolers. Twenty-something Dane with Rex, the elderly resident farm dog, as a puppy, on the tailgate of his truck. She stopped at a picture of Finn, maybe a decade younger than he was now. He had his arm wrapped around a willowy blonde who wore a pair of jeans, a white blouse and a white cowboy hat with a veil tucked into the hatband, and they were standing in front of a little log cabin. In the background, she could see the backside of the big house's porch.

Twisting her lips, she frowned. They couldn't have been a long ways out of high school at this point, just young with the future's promise shining in their eyes. Emma had given her a brief rundown on the family residing at the ranch, touching only briefly on Finn's work with troubled horses, and not much else.

A noise behind her nearly made her jump out of her skin and she turned to find him standing behind her. Close, but not too close. She turned her eyes back to the framed photograph.

"I forgot that was there," he said, his voice quiet in the small space between them.

Chewing her lower lip, she glanced back at him. Resignation read all over his features. Today he'd been a toughened cowboy, heart of leather, and suddenly, he looked vulnerable and heartbroken. The look inside his hardened exterior made her feel like she'd stepped over a line she shouldn't have been anywhere near to begin with. A million questions she didn't have any right to ask raced through her head, and she felt the overwhelming urge to reach out and touch him. She glanced back at the photo, comparing the smiling, self-assured cowboy in the photo to the one standing close enough behind her she could almost feel sorrow rolling off him.

"I'm sorry, I shouldn't be here," she said, looking back at him once more.

"Probably not." Just like that, the man who'd just about wrenched the heart from her chest was gone, replaced once again with the agitated one she'd met this morning. And it felt like he was reiterating his message from earlier. He didn't want her here, and she was wasting her time. A hot flush crept up from her collarbone and she cleared her throat.

"Right, they'll be wondering where we went."

He nodded with a grunt toward the slice of light coming from the kitchen at the end of the hall.

When they came back to the kitchen, Kerri and

Dane had disappeared and Emma and Noah were tidying up.

"Hey, coffee, Lily?" Measuring coffee grinds into the coffee maker, Emma turned to Noah. "You better go before they fall asleep, honey."

Noah smiled and tucked the dish towel he'd been holding into the oven door handle, then slapped hands with Finn as he passed behind Lily and headed into the house.

"Bedtime tag team. It's the only way Gage will go to bed when everyone's here. He gets too excited otherwise. Everybody's gotta have a turn." Emma explained as she assembled the sugar bowl, and a carton of coffee cream from the fridge on the table and began taking mugs from the cupboard. "Couple of weeks and you'll be included. Finn, you staying for coffee?"

Lily glanced over her shoulder to where Finn had edged toward the door. He'd stepped into his boots and held his hat between his hands.

"No, I'm gonna turn in. Long day tomorrow." He cleared his throat, hesitating like he had something else to say.

"Boo, party pooper," Emma chided, arranging everything in the middle of the cleared kitchen table.

Lily glanced at the clock on the stove; it was barely eight o'clock. When she looked back, Finn was gone and Emma was shaking her head.

-FOUR-

FINN braced his hands on the counter, staring down his coffeemaker as it dripped, filling the carafe at a painstakingly slow pace. He *had* wanted coffee, but instead he'd come back to hide in his home like a coward. Any other night, he'd have stayed, shooting the shit with his brothers and their wives until he could barely keep his eyes open. The whole lot of them had always been close, and the relationships had changed and stretched as time and tragedy had taken its course, but they'd finally found that sweet spot again, where they were all on the same page, and he couldn't help but feel like it had been interrupted by the arrival of Lily Jacobs.

The juxtaposition of Lily, who had been present at the back of his mind since she'd climbed out of Nate's truck this morning, in front of the photo of Sunny had been like a shot in the heart, a reminder that she'd produced a little spark where there had been none before, by doing nothing at all.

He'd tried to kindle an interest in pursuing something besides his life of celibacy, but the efforts had never produced success. And here, now that he'd settled into a life he could say he was enjoying, she'd walked onto the ranch with little regard as to whether he wanted her there or not, and he couldn't deny the draw. It had shaken him more than he cared to admit.

And when she'd looked at him in the back hall

of his childhood home—a mix of sympathy and sorrow without pity as she connected the dots about his dead wife—it had nearly undone him.

He'd tried to think about other things after Emma had hauled her away, but he couldn't. It wasn't that she was the first woman he'd met since Sunny's death—no, there had been new arrivals in town, and female clients—some of them rather flirtatious—but not a single one of them had prompted anything but platonic thoughts and business relationships.

Things on the Baylor ranch were simple, and that was how he liked them—quiet and slow. The most excitement they'd recently had was Dane and Ren's wedding. It was easy that way. He could be as social or anti-social as he chose, spending time by himself in his cabin or up at the big house with his brothers and their growing families. And because they were so happy, and so important to him, it was easy not to be jealous.

He'd wanted all of those things at one time. They would have expanded the cabin. Raised a whole slew of kids. Sunny had been kind and maternal toward Gage; she would have been one hell of a mother to their own kids. They'd put off most of their plans to chase a few rodeo dreams, have some adventures before they settled down. And then they'd waited too long. She was sick, and then she was dying, and they couldn't turn that clock back no matter how hard they would try. The cancer had come quick and aggressive, and she'd been brave. It wasn't until the very end she'd let anyone see how much it had taken from her, and even then, he knew she hadn't told the whole story.

He'd never wanted a complicated, fast-paced life. Even during his courtship with Sunny, things had gone slow and steady. She'd been his high school sweetheart, the only woman he'd ever had eyes for. And soon, she'd have been gone for more years than they'd been married in the first place.

The brave, stoic face Sunny had perfected had peeked out of Lily when she'd rope-burnt her hands and barely flinched. He knew the bite of that rope, and it made better men than him curse a blue streak. She'd stuffed it down so quick and so far, it was as though nothing had happened at all.

He shook his head as though that would get thoughts of Lily out of it, and straightened, sliding his hands into the pockets of his jeans. Finally, the green light indicating his coffee was ready flickered to life and he pulled the carafe out of the machine, pouring his mug full and doing his best to put Lily out of his mind.

-FIVE-

BUTTONING her denim jacket, Lily let the door of Emma and Noah's cabin shut quietly behind her. She had woken up with the first lightening of the sky and hadn't been able to go back to sleep. Tucker wiggled gleefully around her feet as she carefully navigated the narrow steps.

Emma's buckskin gelding, Alamo, nickered a greeting to her from the corral behind the cabin and Lily smiled, then shouldered her camera bag and held her hands out, palms up. The rope burns were stiff and sore but didn't sting anymore.

"Sorry, friend. I got nothing." She meandered out the short driveway and Tucker stopped at the property line, sitting and watching as she turned right and headed up the driveway.

It was a half mile walk back into the Baylor property before the big house and barns came into view. The sun was just rising and the golden glow it cast over the ranch was beautiful and soft. A fine mist hung low to the ground, giving the entire place the most ethereal look. *Perfect*. She paused, pulling her one-strapped camera bag around her body until the pouch was in the front, and then unzipped it. The camera was huge and made people feel self-conscious when they saw it, but the truth was she wasn't usually interested in shooting people.

Landscapes and livestock, that was her bread and butter, though she enjoyed the occasional portrait shoot. It was how she'd met Nate Montgomery, taking action shots at the rodeo events around Denver. *He'd* been one of those people intimidated by the big camera with the long zoom lens, and he'd approached her after he'd seen her on the sidelines snapping photos during his eight seconds. She smiled, remembering how he'd invited her for a beer afterwards, thinking he'd take her home. It hadn't worked out that way, but they'd become friends, and since the accident, she'd really appreciated his friendship.

The Baylor ranch was quiet—she wasn't sure what she had expected. Lifting the viewfinder to her eye, she snapped a couple of shots of the way the sun streamed just-so between the roofs of the horse barn and a little log cabin to the left. She hadn't noticed it when she'd first arrived, but then, she'd been busy noticing the way Finn Baylor didn't want her here *at all*. The cabin was small, but bigger than the one Emma and Noah had been living in. Maybe two bedrooms instead of one. And it looked more permanent, too, like it had been around for a while. Probably housing for help before four strapping sons had come along. It was charming, with a covered porch on the front and a red tin roof.

Just as it dawned on her that the cabin was the same one from the photo last night, the front door opened. Lily drew in a quick breath and, without knowing why she did it, stepped behind one of the giant live oaks lining the drive. Finn stepped out onto the tiny porch, hung a flannel work coat on a nail in one of the pillars by the stair and stretched his arms over his head. He had a long sleeved t-shirt on, tucked into a pair of jeans that had clearly seen better days, and a belt buckle glinted at his midsection. His lean body flexed back, then forward as he bent and finished buckling his loosely fastened spur straps, and something low in her belly pulled.

He crossed the yard in a few long, loose strides, to the round pen where Encore had spent the night. She was grateful to the Baylors for being able to accommodate him in an outdoor pen; he needed to move to keep the residual swelling in his legs down. They'd have to figure something else out if they were still here once winter came, but for now, he was a hearty horse that didn't mind the elements and the early fall chill was already burning off with the rising of the sun.

Encore lowered his head over the fence and nickered at Finn, and Lily smiled. He'd been mostly withdrawn for the last year, compared to the big personality she'd come to know and love over the years they'd been together, and seeing him engage again—first with Emma at Renegade and now with Finn—warmed her heart.

As he approached, Finn reached out and let Encore smell his hand. When the horse didn't back away, he reached up and stroked the swirl in the middle of the gelding's forehead. Without thinking, Lily stepped around the tree, lifted her camera, and hit her shutter. She snapped a few more shots as Finn bent and slid between the rails of the round pen. He ran his hand under the Encore's mane, down his neck, over his shoulder, and the horse craned his neck, lipping the back pocket of his jeans.

Her heart thudding in her throat, she watched the cowboy stride confidently into the middle of the round pen and then send the gelding out around him with a flick of his hand. He drove the horse with his body language, first at a walk, and then a trot, testing out his soundness. As if they were connected at a far deeper level, the horse stopped, turned, and changed paces with the simple shifts of Finn's body. Like magic.

She'd seen it before; mostly in videos online. When Emma had told her that her brother-in-law had been doing a variation of natural horsemanship since well before it had become a big-selling business, Lily had been skeptical, but interested. It was one thing to see an imported cowboy from Australia do it for an audience in a packed arena, but it was entirely different to see it in action with her own horse.

When she'd finally realized she was in over her head with Encore's behavior and started looking for a trainer, she'd had lots of offers of the ole yank-and-spur methodology. One cowboy had offered to 'ride the dirt out of him', another offered to lie him down to teach him submission, but Lily knew better. He was scared and unpredictable, not belligerent. Encore had always been what she affectionately called an 'independent thinker' and that quality was what had gotten them out of trouble on the trail more times than she could count. Now it worked against her, and she knew there had to be another way. He'd already been traumatized enough by the long recovery process; it was as long and painful as hers had been, and if she was honest, a little selfish, too.

It was a miracle he'd survived the collision in the first place, the fact that he was now trotting around the outside of the round pen with one ear turned toward the cowboy in the middle and no lameness at all was divine intervention. Intervention she'd needed when she'd been in the hospital recovering from surgery, and then on bed rest. Knowing he was still alive, that as the healing process continued, she would eventually be wheeled into the vet hospital to see him, was what had sustained her.

Lily finally started toward the pen, her shutter clicking every step or two. If Finn or Encore noticed her, neither showed any indication. Finally, she lowered her camera and took in the imagery. Encore's glossy coat rippled in the golden light of the early morning sun, marred by the network of scars on his hindquarters. She still thought he was the most beautiful horse she'd ever seen.

Despite popular belief, with his giant dinner-plate sized feet, abundance of hair, and large, hard-to-fit head, his intelligence and common sense had always attracted her. Since the accident, though, she hardly recognized his personality. Despite their long partnership, they were suddenly more out of sync than they'd ever been, and he was more terrified of everything than *he'd* ever been. Anything approaching from behind sent him into a tailspin. She'd been too frightened to have anyone, including herself, try riding him. It was during a dark moment, when she'd begun to ask herself if it had really been worth it to put him through the agony of recovery that Emma had suggested Finn. And here he was, spinning his magic. He'd told her he didn't want her involved, but she couldn't help it. The horse was engaged and interested for the first time since the accident. She couldn't take her eyes off thcm.

*

It took her just about forever, but when Lily folded her arms on the top rail of the round pen, Finn couldn't help but sigh. Bad enough she'd chased him out of his brother's home the night before. Bad enough he'd been thinking about her the minute he woke up this morning. Bad enough he'd told her she wasn't welcome as a part of his work with the horse. Here she was. There was no way he could focus all of his attention on the horse now. He shifted his body to block the horse's impulsion and Encore stopped up, dropping his head and chewing. Finn smiled briefly.

This was something he knew. Something he could count on to produce consistent results. Different horses took different methods and different spans of time, but the end results were always predictable. This was something he knew, was confident about, while every other aspect of his life could be set into a tailspin, his work with client horses was solid.

As he turned toward Lily, Finn could hear the thud of the horse's big feet in the sand behind him, and he paused about six feet from the rail, without yet speaking to her, while Encore caught up. He turned his back to her, and rubbed the horse's jaw, rewarding him.

"Can I help you?" He thought he'd been clear about his directive the day before, but he obviously hadn't. He turned to her, still leaning over on the fence, watching him interact with the horse.

"Um... no," she said, shifting her weight from one foot to the other, remembering his directive from the day before.

"Seriously, I don't let clients watch sessions, especially the early ones." So far, he couldn't see any need for the 'tough love' methods that upset owners in Encore, but his policy provided a good excuse to try to make Lily out of sight, and hopefully, out of mind.

"I know, I'm sorry. I just thought I'd get an early start on shooting the ranch—" He must have unknowingly made a face, because she frowned. "After you left last night, Dane said I could go wherever I wanted to get shots for the project."

Of course Dane had told her to go and do what

she'd like, because his brother was wonderful at hospitality, and wasn't so bothered by having her poke around. *Because he still has his wife and isn't attracted to Lily.* The bitter thought took him by surprise and felt sour in his head. He wasn't like himself at all—when Sunny had died, he'd cursed every god he could think of—real and imagined—but he'd never begrudged happiness to those he cared about. Not even for a second. Further proof Lily's mere existence on the ranch was problematic.

"I see."

"And I'm not trying to brag myself up, but the photos I take are good."

"Is that so?"

With the challenge, she puffed up with pride, lifting the camera from her chest. She thumbed a button on the back a few times and then slipped the neck strap off over her head, flipping her blond ponytail over her shoulder.

"See for yourself," she said, holding the giant device out to him.

He took the camera from her. On the small viewing screen was a photo of one of Encore doing a rollback in the front end of the pen. The way the shot was angled, Finn could see his own face just above the horse's shoulder. His eyes were focused on the horse, and he could feel the animal's movement even though it was a still shot. She had captured the moment exactly as it *felt*, not just as a sketch of what it looked like.

"I know you said you don't like to have an audience, but I've never seen this stuff before," she continued. "Not in person, anyway."

He raised a brow. "This stuff?"

"Natural horsemanship. I've watched a couple of videos on YouTube, but that's not really the same thing."

"I wouldn't call this natural horsemanship. This is what I like to call common sense horsemanship." Laughing, Finn shook his head and handed the camera back to her. Her talent was undeniable, and she was right—the photo was good. He could let her do her thing to get by if she let him do his thing to get by. "Alright."

"Alright what?"

"Alright, you can watch, take photos, whatever it is you want to do. But I need to focus on your horse while I'm working with him. I'm not interested in a deep, philosophical conversation about this."

Her little frown produced a tiny line between her brow and for a fleeting second, he thought he'd like to smooth it out with his lips. The thought surprised him as much as the thought about Dane, and was gone as quickly as it came. He cleared his throat, uncomfortable, as if she could read his mind. Keeping this kind of thought to himself was paramount to coming out on the other side of this business transaction alive.

"And I need you to trust I know what I'm doing. Whatever you see here is in the best interest of your horse. I'm not being 'mean'."

"Alright," she repeated his earlier word, shifting her ponytail off her neck and drawing his eyes to the silky-looking curve where her shoulder drew up into the delicate column of her throat. *Damnit.*

She needed to go. She'd taken enough photos for one morning, as far as he was concerned, and if she stayed any longer, his stony resolve not to become invested in anything but her horse was going to weaken. He pulled the horse's lead rope off the rail of the fence in front of her. When it wasn't being used for work, he kept the gelding out here to keep him from getting stocked up, but he had a full morning of work, so Encore was heading into the barn for a few hours.

"So we're done here," he prompted, then turned back to the horse, snapping the lead rope into his halter. He didn't turn around until he heard her scuffing away from the round pen. When he did, he watched her back as she headed to the heifer barn, his eyes drawn to her in a way he couldn't explain. It made him feel weak, and anxious. Distraction like this was dangerous, it made mistakes happen, people get hurt; and it was disrespectful to his wife. He couldn't afford it in his day to day life. He hadn't expected her to infiltrate his head, his blood, his bed. She would need to find someone else for her horse. He would have to send her away; find a way to make himself do it.

They weren't even close to done.

-SIX-

"HEY, that's Finn." Emma's voice behind her nearly made Lily jump out of her skin. She was zoomed in on a shot she'd taken that had originally had Encore in it to the left, but she was considering cropping him out altogether because Finn Baylor made such a nice picture, all long legs and cowboy cool. He was turned side on and had one thumb tucked in the belt loop of his jeans. Dust from the round pen's dry sand footing drifted across his boots from Encore's movement. The way the sun hit him hid his eyes behind the brim of his white cowboy hat, but his chiseled, stubbled jaw was visible. A pair of yellow doeskin gloves poked out of his back pocket. It was a good photo—a brilliant photo, maybe, and cropped in on Finn, it made a great portrait of the working cowboy of Colorado. *And* gave her flutters in her stomach despite herself. The minute Emma saw it, it suddenly felt more like voyeurism than art.

Clearing her throat, Lily resisted the urge to slam her Macbook shut, and tilted her head to look at her friend, who had braced her arms on the back of the couch.

"It is, indeed," she said. Emma rounded the end of the couch that separated the eat-in kitchen from the small living room where Lily's stuff was spread out, and flopped down beside her.

"I didn't mean to snoop, I swear. But Finnegan's never looked so good. I guess I've always just seen

38

your promotional material for the bulls and broncs and never anything artistic."

"I don't really do artistic all that often." Lily shrugged, flicking through a couple of other photos in the set without completing the crop on the photo of Finn. "Hey, look at this one."

She clicked on another set of photos, taken later in the day, to one she'd taken of Tucker. The pup was on his back in an uncut row between the hay fields, long strands of grass in his mouth, and Lily had laid down on her stomach to get it. His large ears flopped upside down, all four paws sticking out at awkward angles, and it looked like he was smiling.

"Oh no way, when did you take that?"

"This morning." Lily smiled, thinking of their little adventure. The pup had bounded off like a gazelle, his head only visible as he took long jumps through the grass. "I'm sure Dane will kill me, but it made for a great series of photos."

"I love these. If Dane tries to give you trouble, send him to me."

"He's such a character. And so are these guys." Lily scrolled through a couple more photos, some of them artistic perspective shots of the weathered wood of the snake-rail fence lining one side of the Baylor ranch's driveway, until she got to one of Alamo and Blackjack with their heads hung over the rail of their little corral, all four ears perked forward. It had only taken her about fifty shots to get one where they were both looking at the camera with their ears forward. "They posed like this forever. I might have been making funny noises at them. For quite some time. And actually, I think it was Noah's truck coming in the drive that got me the money shot."

Emma squeezed against Lily's side to get a

better view of the photos, and for what felt like the hundredth time, she was grateful for the opportunity her friends had given her to get out of her head and Denver for a while. It was a new world, and her relationship with her horse's trainer wasn't quite what she'd imagined, but she'd needed a break from the pity and fear and reminders of what had happened.

"You're already getting so many good shots. I don't think I've ever thought of Finn as much as a cowboy as I do now." Emma pointed at the screen to encourage Lily to flick back to the photo she'd been working on, and saw the whole shot with Encore in it, not the crop job she'd done before. She craned her neck to look at her friend and raised a brow.

"What?"

Emma narrowed her eyes and then shook her head, directing her eyes back to the screen. But it was too late, Lily could already see some kind of plan forming.

"Nothing, show me more."

Lily looked at her friend for a moment longer, and then turned back to the computer, but all she had were more photos of Finn with Encore, and Tucker, and the former felt personal. She flipped through a couple, showing one of Tucker bounding up the drive toward the ranch, his ears flopping in the wind with his mouth open, and then shrugged.

"I just did some scouting today, mostly—" Lily's phone buzzed on her hip and she frowned, tugging it out. The call display showed it was her mother and she let out a sigh, setting her computer on Emma's lap and holding up her finger. "Hang on. Hey mom."

"Lily Jacobs, are you alright?" Panic had lifted her mother's voice a couple of decibels.

Dropping her head back, Lily swallowed, waved to Emma and headed out the front door of the cabin. "Yes, mom, I'm fine. You *know* I'm fine, I sent you a text message yesterday when we got in."

"I know, I just..." Her mother trailed off. Julie Jacobs was an incurable worrier, and Lily loved her for her concern, but needed the space Three Rivers would afford her. Though she'd been existing independent of her mother for almost a decade by this point, the accident had caused Julie to revert straight back to mama bear. At first, it had been useful—she'd prod doctors for more information or work when they might have let something slide, but now it was overbearing. Now that her body was mostly healed, she needed time for her heart and her head to do so and her mother's incessant interjection into her life and negativity about Encore was *not* helping. "Is your horse better yet?"

Lily slumped onto the steps in front of the cabin. The daylight had stretched as far as it would go and it was nearing dinnertime. To her right, Alamo and Blackjack watched her with interested expressions; what she wouldn't have given to have had her camera with her. She sat with her feet on the next step and wrapped her free arm around her knees. Her mother had never understood the draw of horses, *especially* the draw of spending hours in the woods with nothing *but* a horse. But to Lily, it was the next best thing to being able to capture the perfect image with her camera. On a bad day, she could feel all the negativity draining out of her by her toes the minute her ass hit the saddle, and that might have been why things had escalated to the point of needing to escape Denver. At least here, they were close. In the backyard, in the barn. In Denver, it was a twenty minute drive to her boarding stable.

"The trainer started working with him, yes."

"And how are you? Feeling okay?"

"Yes, mom, I'm fine," Lily repeated. It had become something of a mantra over the last year. If she answered in any other way, her mother went on high alert, and that was not something she needed right now. Her mother would get in her car and roll in just as she was getting ready for bed, tutting and fussing and making Lily feel like she was ten years old all over again.

"When are you coming home?"

"I don't know for sure, mom. I'd like to stay and watch the work Finn is doing with Encore." Of course, *Finn* didn't want her to stay and watch the work he did with the horse. "I'd like to be here when he makes the breakthrough."

"I don't know why you—"

"Mom."

Julie sighed on the other end of the line. Lily knew what would have come next because she'd heard it a dozen times. *I don't know why you keep trying. I don't know why this is so important to you. He's just a horse.*

But he *wasn't* just a horse. Over the last year, he'd become something of a symbol of the normalcy of her life. If he thrived, so would she. Leaving him with the chaos he experienced now meant she never got any closure.

"I know, honey, I just... I miss you."

Lily sighed. When her parents split up two years ago for her father to upgrade to a younger, prettier wife, she'd become her mother's crutch. She'd known coming to Three Rivers would be hard on Julie, but the last year had taught her that sometimes, to take care of those you care about, you have to take care of yourself first. And besides, her father had been the motivation behind her vow to restore Encore to his former, confident, reliable self. She couldn't justify throwing him away after their years of partnership just because he wasn't what she wanted him to be anymore.

"I know, mama. Maybe once we've made some progress, you can come out and visit for the day."

"Oh, I don't know." There it was—her mother's kindness and concern extended only as far as her daughter, without recognizing the horse was a key factor in it. "We'll talk about it later."

"Right. Later." Emma poked her head out the door, raising a brow as if to ask if everything was okay and Lily nodded, shooing the girl back inside. "Anyways, Emma's fixing to get dinner ready, so I need to give her a hand."

"Okay, Lily." Her mother hesitated a moment and she heard a long breath on the line. She was trying, Lily knew it, but her mother hadn't yet learned that she needed to take care of herself— throwing herself into Lily's recovery had been a convenient way to forgo dealing with the emotional carnage her father had left behind, and while it had hurt to leave her mother alone with that mess, there was no way Julie would have dealt with it otherwise. "I love you, sweetie."

"I love you too, mama. I'll talk to you soon, okay?"

Lily swiped left and disconnected the call, but remained on the steps for a moment longer, letting out a long breath to attempt to calm her nerves. Talking to her mother only served to remind her how desperately important it was that she and Encore could come out on the other side of this okay.

-SEVEN-

"PUT that camera down and come sit next to me, Lily." Caine Baylor's booming voice cut through the din of the entire family preparing a table full of food on the veranda of the big house. Finn watched Lily, who had been crouched down taking photos of Gracie playing with plastic ponies on the floor, straighten and cast a smile over her shoulder at his father.

Every Saturday, his parents showed up for the mid-day meal. It was a good time, everyone coming together, catching up on the week. While he hadn't always appreciated his parents in his youth, he'd come to see them more as equals in the last several years. They were more of a team and a community than parents and children, especially after they'd lost Gage's parents, and it was never more evident than when they gathered together for their weekly meal. Through the week, whoever wasn't tending the store they ran showed up for lunch or dinner, came to keep the kids, or lend a hand on the ranch, but the feeling on Saturday was different. Joyful, relaxed; the one day of the week Finn didn't ride any horses and Emma didn't teach any lessons. More often than not, her parents would cross the snake rail fence separating their properties and join them. It was a day to relax and just enjoy one another's company.

And Finn would have been able to relax—if

there wasn't that little rub every time he saw his family engaging with Lily. His father had always been a harmless flirt, and he'd taken to her right away, with his wife laughing and rolling her eyes at him. Of course, Noah and Emma were comfortable and warm with her, and Dane had taken an interest in seeing her photos of the ranch. The kids loved her already, he observed, as Gracie lifted her arms in the universal signal for 'up' as Lily straightened.

She laughed, swinging her camera under her arm and onto her hip as she lifted Gracie up out of her pile of toys and onto her other hip. "It's a two-fer, Caine."

At the other end of the veranda, Finn took a deep, silent breath and hunched over the bottle of beer Dane had brought him. He watched as Lily crossed the floor, easy and comfortable, and deposited Gracie into his father's lap, sliding onto the bench seat next to him at the table. If he hadn't known any better, he would have guessed she'd been at the Baylor ranch for weeks, not days. It felt that long, too. *Too* long. Too long for her to be turning up in places he didn't expect her, like his thoughts at night when he tried to sleep, and around the ranch, crouched down or even sprawled out on her belly getting an angle he would never in a million years have expected would produce an interesting photo. If she insisted on staying until he was finished with her horse, he'd never survive.

He didn't hear what they said, but he watched his mother attentively ask Lily questions and his father give her shoulder a friendly squeeze, and Finn's chest tightened. She laughed, tipping her head back, and he could see the joy all the way to her eyes. He watched her for a while, interacting with his parents, flicking his eyes away just often enough that he wouldn't get caught staring. She looked completely at home; like she belonged here, and it was clear his family felt the same way.

"You coming to eat?" Ren's voice interrupted his thoughts and he straightened, finally lifting the beer to his lips and taking his first drink. It wasn't all that cold anymore.

"Yeah."

He moved to the bench and took his spot next to his mother, across from his father and Lily. The conversation around the table wasn't all that different from the first night Lily had been with his family. His parents kept firing questions about her riding, and her photos, and Lily answered them with a kind tone in her voice that sounded like she'd known them forever. When Gracie finished her pieces of chicken and corn ahead of everyone else and fussed to get down, Lily insisted Ren sit back down and helped the toddler out of her high chair.

*

After dinner, Finn sat back on one of the padded porch chairs while everyone else assembled on the wide steps to watch a 'show' Gage had decided to put on. He could see everything from his vantage point, including the movement out of the corner of his eye when Lily started to try to discreetly clear the table. She'd been snapping photos from the rail of the porch and when the light started to fade and the 'show' turned into playing in the sandbox while everyone else chatted on the steps, she slipped away, carefully collecting empty bottles from the table and letting herself back into the house.

Against his better judgment, and feeling better with a few beers in him, Finn dragged himself out of the chair. Ren noticed him, and started to get up, but he shook his head. She'd spent the better part of the afternoon putting together the huge meal they were all now in a food coma from eating, and he knew she hadn't been having an easy time with this pregnancy, either.

Lily had stacked a few empty plates onto one of the serving platters and he pinched a couple more empty beer bottles between his fingers on the left hand, and lifted the heavy platter with his right, widening the small gap she'd left in the door with his hip as he backed into the kitchen.

Spotlighted by the fixture over the sink, she had her back turned, rinsing empty beer bottles and setting them aside. She looked completely at home moving around Ren's kitchen. She glanced up and offered him that soft smile that dimpled her cheeks and worked like a line, drawing him straight in.

"Hey," she said, and turned back to the sink, shifting wordlessly to give him space to deposit his bottles into the sink. As he slid the plates onto the counter, she stepped back into the space. So close he could smell her shampoo and feel the warmth emanating from her.

His pulse went from 0 to 60 when she glanced back up at him, that smile still tugging at one corner of her lips and right at the base of his heart. A stray lock of her wheat-gold hair had slipped over her eyes and with her hands full, and wet, she blew upward in a failed attempt to get rid of it. Without thinking, he brushed it back, his fingertips tracing across her brow. Despite his speeding heartbeat, everything else around them slowed and quieted. With her big, dark eyes locked on his, she wet her lips and Finn thought he felt his knees go weak.

He tucked her hair behind her ear, hearing blood rushing in his own, and let his fingers linger on the soft spot behind the delicate shell of her ear. A little bit of alcohol in his blood made him braver than he expected, especially now that he'd touched her silky skin, standing so close he could pick out the scent of coconut and brown sugar. She could easily taste as good as she smelled. And what would it hurt to find out?

*

Finn's fingertips felt like fire on her skin. A chaste, platonic touch, but it felt more intimate than it should have. Lily held perfectly still, balanced on the balls of her feet, trying not to let herself lean forward into his touch.

They'd barely exchanged a civil word between them, and he'd watched her like a hawk the entire afternoon. Somewhere between sitting across the table from one another and this very moment, the entire feel of his gaze changed from distrust to something much warmer. Fuzzier around the edges. And now that he'd locked her in with those dark eyes of his, she just wanted to rest inside this moment for a little bit longer, wherever it went. He let out a breath that sounded like a decision and tipped his head forward.

"Hey, thank you guys—" Ren's voice startled Lily and made Finn jump back nearly a foot, dropping his hand. Her heart raced wildly as she turned back to the sink and shut off the tap she'd left running.

"Don't be silly, think nothing of it," she said to the sink full of bottles, and possibly herself.

Ren had paused inside the door, like she realized she'd walked in on something, she just wasn't sure what it was. Neither was Lily. Finn mumbled something about his beer and let himself back out onto the porch.

The pregnant woman took a spot beside Lily at the sink, opening the dishwasher and separating the dirty plates Finn had left behind to load it.

"I know you haven't been here long, but it's nice

having another woman around." Ren said, as she worked. "We'll never truly outnumber them, but it's nice to have a little more backup."

"You guys are wonderful, honestly. I feel like I'm with my own family," Lily replied, and she meant it. They'd so quickly opened their home and their hearts to her, she wondered why she hadn't taken Emma up on her offer to stay sooner. She turned and leaned back against the counter, crossing one arm over her waist and touching her lips with the fingertips of her other hand. She wished Ren had been just a few minutes later, so maybe it would have been Finn's lips on hers instead of her fingers. "I don't know how long I'll be here, though. The second I outstay my welcome, you'll let me know?"

Up until about ten minutes ago, she thought she might have already outstayed Finn's—hell, he hadn't acted like he welcomed her at all from the beginning, and they'd only made an uneasy truce.

Ren straightened, chuckling, and shook her head as she closed the dishwasher and grabbed a handful of bottles. "That doesn't tend to happen around here."

-EIGHT-

"TUCKER!" Lily heard Emma hiss at the pup two seconds before she felt the cold, wet nose on her forehead, immediately followed by the long slurp of his tongue across her face. "Ugh, sorry."

Burrowing her face in the worn quilt covering her, Lily groaned. She loved the goofy pup, but they *had* to stop greeting one another this way. She uncovered her face and tucked the blankets under her arms, looking at her watch. They kept the dog closed up in their bedroom during the night, and he usually went straight outside with Noah in the morning when he got up to feed.

"Sorry... sorry," Emma repeated as she tugged the dog away. "I had to get a jump start on today and get some horses worked before a new arrival. He just loves you so damn much."

Lily chuckled and shifted into a sitting position. The ache in her bones told her she had a couple more nights of couch sleeping, max, before it was more couch laying than sleeping.

"Good thing the feeling is mutual, Tuck." Stroking the pup's ears, she swung her legs over the edge of the couch and tossed the quilt aside. She twisted slowly at the waist, stretching her arms over her head and working some of the stiffness out of her body before she rose to her feet. It would be a painkiller day she decided as she wandered into the kitchen. Emma handed her a mug of coffee.

"You wanna come up with me?"

Lily yawned and nodded, rummaging in her camera bag hanging by the door for her bottle of painkillers. She shook out two, then three of the white over-the-counter pills and popped them in her mouth, washing them down with the black coffee. Emma set a pair of empty travel mugs on the counter top side by side.

"Sure, I've just got to get dressed." She poured her coffee into one of the mugs and went to her duffle bag at the end of the couch. Living like this out of her bag wasn't convenient—she wasn't sure what she had expected—she'd known their place was small, but she couldn't imagine sending Encore alone and just hoping for the best. She'd been with him this far, she couldn't just abandon him when it came to the hardest part.

Ten minutes later, the two friends climbed into Noah's pickup truck and headed for the big house with Tucker sandwiched between them. Lily could see Finn in the round pen with Encore before they'd even pulled up in front of Dane's house.

"Hey, he looks good!" Emma said as they climbed out of the truck. "He's moving really well, Lily. I think we did a mighty fine job with his rehab."

Lily crossed in front of the Ford with a smile, Tucker hot on her heels.

"Couldn't have done it without you." She shrugged her camera bag higher on her shoulder. She had meant to go into the West pasture today to check out a big live oak Dane had told her about, but seeing Finn in the pen with Encore drew her like a moth to a flame. And Emma was already heading in that direction, striding confidently across the yard toward them. Lily had to jog a couple of steps to catch up with her friend's long legs, and Finn had already pulled up the horse by the time they got to the work space.

"'Morning Finnegan," Emma greeted him as Finn took his gloves off, tucking them into his back pocket.

"You're up early, Champ." He nodded to Emma, his eyes not straying from her face.

Lily didn't know if he was purposefully ignoring her or not. After the way their interaction had ended the last time, she wasn't sure, despite their conversation, she *was* welcome.

"I have a bunch of horses to work before Sandy Ray's mare comes in."

"Oh yeah? What's she sending Cocoa over for?"

"Just some fine tuning and hours. Her little boy is ready for small fry and they want to make sure all the kinks are worked out. He'll come over for lessons in a couple of weeks."

Clearly having been left out of the conversation, Lily tugged her camera bag around herself and removed the device. Encore had already lost interest in the humans and was watching a pen of calves by the heifer barn with interest. At Nate's prompting, they had done a couple of cattle penning weekends and they'd been fun, but the thrifty draft cross had no real cow sense, and neither did Lily. She made the round of the outside of the pen while Finn and Emma chattered about which horses were doing what, and took a couple of profile shots of her gelding, then crouched for a different angle, backed herself up against the panels of the pen to take a shot of what Encore was seeing, and then, just for good measure, put her head against his and turned the camera toward themselves for a selfie.

Before long, she saw Emma heading off for the horse barn. Her friend waved at her as she went, and just as Lily was about to follow, she heard Finn's voice behind her.

"We need to talk about your horse."

Because that phrase had been used in the darkest of times, Lily struggled with the jolt of anxious adrenaline coursing through her for a moment before she turned. She had to remind herself sometimes Encore was perfectly fine—physically, anyways—there was no chance of things taking a turn for the worse at this point, but it was hard to forget the memory of it.

When she looked up at Finn, he was scowling; a far cry from how he'd looked when he'd been making small talk with Emma earlier. She thought they'd come to an uneasy agreement yesterday, but his expression said otherwise. He was wedged in between the horse and the fence, closer than he'd let himself get to her since they'd arrived.

"What about him?" She sounded at least fifty percent braver than she felt when it came to facing down the thundercloud that was Finn Baylor.

"I mean, he works well, he's respectful. He's a far cry from the fire-breathing dragon Emma promised me."

She did her best to keep her jaw from dropping open, but a short, tight laugh escaped instead. She shook her head with a smile. She knew there was no way in hell that was how Emma had described Encore to Finn, and to hear him described as such was almost comical.

"He's *not* a fire breathing dragon." She watched him for a second, her brow furrowing. What was he getting at? "Would it really be better if he was wild and crazy up front?"

"An honest crazy horse is better than a sneaky one. 'Least then you know what to expect."

Was he really implying her horse was dirty? She

frowned, backing up a step. "He's not sneaky. He's scared."

"With all due respect, I need a little more information than 'he's scared' to know how I'm supposed to proceed, since he seems perfectly fine to me." Finn's voice was hard, his gaze unyielding. His grumpy-old-cowboy face had been easier to handle than this. He seemed... angry, and she wasn't sure what she'd done. She hadn't lied to him—she hadn't talked to him about the horse at all—but suddenly she felt like she'd done something to upset him.

"If he's going to try to kill me when I saddle him up, I'd rather know now," Finn pressed when she didn't reply.

Lily's tongue felt like it was glued to the roof of her mouth. Her heart rate increased without warning. Any other day, with any other person, she'd have cut them down in a heartbeat. But Finn stopped her up. Maybe because she still half-believed the people who told her Encore wasn't worth saving, maybe because he was her last hope and he'd spoken her deepest fears.

"H-he's not going to try to kill you," she finally stammered out, but she suddenly wasn't sure. Nobody had saddled him since the accident. He had shocked the hell out of her more than once since he'd recovered enough not to be regularly sedated for healing.

"Then what the hell are you doing here, Lily?"

She crossed her arms over her chest as if to protect herself from Finn's words, but it didn't do any good. Twisting her lips together, she willed herself not to cry. What *was* she doing here? This wasn't how she would have picked a trainer any other time. She'd taken Emma's word for it, hadn't even contacted the trainer to discuss her horse's issues or what the plan of attack would be for his progress. Truthfully, she'd done a disservice to the horse she'd been working so hard to fix. And she'd done a disservice to herself. It was hard to believe any part of the Baylor clan could be anything like Finn when Noah and Emma and all the rest of the family were so wonderful, but this was the last thing she needed right now.

Widening her eyes to try to avoid the tears from spilling over, Lily took another step back.

"The wrong thing, apparently."

*

Finn watched Lily's back as she retreated to the horse barn. He couldn't have felt lower if he'd gotten down in the dirt and crawled around on his belly. It wasn't her fault he'd replayed that moment he'd almost kissed her in Dane's kitchen over a hundred times in his mind in the last twelve hours. But he couldn't go on this way, distracted, half pissed, entertaining ideas that hadn't crossed his mind in *years*.

After this session, where Encore had behaved perfectly, he suspected Lily was actually here more for herself than her horse. Based on Nate and Emma's reports, he'd expected a wall-climbing, aggressive bastard of a gelding that needed a little tough love, but found the horse in his round pen was none of the above. He didn't know if he'd really been lied to, but he did know this woman and her horse needed to go. There had to be any number of trainers in Denver who could help her; hell, *he'd* help her find them. He just couldn't do this. *This is just self-preservation,* he promised himself.

If he'd been ready to feel more than indifferent about any woman, he would have actively sought someone out, but as it stood, the fear kicking at the backside of his heart told him there was no way he was ready to go down this road. Not this close, and not this intense.

He was still considering the situation when Emma came bursting out of the barn like a fiery tornado.

"Shit," he muttered, assessing his escape options. He'd have to slip out of the round pen and cross Emma's path to get to either his truck or his house, and the rate of speed with which she was coming at him meant there was no way in hell he'd make it. "Damnit."

"What the hell did you say to Lily?"

"My relationship with my clients—"

"She's not just your client, she's *my* friend," Emma said resolutely. "So don't give me bullshit about 'clients'."

There was no way he was going to win this one. He took a step back, aiming for a softer approach.

"What did she tell you I said?" he asked.

"She didn't have to tell me anything. The poor girl looked shattered."

Finn wet his lips, and movement caught his eye as Lily walked out of the horse barn without looking back and headed out the gate toward the West pasture, camera bag in tow.

"Well?" Emma demanded, undeterred by his momentary distraction. There it was again—distraction he couldn't afford.

"I asked what she was doing here with a horse that clearly could have gone anywhere."

"That horse *cannot* go 'anywhere' and neither can that girl." Emma hissed. "If you had bothered to treat Lily like a normal client instead of a leper, you might know Encore has issues being approached from behind. *And* if you had given the horse more than a couple sessions, you might have discovered that yourself if you still couldn't find the decency to talk to his owner about his issues."

Finn raised a brow, looking over his shoulder at the horse that was to his left, craning his head under the edge of the round pen panels to get the last shoots of grass he hadn't grazed down. He *hadn't* approached the horse from behind yet, but it would explain, at least in part, what had happened when he'd gotten off the trailer and panicked.

"That girl didn't do anything to you," she continued while he watched the horse grazing. "If you're going to be mad at anyone, be mad at Noah and me. But don't take it out on her. She's fragile and she needs some goodness in her life for a while. And we're going to give it to her. *You* are going to fix her horse. And *we're* going to fix her confidence. Got it?"

Finn held his breath for a moment, watching his sister-in-law. She'd come a long way from the bossy little girl crossing the fence line to play with her 'brothers'. Most days he was proud she'd grown up a strong enough woman to handle Noah, but days like today, he wished she'd mind her own business. He could have argued with her, told her he wasn't willing to work with the horse anymore, but he didn't want to be here all day fighting with her just to lose anyway. He let out the long breath in a loud rush. Suddenly, Encore, who had been stealing grass under the bottom rail with his hindquarters turned toward them, took three great leaps forward before careening around the sand pen to get away from the noise. Without hesitation, Finn stepped out of the pen between the planks of the fence. Standing beside Emma, he watched the gelding race a couple laps around the circle before he settled enough to gear down.

When Finn tore his eyes away from the horse and looked over at Emma, she was staring back with a brow raised as if to say 'told ya so'. Story of his life.

Clearly, he had another angle to work with this horse. If he hadn't been so concerned over whether his owner was here or not, he would have figured that one out a lot quicker.

"Damnit."

"You're not a quitter, Finn. Tell me you'll finish this job, however it ends."

"I'll finish the job."

-NINE-

"GOOD morning, Finn."

Warmth filled Finn at the sight of Aida Montgomery. Technically, she was Banks and Nate's grandmother, but she served as surrogate grandma to the entire town. He had memories of her as far back as he could remember, and she was unchanged—silver hair, twill work pants and a short-sleeved plaid button-down. It was her standard uniform when it came to anything from volunteering at the high school football games to gardening in her own backyard, which she was doing right now. She'd known it was him without even looking up.

"'Morning, Nan. Nate around?"

She straightened, slowly, and he resisted the urge to reach out and help her because he knew she'd only slap his hands away. He'd never known her husband; there were times he wasn't even sure she'd ever had one. She was as capable and handy as any man he knew—she sure wouldn't have ever *needed* one. She'd singlehandedly raised the Montgomery boys when their parents had taken off, and she'd done a fine job of it, too. They were men he was happy to call his friends.

With a twinkle in her eye, she shook her head. "I thought he'd come home to visit me, but apparently not."

Finn looked pointedly to the back of her house

where the gooseneck trailer Nate had brought Encore in was parked. He knew there was a horse somewhere between Three Rivers and Denver counting on him for a ride back to the Renegade Racing outfit. Which meant one thing: Nate had gone to town and found himself some pretty little thing to hold his attention and bide his time with.

"You want me to go drag him up?"

"Oh no, don't be silly." Nan brushed his offer off, shaking her head, and then winked at him. "Maybe he's out there finding something that'll hold his interest here."

Finn chuckled; she was always lamenting that while she had Banks nice and close, Nate had settled in Denver. The boys were her pride and joy, and she never tired of talking about them.

"He'll be back for dinner," she stage-whispered conspiratorially as she gathered her gardening tools in a bucket and moved toward the house. "He always is."

With a few quick steps, Finn got ahead of her and held open the sun porch door. A bistro table sat in the corner with two chairs pulled out, topped by a ceramic jug with a half dozen tulips, a coffee carafe, and a couple of mugs. While Nan kept herself busy with town business just about all day, every day, she had kept Sunday mornings open for him since shortly after Sunny's funeral. They would talk about just about anything; from client horses to Dane's children to the price of feed—anything that would take his mind off his pain, and he'd leave with something to put on Sunny's grave. It was coming to the end of the season for fresh garden flowers; soon she would peel the supermarket price tag stickers off of small bouquets she picked up at Sawyer's, and when he'd try to pay her, she'd deny all day long that she hadn't just had them 'laying around'. The woman was one of the most normal, dependable things in his life these days.

"Come in, sit down."

Nan always said the same thing, and Finn always did as he was told. Because somewhere in the midst of all the catch-up talk, there were nuggets of wisdom, lines of sage advice he could repeat back to himself when things were hard. He'd hang on every word this woman said, because she'd had at least twice the life experience he had at this point. He took his seat and started to pour the coffee for the two of them.

"So tell me about the new girl." The woman leaned forward on her elbows.

He should have been surprised she wanted to talk about Lily, but then nothing Nan said ever surprised him. Nate would have mentioned the reason for his visit, and Nan collected information about people the same way some women collected jewelry. She wasn't the hub of the rumor mill, though; she was the person who sent the unexpected birthday card or dropped by with chicken soup when you weren't feeling well. Her knowledge was always used for good, for making others feel good, and he supposed that was why, even years after Sunny's death, he maintained these Sunday morning visits. Invariably, Nan said the right thing and made him feel good. And maybe he was a little desperate for that today, when he was feeling nearly as bad as he had in the early days.

It had been a long time since he'd felt so out of sorts. Especially after seeing the way Lily had slid right into his family unit, his family home, and seemed like she belonged there.

"Well, she isn't supposed to be here."

"But Nate brought her," Nan supplied.

"But Nate brought her." Finn sat back with his

coffee cup in hand, stretching his long legs out under the table, unable to keep the irritation out of his voice. Because Nan wanted to talk about Lily wasn't a good enough reason for Finn to want to.

"You don't sound pleased."

"You know I don't like clients hanging around while I'm working with their horses. I mean, the horses I get in are usually rough, sometimes dangerous. Sometimes the owners think I'm being 'mean' and all I'm really doing is saving my hide. And theirs." At least, this had been his line of defense so far. It was easier than admitting his heart rate sped up when he saw her, his mind wandered to her when he didn't want it to, and it was easier if she didn't come around.

"I know, Finn." Nan smiled knowingly and Finn wanted to curse. Was he that obvious?

"It's just... it messes up the rhythm of the ranch to have an extra body coming and going as they please."

"*Now* you're grasping at straws, darling." The woman sat back with her cup of coffee in hand and watched him over the rim without taking a sip. "Did it ever occur to you that maybe she needs to be at the ranch as much as her horse does?"

It *hadn't* occurred to him, not until Emma had cussed him out. Sure, Emma had told him Lily needed some time away from Denver, but the girl seemed sound of body and mind, as far as he could tell.

He scratched his head and set his coffee mug down. "We don't run a guest ranch."

The stern look she directed at him told him he hadn't earned points with *any* of the women in his life today. *Damnit.*

"But the Baylors don't turn away folks in need. You've always taken care of your own, but look at

Ren and Kerri. Look at how you brought Emma into the fold. And my boys, too.

"Sometimes, the deepest hurts are invisible on the outside, Finny." When she nodded her head toward him, he knew she wasn't just talking about Lily. "But they're still pretty significant cracks in the foundation of who a person is. I think you know that."

"Yeah." He swallowed, rotating his coffee cup on the top of the table, his eyes focused on the way the liquid inside stayed rooted even though the world was spinning around it. "Yeah, I do know that."

"And you know, sometimes the best way to repair the cracks in your own foundation is to help someone else mend theirs."

He finally looked up, giving her a long, thorough look. He'd always figured himself to be a private kind of man, not the sort to wear his heart on his sleeve, but here Nan was, cutting straight to the crux of the issue when he hadn't even told her about it.

"I don't know what to do, Nan." Lily's sudden appearance had dredged up feelings and memories he'd long ago buried; pain that hadn't needed to resurface, but told him now that he was in a whole world of trouble. He didn't know what to do with her horse. He didn't know what to do with that girl.

Maybe he could help her Encore, but he couldn't help *her*. He'd gone down that road once, doing all the things, and saying all the words that were supposed to make things better. He'd invested himself so deep in trying to make Sunny well that he'd almost forgotten who he was when she died.

"Here's what you do, love," she continued. "You keep working with that horse. And that girl will tell you what she needs soon enough."

That was what he was most afraid of.

-TEN-

LILY shifted Emma's economy car into park in front of Hinkley's diner. Because she didn't want to shoot everything on the ranch before the first week was over and her hosts were busy with client horses all day, Emma had suggested she take a drive into town. It wasn't a bad idea, if the town was half as friendly as the majority of the Baylor ranch had been, she shouldn't have any problems finding someone to chat with. Plus, the added bonus of clearing her head after the run-in with Finn that morning practically begged for her to get off the ranch. She hadn't expected him to be cruel like that—they were supposed to have a professional relationship—but a long walk out to the West pasture and then a chat with Noah before she'd left the ranch convinced her not to pack her bags then and there. Regardless of how Finn treated her, he really only had to fix her horse. She wasn't paying him for his friendship. It would have been nice to have a working relationship, but it wasn't necessary for the same end result to be achieved.

Primary businesses huddled together on the short main drag; the diner in a building adjoining the grocery store. Across the street was what looked like a doctor's office, the Baylor general store, and a gas station. Less than a quarter mile back, she'd passed a bar with a few cars already in the lot. The transition from ranches to residential to commercial was gradual and Lily had barely noticed she was in town until she was right there.

On the passenger seat, her phone buzzed and she picked it up to find a text from Nate.

Heading out, thought I'd stop by and say bye.

She tapped in her reply quickly.

Not at the ranch, I'm at the diner for coffee.

Great, I'll come by. Be there in 5.

She slipped the phone into one of the many utility pockets on her camera bag and climbed out of the car, shouldering the bag. She carried it everywhere—when one made their money from taking photos, they couldn't risk missing an opportunity to do so. She assessed the buildings around her for a moment, and then went into the diner.

"Hey hun!" A red-haired waitress greeted her from behind the counter, where she was refilling a display of donuts. It was a small spot, and most of the booths lining the walls, as well as the stools at the counter were vacant; the breakfast rush gone and too early for the lunch crowd. Tall windows threw long slices of sunlight along the floor. It looked like something straight out of the movies.

"Good morning," Lily said, smiling, as she decided the town was, indeed, at least half as friendly as the Baylor family, Finn excluded.

"You go on ahead and seat yourself, I'll be right along. Coffee?"

"Yes, please."

She slid onto the warmed vinyl seat of one of the booths, pushing her camera bag in ahead of her. Soon, the waitress appeared with a carafe of coffee and a chipped ceramic mug. She set the mug down and filled it up, then pulled a menu out of the back of her apron and set it in front of Lily.

"I'm Tina, you just holler for me when you're ready." The bubbly waitress made to leave but then did a double take, narrowing her eyes at Lily. "I don't think I've seen you around. Are you new or just passing through?"

Lily considered her response for a minute before speaking. "An extended guest, I guess you'd say. I'm staying at the Baylor ranch with Emma and Noah. Finn is working with my horse."

"Oh those Baylors! Isn't Emma just the greatest? She worked here with me before she went to Denver. What a sweet girl. And that Finn, poor soul."

Smiling at the way the waitress lit up when she talked about Emma, Lily tipped her head. It was none of her business, but she might get some answers here. She didn't think for a second Noah or Emma wouldn't tell her about Finn's wife if she asked, but this seemed like a convenient segue into the conversation she was interested in.

"Yes, his wife went quickly, didn't she?" It wasn't inappropriate to ask. At least, that's what she told herself, anyway. She'd seen the picture, his vulnerability; there was no existing wife, and he still wore a wedding band—*that* she'd noticed yesterday morning when she'd been shooting the session.

"Yes, she did, that poor sweet girl. Cancer. They barely had the diagnosis before she was so sick she couldn't do much. He took care of her right in his house. Hired a nurse to come in when he couldn't look after her. They never even had a chance to make babies." She tutted and shook her head. "High school sweethearts, they were. He used to bring her in here for a milkshake every week."

Sympathy pushed at her heart, clearing out her own agitation with Finn's behavior this morning quicker than she expected. She could understand someone doing everything they could to keep every unnecessary person out of their lives to protect their heart. In fact, wasn't that sort of what she was doing here in Three Rivers herself?

"Tina, you do get better looking every time I see you." Nate saved her from the spiral of pity that had started to claim her as he interrupted her thoughts, sweeping the waitress into a playful hug, careful of the half-full carafe of coffee she was still holding.

"Nate Montgomery." It was half a careful attempt at disapproval and half trying to keep a pleased flush from taking over her fair complexion. "Coffee for you, too?"

"Yes. And two slices of banana cream pie." Nate slid into the booth opposite Lily and handed the menu she'd been looking at back to Tina, who nodded and headed for the kitchen.

"It's *way* too early—" Lily started, but Nate cut her off, holding a finger up.

"It is *never* too early for a slice of banana cream pie from Hinkley's. The stuff hasn't changed since I was a kid, and I get a piece every time I'm in town. Ask Emma. There's nothing better."

Lily wrinkled her nose and slumped back in her seat, clearly having lost the battle before it had even begun.

"So?" Nate asked, leaning forward on his elbows on the table between them.

"So, what?"

"So, am I taking you back to Denver this morning or has Finn softened up a little?"

She thought of the way he'd gotten all hot under the collar this morning with her. He'd cut straight to the heart of the issue—her fear—with frightening precision, and she suspected he was better at people than everyone, including himself, gave him credit for. Even though he'd been nothing but a perplexing thorn in her side over the last few days, she hesitated to say anything to Nate about it. Especially now that she knew more about the situation with his wife. She'd be prickly, too, if she was dealing with a sudden loss like that. It was terrifying, the idea of loving someone so completely and so endlessly, and then suddenly, and almost without warning, they were taken from you. It was almost enough to put her off of the idea of love completely.

"Out with it, Lilypad." Nate prompted when she took too long to speak again.

"It's fine." She hoped she was making it clear there would be no more discussion here, like he hadn't wanted anymore discussion about the pie. And like she'd been summoned, Tina showed up with two dessert plates. On each sat a slice of banana cream pie almost a half foot tall, stacks of real sliced bananas topped with a heap of cream. Maybe he'd been right. Maybe there *was* no bad time for banana cream pie.

"If you say so," Nate said as he took up his fork and cut a generous wedge off his piece of pie with the side of it.

"*You* are the reason I have never been able to get rid of the weight I gained when I was laid up," she laughed as she stuck a forkful into her mouth. "Hold the phone. This is incredible."

Her companion wiggled his eyebrows at her with his mouth full. They ate in silence for a few more minutes. Tina came by to refill their coffee mugs, and finally, washing a mouthful of bananas down with the hot black liquid, she pressed her lips together and continued.

"You didn't tell me his wife died."

Nate shrugged, spearing another piece of pie

without looking up. "I didn't figure it was important, seeing as he's working on your relationship with your horse, not your relationship with him."

"No, I know." A little niggling in the back of her mind told her it was time to drop it now. She had no right to pry into Finn's life more than she already accidentally-on-purpose had.

"Unless..." Nate narrowed his eyes at her. Her heart skipped two beats. In another time or place, she might have actively pursued someone like Finn Baylor, but she had bigger fish to fry right now. But she *could*. He was straight up her alley.

"Nevermind, Nate. Anyways...how was your time with Nan? You look like you hardly slept since I last saw you."

It was his turn to dance around her question, and he hesitated, rubbing a hand on the back of his neck.

"I had to catch up on the night life."

"This town has night life?" She asked incredulously, but she wasn't surprised. The opposite of his brother, the straight-laced sheriff of Three Rivers, Nate was always looking for a good time. If there was one to be had, he'd sniff it out quicker than a bloodhound on a scent. She'd seen that a mile away the first time she met him. It had been both the reason she'd declined to go home with him, and the reason she kept him around. Three years later, they made better friends anyway.

"Well. It has a bar. And a dance hall."

"And there are enough people to support these things?"

He shrugged with a secretive smile on his face that suggested to Lily he hadn't spent *all* of his nights in the bar and the dance hall since she'd last seen him, then polished off his piece of pie. Lily still had half of hers left. He wiped his mouth with the paper napkin then crumpled it and tossed it onto his empty plate as he moved to rise.

"You're leaving already? You just got here."

"I ate a piece of pie and had a coffee with you."

"You *inhaled* that pie," she said pointedly, but sat back.

"I've got a horse to pick up an hour out, and they're expecting me..." He glanced at the clock over the counter. "...in about an hour. I just wanted to make sure you didn't need to get out of Dodge."

She slipped out of the booth when he did, and he bent to wrap her in a big, warm hug. Nate had taken the place of her brother in her life, and for just a second, she thought maybe she should go with him. But she knew she couldn't leave Encore behind. He rubbed his big hand over her back and spoke in her ear.

"I know you're scared of moving forward, but let these people help you, okay? You deserve it."

He was right. Two years ago, a doctor's recommendation wouldn't have kept her from riding. Nothing would have. After the accident, she'd waited anxiously for the day she'd be told she could ride again—that was nearly six months ago, now. Instead of the joy and excitement she'd expected, she'd been taken over by the same cold shards of fear she'd known when they'd suggested she may have difficulty walking again. It should have been a triumphant success, but instead it had sparked anxiety and panic.

"I gotta hit the road, but I wanted to check in with you. You know you can call me anytime." He held her out at arm's length for one appraising minute, then released her. "But I don't think you'll have to."

"Later Nater."

He dropped a twenty on the table and she started to stop him, but he winked at her and reached out to squeeze her shoulder. "You got this, Lilypad. I believe in you."

He swaggered out of the diner, tipping his hat at Tina as he went, and she watched his back for a moment, and then, with renewed butterflies in her stomach, slid back into the booth to finish her pie.

-ELEVEN-

LILY made her way across the yard carefully the next morning. She hadn't been comfortable on the couch at any point, but now there was pain. Nothing she couldn't handle—as long as she could walk, she would, pain be damned—but enough to shorten her stride and require her to down a couple of painkillers before she'd started the long trek up the driveway.

She'd have been lying if she said there weren't butterflies banging around in her rib cage as she headed up toward the big house. Dane *had* given her permission to come and go as she pleased to shoot the ranch. And Finn hadn't said she couldn't shoot his sessions with Encore. The rest of the Baylors felt like her family by now, she'd be damned if she'd let him get away this easy. The least they could do is develop a reasonable, professional relationship when it came to his work with her horse. She was, after all, paying him. And despite his best efforts, she was staying. He'd have to get over it.

Finn was stripping a young gray mare of her tack in the round pen. As he swung the saddle over the fence rail, the filly folded her knees and dropped into the sand, rolling to rub her itchy sweat marks. Lily smiled as the horse made a complete turn over twice, and then floundered on one side for a few seconds before she jumped to her feet, shook, and made two bucking, farting victory laps around the pen. He shook his head and laughed, and then turned those charcoal eyes on her. She tucked her lower lip between her teeth; this could go either way.

"'Morning."

Finn's tone was friendlier than she expected, and her footsteps faltered as she reached the rail. She'd been halfway ready for a fight, and he'd disarmed her in two seconds flat.

"Good morning." Tentatively, she offered him a smile, and he returned it. She couldn't figure out what any of this meant, so she decided to just tread lightly. Essentially, they were business partners, investing time and energy into the same project— Encore. It was essential they had a civil relationship, at least.

"I forgot what your face looked like, I'm so used to seeing it with a camera in front of it." Was that...was that *teasing*? Lily laughed a bit and shook her head. Her camera hung around her neck, *that much* rarely changed. Even in the height of her racing days, she always had a high tech compact point-and-shoot in her saddlebags, just in case.

"You are definitely not the first person who's said that to me."

He looked at her for a long moment, and since he'd already been surprising this morning, she held her breath.

"Look, Lily...I haven't been particularly nice to you, and I'm sorry." Well *that* was another surprise. "You did nothing to deserve it; you're a friend of Emma's, which makes you a friend of mine, and I'm gonna start treating you that way."

Lily rocked back on her heels and raised a brow at him, pressing her lips together. He might have been a lot of things, but she didn't think insincere was one of them; he wouldn't have been a good horseman if he was, and he'd clearly been getting along well with Encore. He'd told her that much the last time they'd seen each other.

Finally, she shrugged, smiling. "Water under the bridge." She nodded to the filly, who had taken up a spot gazing out over the fence at a pen of cattle. "So who's this?"

"This is Kerri's new horse, Kit. We're just getting her started."

"She's cute."

"Smart as a whip, too. Little mare-ish but nothing she can't handle."

Lily appraised the horse—she was leggy and had a ground covering trot, a body like a tank, and a delicate, feminine head with bright, calculating eyes. Kit would make a fine barrel horse, but then, she was the type that would be athletic and excel at anything, distance included.

"Mare-ish is a term some man made up that means 'smarter than me'." She chuckled.

Finn rolled his eyes. "Good Lord. Women."

"Hey, I'm not saying it's a bad thing. Why do you think I ride a gelding? I don't have the energy to ride fifty miles *and* stay ahead of a mare."

The look on his face told her he wanted to say more, but he didn't, though she saw his eyes drift down her body. And not in a sexy way either, to her dismay. She could get used to this softer, more humorous, human side of Finn.

"Of course, I can't ride fifty miles anymore. I can't ride five." She didn't need to explain herself to him, but she felt compelled to. She didn't know how much Emma might have told him about the accident—talking about it wasn't high on her list of priorities. She could talk about the injuries all day long, but the actual *accident*, the moment that had robbed her and Encore of their normalcy, and nearly robbed them of their lives...no, talking about that didn't come easy.

"I noticed a little hitch in your getalong." He nodded to her midsection and she cringed. She knew she was moving slow today but she'd hoped it hadn't been noticeable—always hoped it wasn't noticeable. The last thing she wanted or needed was pity.

"Yeah. Some days are better than others," she admitted.

"Anything in particular help or harm?" he asked. His conversational tone and personal interest shocked the hell out of her. It might have been the first time he'd asked her a sincere question.

Kit crossed the ring, having lost interest in the cattle, now much more interested in the two of them and their conversation. Lily was grateful for the distraction, and when the gray hung her head over the fence, she stroked her nose, focusing on the multiple swirls in the hair on her face. Old wives tales said the whorls meant something about a horse's demeanor but she'd been around the block enough times to know it was a lot like mares being mare-ish.

"The weather, the way I sleep, which direction the wind is blowing." She chuckled; people felt most comfortable if she could make a joke about it. "Sometimes it doesn't bother me for days and then all of a sudden I can barely move, everything's so locked up."

"If you don't mind my asking..."

"I do, but people ask anyways." She looked up and was surprised by the soft, interested expression in response to her prickly words. She didn't have to tell him, but she would, because maybe then he'd understand why she couldn't leave. Why she couldn't just find someone else to help her. "I'm held together with plates and screws. The car pushed Encore out from under me and I landed on the bumper. A couple inches higher and the prognosis would have been 'won't walk', not 'probably won't walk'."

If she talked about the prognosis, the hospital stay, the physical therapy; if she kept it all in a neat box of recovery, it helped her not to think about the blood, the screaming, the panic. It helped her not to remember the feelings of desperation as she'd watched them sedate her thrashing horse to coax her into an ambulance, not knowing if he would live or die. Not knowing if *she* would live or die. But it was always there, all of it, at the back of her mind. She was lucky to walk; painful or not.

"Shit."

"Shit," she agreed.

"Well, if there is anything I can do to make your stay more comfortable in that respect, let me know."

"Recommend a bed and breakfast?" She offered a smile. She hadn't yet been brave enough to broach the subject with Emma; they had offered up their couch and it was great, but the inability to easily shift to more comfortable positions during the night was taking its toll, and was almost certainly the cause of the 'hitch' this morning.

Finn raised a brow, took off his gloves and tucked them into his back pocket. "Tiny cabin's not doing it for you?"

"You know 'how I sleep'? I don't want to offend Emma and Noah, but couches cause problems."

Finn winced.

"Ah. Well...there's nothing formal this time of year, but Nate's Nan has a basement apartment she rents out from time to time that might be available. I'm sure they won't be offended if you explain it to them the way you just did to me."

"Great. I'll see if Noah can get me in touch with her today." She rocked back on her heels, sensing something unsaid in the air between them.

*

"Great," Finn swallowed. The words were on the tip of his tongue but he couldn't bring himself to say them. He had a spare room in the cabin, with a bed, and a desk, and everything she'd need to be comfortable. And it had housed its fair share of guests since Sunny had been gone. But this felt dangerous. He cleared his throat to keep the words at bay. No bother. She would ask about Nan's place.

For days now, she had been watching him through the viewfinder of her camera, and even though she was creating images that would last forever, it somehow seemed less intrusive. This was direct, and he felt vulnerable, the same way he did when they'd been standing in the hall at Dane's and she had put two and two together about Sunny.

He couldn't figure out how this girl was getting under his skin so easily, like he'd opened it up and let her right in. Except he hadn't. She was best at an arm's length, but it was hard to keep her at an arm's length when she was in his head. She'd been there right from that first night. He had never thought about another woman this much since Sunny, and he hadn't missed Sunny this much in a long time, either. It was a double-edged blade.

He'd done everything he could to deflect her since she'd arrived but she kept coming back for more, barging right into his day the same way she'd barged right into his life—without permission or apology. Unexpectedly sweet; soft where he'd been hard. Still generous with her smiles and her gentle words when he didn't deserve them. In truth, she hadn't done a thing wrong except show up here with her horse. It wasn't her fault he couldn't work his head and his heart out enough to be civil. Distraction was dangerous, and he couldn't afford it. Especially not in his house.

"I actually didn't come up here to make you feel bad about my couch-sleeping arrangement," she said. "I actually thought since I'm *going to be here for a while...*" she made direct eye contact with him then, which told him the way he'd treated her yesterday hadn't made a difference in her decision to continue with Encore's training. "I'd like to make myself useful."

"And how's that?" he asked, intrigued.

"Well, the shooting and editing I'm doing only takes a few hours a day. I thought I could earn my keep helping out."

Raising a brow, Finn looked at her, remembering the obviously pained way she'd approached. Though she might have wished differently, her body wouldn't hold up to the kind of rigorous day-to-day stuff the rest of them did. Even *if* she was sleeping in a bed instead of on a couch.

"Like what?"

"Stalls, clean tack, whatever little stuff you guys are too busy to get to. I'm your girl."

He rubbed the back of his neck, considering. She'd be underfoot, basically. At least the way things were now, she could be tucked away at Emma and Noah's all day, and the odds of running into her, except when she headed out to shoot, were low. He was sorry for the way he'd treated her, but not sorry enough to want to rub up against all that temptation all day long. But the fact that she obstinately showed up every morning, swinging by the round pen to snap a couple photos even though he'd all but chased her off with bared teeth early on, meant she wasn't going to give up until he gave her something to do.

"Come on, I *saw* that dusty tack room, Finn."

She sounded like she'd taken a page right out of Emma's book and he couldn't resist the little laugh that came out of him.

"Alright, alright. You got me there." He dropped his hand, defeated, and shrugged. "The only person that bothers is Emma, but she's too busy to clean it."

"Then it's a good thing I came along."

A genuine smile quirked one corner of his lips. "Jury's still out on that one."

-TWELVE-

THE next morning, Lily woke with a new found purpose before Tucker even found her eyes open, and snuck out of the house. The fresh morning air was chilly, but welcome, filling her lungs as she walked up the driveway toward the big house, slowly loosening up sore muscles and joints. When she'd asked Emma about Nan's place the night before, her friend had promised to look into it but Lily recognized the doubt in her expression. She'd have to figure something else out sooner rather than later, but she'd be damned if she'd leave Three Rivers before her horse. Especially now she and Finn had found some kind of ease in the friction between them.

She'd brought her camera, just in case. She liked to think she was documenting the work Finn was doing with Encore but she knew it was more than that. He made a pretty damn compelling study of a cowboy. But it was more than that, too. He was a good man—anyone in his family would attest to that—and she could see it in the photos. She'd seen a little bit of it yesterday, and she wondered how long it would take for him to open that side to her.

"Good morning."

The soft voice took Lily by surprise as she passed by the big house, but when she looked up and saw Ren sitting peacefully on the porch in a sunbeam, all fiery halo of messy sleep hair and a steaming mug clasped between her hands, she wondered how she'd missed her. The urge to pull out her camera tugged at her. This wasn't the rough and tumble cowboy of Colorado, but it said something about the women who stood behind those men.

"Good morning." She slipped her camera bag around her body, unzipping. "I know this is silly, but would you mind if I take your photo?"

Ren shook her head and smiled, straightening from her hunched over position. Lily stopped her.

"As you were, please." Ren resumed her position, and Lily snapped a few shots, getting closer, before she put her camera away. The other woman gestured for Lily to join her. Crossing the lawn, Lily pulled her camera bag off her shoulder, and then settled in next to Ren.

"It's quiet this morning."

Smiling, Ren checked her watch, then tugged her open coat around her belly. "For a few more minutes. All hell will break loose in about ten." She winked. "I like to take this time to prepare myself for the day. How's the shooting going?"

"Well, your husband was right. There's no shortage of places to take photos on the ranch." She chuckled, unzipping her bag to pull the camera back out. She flicked it to the 'play' setting to show Ren some of the photos she'd taken. "This tiny screen doesn't really do them justice before editing, but..." Shrugging, she handed the camera to Ren.

"Wow..." The other woman sucked in a breath as she slowly scrolled through the selection of photos Lily had taken. Some of them featured the Baylor men doing their day-to-day ranch work, some of them showcased the livestock on the ranch, and there were a few landscape shots scattered amongst photos of Ren's own children. "You truly have a talent for this, Lily."

Ren looked up, smiling, and handed the camera back. "I'd love to see the finished product. When it's ready, of course."

"Of course. You've all been so kind opening the ranch up to me. It'd be the least I can do." She was sure she'd need to source canvas prints from Denver, but she'd already decided she'd set everything up in advance for them to see the Baylor ranch through her eyes. "Your family is great, Ren, really. I mean, I knew Emma and Noah were good people, but you guys are better than my own."

The other woman's smile warmed the chill out of the fall air around them. "I can't take the credit. I was once somebody who needed a place to go, and the Baylors opened up their home to me, too."

Lily smiled and shook her head, folding over her lap to rest her elbows on her knees. "Funny how they always seem to know what it is you need. I called up Emma and she had a plan cooked up within a couple of days."

"Emma and her plans." Ren shook her head with a smile, then took a sip of her tea. The smell of the strong peppermint hung between them.

Lily nodded toward the mug.

"Morning sickness?"

"God, yes." Ren grinned. "Caught me. That's what wakes me up before everyone else. Speaking of..." The woman checked her watch again and stretched back, her belly protruding. "Gage takes forever to roll out of bed. I've got to go get him up."

Lily slipped her cell out of the front pocket on her camera bag, surprised at how much time she'd spent with the other woman. Noah and Emma were great support, but she felt her spirit quiet in Ren's presence.

"Yeah, I should get to the barn. Finn's agreed to

let me help out a little."

Ren raised a brow as she struggled to her feet. "Well, good." She paused, pressing her lips together, hesitating as Lily got up. "I know he can be a little gruff, but he's a good man. Don't let him let you think otherwise."

Word of their little run-in must have spread. Lily offered Ren a gentle smile and went down the stairs, stopping at the bottom. "Don't worry, it takes more than a little growl to scare me off."

Ren's words resonated in her mind as she crossed the yard. There was nobody around, but Finn's truck was parked in front of his cabin. Her footsteps stuttered as she scanned the yard for him, but he was nowhere in sight. She moved on to the barn, slipping into the tack room.

With her hands on her hips, she frowned at the jumble of dusty leather. It was a bigger job than her body was up to—she'd have to take her time. Do a little today, do some more tomorrow. It might even take a third day, she decided.

Rummaging through a cupboard of liniments and wound treatments for the horses, she found some leather soap and conditioner, gathered a rag and a bucket, and started working.

With her head buried in dusty leather and her back to the door, she didn't hear Finn until he spoke. "Boy, you've got 'er torn apart good."

Twisting to look over her shoulder, she saw him standing in the doorway of the room, his arms crossed over his chest.

"Good morning."

"How long have you been in here?" he asked.

"Oh..." She looked around as if for a clock but didn't find one. Her camera bag and phone were across the room. She shrugged. "Since before the kids got up for school. Twenty minutes? Half an hour? What time is it?"

He chuckled. "Eleven."

"That would explain why my stomach is grumbling." She got to her feet carefully, shifting her weight from one foot to the other to stretch out her hips. "Did you work Encore yet?"

He nodded. "I figured you slept in."

She laughed tersely. If only her body would have let her.

"I'm about to quit for lunch. You want to come? A bit early, but I've got something else planned for you this afternoon."

She raised a brow, appraising the work still left to be done in the tack room.

"I still have a lot of work left in here."

"It can wait." He nodded to the working saddles that had the least amount of dust on them. "I can still find my colt saddle, that's the important part."

She shook her head. It was the sort of job that needed a good gutting in order to put things right. It had been her first instinct to offer to help with the room, but she hadn't realized what a big job it would be until she got started at it.

"This..." she rested her fists on her hips as she looked around the room and blew out a breath. "...is going to take a while."

"Why do you think it went this long without getting done?" He laughed, and it was a good sound. It made her want to draw a bit closer. And she did, but he stepped out of the doorway to let her through, keeping a good buffer of space between them.

Together, they walked up to the big house, where Ren had a big pot of beef chili on the stove, with fresh rolls. Gage and Kerri were at school but Noah, Emma, Dane and Ren were all present, as well as Ella Baylor, who turned to greet them after depositing Gracie into her seat at the table.

The matriarch of the family held her arms out to Lily and wrapped her in a warm hug, as if they hadn't just seen one another a couple days before. The woman's embrace was comforting, a reassurance about Lily's decision to stay.

Finn pressed a kiss to her cheek. "Hey mama, I didn't expect you."

"I wasn't aware I needed to wait for an invitation." Ella raised a sharp brow at her son, her tone teasing, before she took her seat at the head of the table. Noah slid into the chair next to Emma, the one Lily had been eyeballing. There was a chair missing, and another with a booster seat and toddler strapped onto it, and as everyone fell into their typical places, she realized the only remaining seat was next to Finn. She paused for just a minute, and he glanced up, winking so quickly she thought she might have imagined it. It was an action that, in light of the newfound ease between them, made her heart skip a couple beats. She sat down.

"I was over at Nan's, she was telling me about Nate's visit," Ella explained.

"You know Nate?" Lily asked, plucking a roll out of the basket Dane handed her before passing it off to Finn.

"Everybody knows everybody around here. *And* their business." Ella laughed and Lily didn't know if her last words were a warning or not. With a stack of bowls beside her, the older woman started dishing up everyone's food. It was clear that while Ren ran the big house at the Baylor ranch, everyone ceded to mama when she came to visit. "Nate and Banks practically grew up here, like Emma. Sometimes I felt like I had a lot more than my four boys."

She hadn't known Emma and Nate when they

were children, and she was fascinated. "Tell me what little Nater was like, then."

Ella launched into tales of the boys' shenanigans as they tucked into the meal and everyone had something to add. Lily sank back in her chair and took it all in.

*

After lunch, Lily headed back to the barn but Ella motioned for Finn to hang back. He'd known he was in trouble the minute he saw his mother's car in the yard. Especially once she revealed she'd been visiting with Nan. Ella did visit often, but he knew this visit had a purpose—she was an intuitive woman and he hadn't covered his tracks well enough. She was mining for potential.

She fixed a couple mugs of coffee and motioned for the front porch, leaving Emma and Ren with the cleanup and the baby. He had more than he could manage on his plate today, including a nice little surprise he'd planned for Lily, but when mama spoke, you listened, so he took his coffee and settled in beside her on the steps looking out over the lawn and the garden Ren had been tending all summer.

"She's really nice, Finn." Ella smiled, taking a sip of her coffee.

Even though she wasn't looking, he shook his head. This wasn't something open for discussion. He barely knew what it was himself, let alone being able to articulate that to his mother. And he'd only just made up his mind that he ought not resist it so aggressively—for Lily's sake, if nothing else.

Ella Baylor was the cornerstone of the family, there was no doubt about it. And she'd been a tremendous support to Finn when he'd lost Sunny. But the last couple of years, she'd latched onto any foothold she found to encourage him to love again. *Be happy*, she said, as if it was just that easy to make the conscious decision to forget about his wife and move on.

Over the years, it had always been Ella who had pushed him out of his comfort zone, and he was usually grateful, but this was one place he'd dig his heels in. That kind of happiness only came around once in a lifetime, and it wasn't right to try to recreate it with something lackluster. Not fair to anyone involved. At least that's what he told himself.

"She's a good *client*," he underlined the word. Because that's all she was, and that's all anyone needed to know. At least until he could figure out the tangle in his head and his heart.

"Right. She's taken some lovely photos of the ranch." Ella ignored Finn's insistence, sipping her coffee. He had to hand it to her—she had a way of changing one's thinking without them even realizing it. He'd always figured it was the finest notion of horse training; you make a twelve hundred pound beast do things not through force, but by convincing them it was their idea in the first place, without them even realizing it. He had learned that from his mother, but it didn't make him immune to the tactic, even when he recognized it in play.

And she was right about the photos. What little Lily had shown him had been great. She clearly had an eye for the work that couldn't be trained or taught.

"She *is* very good. You should ask her to show you more before she leaves."

"Oh, I will." Ella's knowing smile told him she thought she had more than enough time. "But I'm not here to talk about your new 'client', honey. How are you doing?"

Finn took a sip of his coffee and shook his head.

Five years was too long to still have to be asking how he was doing. He straightened and set his coffee cup aside.

"Busy," he said, leaning to press a kiss to his mother's cheek before he got to his feet. "I actually have a pretty busy afternoon scheduled, mama."

"I know, you're always busy." She smiled up at him warmly. "But a mother can worry about her sons once in a while, can't she?"

"Nothing to worry about, I promise." He laughed, helping her to her feet.

"Alright, honey. I'll see you on the weekend."

"I'll see you."

He took the two steps off the porch and headed toward the barn, but couldn't shake his mother's knowing smile. At the end of the day, she'd known Dane loved Ren before either one of *them* had realized it, and she had been Noah's voice of reason when it came to Emma. She had a history of being in the right place at the right time to give things the nudge they needed to fall into place. And that worried him almost more than Lily's presence.

He found Lily in the same position he'd found her earlier, crouched over a dusty pile of leather. She was nothing if not a hard worker, especially considering the hitch in her getalong he'd been noticing had become more pronounced. She might have been overdoing it, but he guessed, based on what he knew of her already, she'd stick with this job until it was finished and not complain. He made a mental note to replace the overturned bucket she was sitting on with a camp chair, if nothing else. He sure as hell wasn't going to get her to give it a rest for a couple days.

"Come with me a minute."

She quirked a brow at him but got up, doing the same careful stretch he'd seen her do earlier. He suspected her physical issues were deeper than she suggested, but she kept quiet.

"I'm never going to finish at this rate."

"You have lots of time for that," he said as he laughed, stepping past her to grab his colt training saddle and a bridle with a snaffle bit she'd hung on the wall. It was time to treat her with the standard Baylor hospitality they were known for, whether he was conflicted inside or not. "But you only have ten minutes to get ready to ride."

-THIRTEEN-

There would have been a time when Lily would have jumped at the opportunity to ride. Today, her heart jack-hammered in her chest at the prospect. She would have told him no, but Finn was already at the other end of the barn, pulling a horse out. She slipped out of the tack room and then out of the barn to get some air. She'd actually brought all of her gear because Emma had promised they'd ride together. And that had been okay. Because she could fail in front of Emma—she'd done it enough times. But riding with Finn meant she could fail in front of someone who didn't already know her weaknesses intimately. And trying to put him off meant she'd have to admit she was afraid, and she wasn't ready for that.

There were a lot of ways her body didn't work how it used to, and that was the most fearsome. Then, there was re-injury. She couldn't go back to crutches or a cane; she wanted *that* chapter of her life to be closed until she was old and gray.

After a few minutes, she steadied her breathing and went back into the barn, pulling her lightweight helmet out of the bag. At the end of the aisle, Finn and a big, shark-withered gray horse waited, already saddled. She wasn't sure if her ten minutes had already passed.

"You've met Buckshot?"

"Gage has told me about him," she said,

smiling. There didn't seem to be a person on the ranch who didn't have a good memory of the old horse. Even Emma had a comical tale about a barrel racing bet against Noah in which Buckshot starred. She reached out to stroke the horse's nose. "He's a bit of a celebrity around here, isn't he?"

"He's played a pretty big part in everybody's lives, that's for sure. We'll miss him when he's gone." His adam's apple bobbed as he swallowed hard, and a rare softness crossed Finn's face as he stroked the horse's neck. "I'm convinced he'll live forever."

"I get that. I'm pretty sure Encore will, too. Especially after the accident. I have Nate to thank for that, though. He was about the only person who stood by my decision when everyone else thought I should put him down."

Finn absorbed her words, one corner of his mouth tipping up when she mentioned Nate.

"You know, I thought you were Nate's girl when you showed up."

"Nate? No." Nearly choking on her laughter, Lily shook her head. "Don't get me wrong, I love the man. He's been a good friend. But we are *not* compatible like that. He's more like a brother to me."

More than her own brother, even. Her family had never really been into horses or the rodeo; she'd found her own way there, so there was no common ground. Nate had encouraged her to step outside of her comfort zone, and it was because of him she'd had opportunities to try cattle penning and barrel racing, and even a laughably terrible attempt at roping. He was her go-to when she needed advice, or an unbiased opinion, or a cold beer and a long talk. She'd seen every shade of doubt in his eyes during Encore's recovery, but he had also been the one who connected her with Emma when Encore was ready for rehab.

"Same," Finn said. "It's strange we've never crossed paths before."

"Oh, you know, Denver is a pretty long haul," she teased. The easy banter between them was strange, but welcome. She had no idea what had made him change his mind, but she thanked whatever deity was listening that they were making some headway, especially if she was going to be here for a while. And more than slowly building a bridge between two of them, their small talk helped to calm the burst of butterflies that had been flittering around in her stomach since he'd announced she'd be riding.

*

"Why don't we get started?" he asked, his voice gentle. She let out a breath and nodded, and he unhooked Buckshot from the cross-ties and led the way to the round pen.

"Do you trust me?" Finn asked Lily as she closed the gate behind them.

"No," she said flatly. He laughed, but ignored the sentiment.

"You know Buckshot's our babysitter. So you'll have a chance to figure out how to sit, how to use your body in this role again, and he won't move a muscle." He guessed that was the main issue here— any length of time away from riding meant those muscles you used in the saddle needed some gentle reminding when you got back into it—and adding injury only made it worse.

She let out a breath, her fingers twisted together in front of her as she looked at the horse. "Okay."

"There's no reason why this won't work, Lily."

The straps of her helmet swung around her ears as she looked back at the horse one more time and nodded to herself. His first instinct had been to rib her about the helmet a little bit—he'd never worn one and he'd gotten through thirty years just fine—but it was clearly something important to her, so he'd reconsidered. By his estimation, that flimsy little brain bucket wouldn't do much if she decided to fall off, but he still found himself reaching out to buckle it under her chin. She stopped moving, drawing in a breath as the backs of his fingers brushed her jawline.

They'd barely touched one another since she'd arrived, but the little shock of electricity that passed between them now was undeniable. He was an effective communicator when it came to his work with the horses but apparently, he got his signals all mixed up with women. In the ring with a horse, you couldn't let your emotions control your actions—they'd pick up on it in a heartbeat—so you played your cards close to your vest. Consistency was the key when it came to horse training, and he couldn't seem to get his emotions under control enough to be consistent when it came to Lily.

But now he was more nervous than she looked, and he could only attribute that to the fact he cared too much, already; he admired her pluck and courage, she had a hell of a poker face, and he was getting used to having her around. It was one thing for him, with his long legs and years of experience, to sit a challenging ride, but it was an entirely different thing for a girl with half a hardware store bolted to her bone structure to stick with anything aside from a little plod around the ring. While Buckshot was pretty much bombproof by nature, anything could happen with a 1200lb creature with a mind of its own. He nodded toward the saddle, though the part of him that tugged at the stubborn tilt of her chin wanted to tell her to take the horse back to the barn, just to be safe. "You ready?"

Letting out a swift breath through her lips, she nodded, reaching for the horn and cantle of the saddle.

She lifted her left foot to lever herself into the saddle but came up short. The grimace on her face told him she didn't have the range of motion in her hip to get her foot into the high stirrup on the tall horse, never mind the stability to torque her body up onto the horse even if she *could* get her foot into it.

"We can put him up to the fence, if you want." Finn said, quietly. Though there wasn't another soul around to see it, she was blushing. A little sweat had broken out over her pretty features; in the chill of the fall air, he knew it wasn't because of overexertion. "Or I can give you a lift."

Without turning to look at him, she shook her head, staring down the fender of the saddle as if it owed her. "No. I can do this."

She couldn't, but he wouldn't say that out loud to her. He had a feeling there was little in life she ever admitted she couldn't do. She had, after all, healed broken bones, and a broken horse, by sheer force of will alone.

But it was painful to watch her try again. She was close, her toe hitting the bottom of the stirrup but unable to get into it. Finally he stepped sideways, curled his arm around her leg, grasped her ankle, and rooted his shoulder under her bottom, hoisting her up and into the saddle before she had a chance to decline his help.

The look she gave him from atop the horse was a perfect blend of bewildered, embarrassed, and grateful. She slipped her feet into the stirrups, and gathered up the reins, then closed her eyes and let out a long, slow breath. With each second of her exhalation, a soft smile grew. When she opened her eyes again, she looked at peace.

"Ready?" he asked, smoothing his palm over the horse's neck. The big gelding had been a rock while she'd tried to mount up, just as he'd expected. Buckshot was his go-to horse for anyone who needed a little safe confidence boost; he always came through. Finn turned so he could walk backwards and watch her as he led the horse the first couple of steps. She sat straight, but jerked like she'd been burnt when the horse took his first easy step forward.

"Whoa." Finn spoke and the horse stopped. "You okay?"

"Better than ever." The smile that slanted over her lips was not the same as the one she'd flashed him before she'd mounted up. Not nearly as sincere.

"Does anything hurt?"

*

Lily considered the question, taking a mental inventory of her body parts the way she had almost every day since the accident. She wiggled her toes in her boots, and tilted her pelvis. There was soreness—there had been since she'd started sleeping on Emma and Noah's couch—but nothing she couldn't handle. Her pain tolerance had changed dramatically in the last year.

"No more than normal."

"Good." Finn turned his back to her, urging the horse back into motion. He checked back with her every few strides, and they made a couple of laps around the round pen. He kept a hand on the chin strap of the bridle the entire time, and while she wanted to make a comment about how she'd outgrown pony rides, she was grateful for that extra little bit of security.

It took more time than she expected to convince her hips to relax into the gentle movement of the horse's walk, but before long, her body was fluid, the way she wanted it. And then Finn turned to walk backwards, tipping his head down in an unasked question. Pressing her lips together, she drew in a breath and nodded.

His hand dropped to his side and he took a step in toward the middle of the round pen, and she was on her own. The gelding plodded along like nothing had changed, but for Lily, everything had.

"He's fine to direct rein," Finn reassured her, backing off until he was several feet away. He was telling her the horse could be steered without the use of her legs if necessary, but she knew the better way was to ride with her seat. Consciously, she pushed her heels down, imagining her legs long and draped down the horse's side. And then she attempted to apply pressure to his side with her right calf. Buckshot bent around her leg, moving away from the pressure. Feeling a rush of relief, Lily smiled, and looked to Finn. His own smile told her she hadn't imagined her body had actually worked the way she expected it to.

"The other direction?" Finn asked, circling a finger in the air to indicate she turn. She reined the gelding around and pressed her left leg to his side. The gelding hardly flinched. It was the first time she'd really noticed the weakness and she frowned. It wasn't painful, just not effective. Frustrating. "Okay, try and bend him again?"

"I'm trying." She could feel her face reddening. If she couldn't ride a sensitive school horse effectively, how would she ever ride Encore?

She wouldn't. The certainty echoed in her heart, more terrifying than the fear she could never ride again. If she couldn't ride Encore, none of this was worth it. Swallowing tears, she scolded herself for being unrealistic. She was lucky to walk, being able to ride was otherworldly—she'd proven her mother wrong—but she had her heart set on an idea of perfect she might not ever accomplish.

"Lily?"

She glanced at Finn, concern forming two lines between his eyebrows that she could see even through the glaze of tears in her eyes.

"Are you okay?" he asked, that same gentle note in his voice as when he'd thought about Buckshot in the barn. She could barely stand it when it was directed at her.

She sniffed, slipping both reins into one hand so she could swipe at her eyes. It was bittersweet. They'd thought maybe she'd have trouble *walking*, and here she was riding, defying odds... just not the odds she wanted to defy. She hated that she'd failed in front of Finn, and hated that it had brought tears to her eyes.

"Yeah."

"What's wrong? Are you hurting?" He stepped toward Buckshot and she shook her head, holding her hand out to stop him. She'd had enough pity to last the rest of her life over the last year. That wasn't what she wanted right now.

"It's fine, I'm just weak. The physical therapist mentioned it. I don't know why I thought it would be different."

"Well, can we build it up?"

She glanced at him and saw a man more invested than he ought to be. He was talking about a lot more than just the work she was paying him to do with Encore. She pressed her lips together and shrugged.

"I don't know."

"I mean, we could make you an appointment

with Dr. Fields and see if he could refer you while you're here."

"That's thoughtful, but it's fine." She tried to enjoy the fact that she was just sitting astride a horse but the realization that her body had betrayed her sucked all the joy out of it. Steering the gelding to the middle of the ring, she stopped in front of Finn. There was no sense in continuing.

"Do you think you could be weaker because you're so sore?" he asked next. She wanted to tell him it wasn't any of his business and that she'd make do. That's what she'd been doing for the last year. Making do, adjusting her lifestyle to fit her limitations, and deflecting pity.

"I don't know." Pressing her lips together, she put all her focus into swinging her right leg over the horse's back and dismounting. Normally, she'd jump clear, but not sure what the shock of impact would do, she held on, sliding her body down the side of the saddle. Her feet dangling in the air, she felt Finn's hand on her back, his palm warming her skin even through the layers of clothes she wore. Finally, she found herself on the ground, too close to him.

She managed just fine if she kept her distance, but when their bodies got within a couple feet of one another, she felt an inexplicable warmth, a magnetic draw that should have been a deflection based on how their relationship had progressed. But he'd been kind to try to help her ride. He was trying to be kind now.

"I have a spare room, you know. I mean, until you can get something worked out at Nan's."

"Oh...Noah called her. I guess one of her grandsons has a guest staying in that apartment." She shook her head, offering him a smile as she unbuckled her helmet. "I'll deal."

The truth was that the softness of Finn she was seeing was too much, too enticing. He was a man with a history, with a wife he hadn't moved on from. And she was a resilient woman, but she wasn't strong enough for that.

-FOURTEEN-

FINN rounded the corner of the barn and headed for the round pen. It was mid-morning and he hadn't gotten to Encore yet. He liked to get the gelding out of the way as early on as possible so he could try to compartmentalize Lily and all the feelings he had about her being here. This way he didn't have to sort them out, he could be distracted for the morning and then move on.

She was there, this morning. Leaning over the rail of the round pen watching Encore eat a flake of hay. Her back was to him so she didn't see him approaching, and she was talking on her cell phone. His step faltered for a moment, torn between the idea of giving her some privacy and knowing his day was already running behind and was about to get further so.

"Yes, I still want to ride." Lily's voice was tight and thick, like she was holding back tears. Finn pressed his lips together and went to the gate of the pen, making noise with the chain that held it shut to signal his presence. When she looked over, he lifted a hand in greeting and she swiped at her cheek. Maybe not holding back those tears after all.

"Mom, I can't have this conversation right now. Finn is here to work with Encore. I love you. Bye." Her words were so close together, he could tell she was offering no room for conversation as she swiftly disconnected the call. She shook her head as she directed her gaze to him, a crooked smile tipping her lips. "Twenty six years old and I still feel like I'm fourteen sometimes."

He chuckled, still paused at the gate. "Thirty this year and my own mama can make me feel the same way."

Lily's chest rose with a silent laugh, and she slid her phone into her pocket. "So what's on the agenda for today?"

"Well, I could use a hand."

"Oh? I'm not supposed to be watching, even, nevermind helping." She raised a brow in his direction but her tone was teasing.

"Yeah, yeah." If he was truthful, he'd never had a client for a problem horse so invested in his success, so clearly attached to the final outcome. Usually by the time horses like this landed on the Baylor ranch, there was an ultimatum to fix them or send them up the road. But Encore was different. She'd already stood by him for the year it had taken him to come right physically, he had a feeling she'd stand with him til the bitter end, no matter what the outcome. "I changed my mind. Wait here."

He jogged back into the barn, grabbing his colt training saddle from the tack room. They didn't make them like this anymore. The saddle was almost as old as he was, and well-constructed; designed to take a beating, just in case an unruly young horse decided to roll on it or try to scrape it off on the round pen rails. Holding it by the horn, he braced the skirt of it against his hip and grabbed a wool saddle pad from a standing rack. She'd gotten a lot of work done in the tack room, but she still had some parts to organize. He kept taking her away from her work and she'd be here forever.

When he emerged from the barn for the second time, Encore had finished cleaning up all the leftover hay. Lily leaned on her hip against the rail of the pen, but he could see the stiffness in her when she straightened.

"You're gonna ride my horse?" she asked, incredulously.

"Let's not get ahead of ourselves, here." He laughed, swinging the saddle up onto the top rail, and then unknotted the lead rope that had been hanging from the gate for transporting horses back and forth between the pen and the barn. "We'll saddle him up and see how he does."

*

He was crazy, that was all there was to it. But she'd go along. This would be tangible progress. She'd watched him send the horse around the pen, but it was hard to discern if what was happening was good, bad or none of the above, since she had no experience with it and they weren't working on a specific behavior, but an entire mindset. Finn seemed to know exactly what a horse would think before it even thought it, and despite her long history with Encore, she was completely oblivious to the state of the horse's mind these days.

Encore came to the fence with his ears forward. Clearly, the cowboy had cemented a good relationship with the horse, and when she thought of the other offers to 'break' him she'd had, she was grateful for Emma's suggestion.

"Hey, buddy," Finn breathed quietly, rubbing a hand over the broad spot on his forehead. The horse whickered, and dropped his head. Movement on the other side of Finn caught Lily's eye, and suddenly, the gelding was chewing, a treat crunching between his flat molars.

"You've been bribing my horse!" she accused with a laugh.

Finn's hand dropped from where he'd been

rubbing Encore and his shoulders lifted in a shrug. "You get more flies with honey."

"What would the old cowboys say?"

"They'd say it's stupid to get your boots wet crossing the river when the bridge is right there." He smiled, and stepped back, letting himself into the round pen with the horse. "Give me a minute to see where his brain is."

Finn sent Encore around the pen, the same as she'd seen him do before. It never got old, watching the way the horse responded to the slightest change in Finn's body; or maybe just watching the way the cowboy's lean figure shifted. There was something about the subtle, long muscle of a man who used his body every day for work, and she guessed, by the slice of skin she'd seen at his abdomen when he'd lifted the saddle onto the rail and his long sleeved tee lifted ever-so-slightly, Finn Baylor was no exception. She tightened her jaw and tried to focus on the horse. So far, she'd seen him only walk and jog, switching directions, changing the size of his circle. Today, Finn stepped in toward his hip and the horse shifted up a gear into a long legged, fluid lope.

Lily loved that lope. She watched for a minute, and then closed her eyes, savoring the sound of the rhythmic three-beat gait. She could almost remember how it felt under her, a rocking horse canter that was easy to ride and barely jostled her. It was their favorite speed on the mossy flat terrain they normally trained on. Drawing a long breath in, she released it through her nose, feeling every nerve in her body that had been wound so tight since the accident begin to loosen.

When she opened her eyes again, they came into focus on Finn. As prickly as he was, she was grateful she'd walked into his life and chosen to stay. It had taken some time to smooth the rocky relations between the two of them, but they were at least cordial now.

Finn let the horse slow to a walk, and then closed down his body language so Encore would approach. The smile on the cowboy's face told her it was successful, though it looked the way all the other sessions had; like a dance between man and horse, only she didn't know the steps and couldn't hear the music.

"Next step. Come on in, Lily."

She bent and slid through the rails of the round pen. Encore's ears pricked forward, and she smiled.

"You don't look half bad, buddy," she told the horse, smoothing a hand over his neck. He was barely heated up. The work Finn had been doing with him was slowly, but surely, bringing his physical fitness back.

"I'm impressed," Finn said, his voice close at her ear. "With those scars, you'd guess he'd be sore, or short stride, or something. I gotta say, the team you had working on him did one hell of a job."

She nodded, swallowing, but didn't look back at him yet. How many times had she been told she was wasting her time? How grateful had she been when they'd taken him in at Renegade Racing and Emma had started with the hyperbaric chamber and water therapy? She'd made referrals to chiropractors and massage therapists that had helped make his body work again. It was a long road, and she'd been grateful for the team that had stood beside her; namely Emma, Noah, and Nate.

"They're the best. When I got to Renegade, your sister-in-law was as much of an advocate for him as I had been all along." It had been nice to be able to back off and let someone else be aggressive about the horse's treatment. It allowed Lily to focus on her own healing; physically, anyway.

"Emma can be a bulldog." She heard the smile in his face, and when she glanced up, a crooked grin graced his features. She hadn't seen him looking happy since she showed up; and she couldn't say it was this moment that had made him happy, but it was interesting to see the way his handsome face lit, the corners of his eyes crinkling with laugh lines; testament that at *some* point, Finn Baylor had been a happy man. "Anyway...you ready?"

He lifted the looped up lead rope he'd been holding and she took it from him, snapping the rope to Encore's halter.

"I'm assuming you know the rule; if anything happens, let go."

She laughed and shook her head. "In the woods, letting go means you have a long walk back to your trailer."

Or worse, a lost horse. A nightmare she'd never had to endure, but she'd had experience helping other riders search. Best case scenarios, gear got caught in brush somewhere near the edge of the trail and the horse waited until someone came to get them. Worst case was... worse than her accident.

"You're crazy," he laughed, shaking his head. "But for serious, let go if anything happens."

"Nothing will happen," she said with more confidence in her voice than she felt in her whole body. She petted Encore's nose while Finn went for the saddle.

Riding competitive distance, she'd long ago abandoned cumbersome western saddles, and she still couldn't put her finger on why anyone would want to lug one of the giant beasts around. Shrugging, she held Encore while, with one swing, Finn settled the saddle onto his back as though it was as light as air. Clearly, with his height and build, he wasn't as overwhelmed as she tended to get, trying to maneuver tack onto the tall horse's back.

Encore shifted his weight, his eyes widening as Finn worked around him. He expelled a long, loud breath and Lily took a step back, but rested her hand on his muzzle gently. "Easy, buddy."

Finn paused as he pulled the latigo through the saddle's girth, then checked with the horse, gauging his reaction. "You're alright, brother."

He looped the leather strap twice, then a third time, with the girth hanging loose around the horse's barrel, then slowly began to tighten it. Without warning, Encore dropped his head, jerking the rope out of Lily's hands, let out a grunt, and set off bucking like the best bronc stock she'd seen at the Denver rodeos. Suddenly, his hind hooves were so close to her face, she could feel a rift of moving air, and then she was being plowed over, pushed quickly to the edge of the round pen while she watched her horse root his head and lift his hind end over and over while he tore around the sand footing. Even from across the pen, she could see the whites of his eyes. Finn stood behind her while she slipped to safety between the rails of the pen, and then followed her. The girth got looser with every buck until, almost in slow motion, the saddle slipped off over his hind quarters and landed in a heap in the middle of the pen, dust billowing up around it.

Her heart racing, Lily braced with both hands against the rough rail of the fence, trying to calm her harsh breathing and her spinning head.

"Shit." She felt Finn's hand on her shoulder, his touch light, and suddenly, she found the ground again. Releasing a long, slow breath, she straightened a little, hoping he would keep that point of contact. She felt the warmth in his palm through the thin fabric of her long sleeved tee and it comforted her. "I'm so sorry. I didn't... I should have saddled him myself, first."

A hard lump three quarters of the way up her raw throat formed a dam for the words she wanted to say. In that moment, she had seen not only Encore bucking a blue streak across the pen, but been back inside that moment a year and a half ago, with Encore on his side in a ditch, the rigging on his saddle caught up in some alders. He was struggling, his long legs paddling the air and finding no purchase. There was blood everywhere, the air filled with screams she didn't know the origin of, and so much excruciating pain. It had been difficult to separate the accident from the present.

"Hey." Finn ducked under her arm and tried to catch her eyes and without thinking a second more about their business arrangement, Lily anchored herself with her arms around his neck and he eased her into his grip. It was only once his arms were around her that she let her rigid body relax, pressing her face against his shoulder. One of his hands drifted a lazy pace up and down the middle of her back, soothing. "You're alright."

But she wasn't. She had been protecting herself from this very thing, and while she'd thought she'd be able to completely avoid it by having a professional work with her horse, it was clear she couldn't go over, under, or around the trauma. She'd have to go straight through. At least she had company.

-FIFTEEN-

IT wasn't until later, when he'd safely delivered Lily to Noah and gotten Encore put away and everything cleaned up that Finn's hands started shaking. It had been a close call. Too damn close. He'd let his guard down, gotten a little cocky, and Lily had nearly had to pay the price. He couldn't get the image of flying hooves just narrowly missing her face out of his head.

It was the time of night he'd normally sit in his recliner and watch the news until he dozed off, but he couldn't sit still. His whole body buzzed with the adrenaline dump and he paced a square between the kitchen, dining area and living room. Almost worse than the fear he felt was the memory of the way her body felt pressed against his, and the feelings that stirred up. Rubbing one hand on the back of his neck to try to calm the trembling, he made a ninety degree turn at his kitchen table and walked straight out the door to his pickup parked out front.

Daylight waned; the days had become shorter and the nights got crisp a lot quicker than they used to. He turned the key in the ignition and the old truck roared to life. There were still pieces of every single day that made him think of Sunny, including the F150. She'd helped him pick it off the lot the summer before they'd married. Dane had traded in his truck twice since, but Finn just kept fixing the problems and running his because if he let himself relax enough, he could still see Sunny in the passenger's seat on the way home from the dealership, the window down, her long blonde hair whipping in the wind, and her laughter carrying through the main street shops of Three Rivers. He couldn't relax enough for that right now, but the thought of her put a knot the size of a bowling ball right at the bottom of his gut. *Go back in the house,* he told himself.

"Screw it," he muttered, jamming the truck into drive and making a wide turn in the yard.

The drive to the cabin Noah had built wasn't long enough for him to change his mind, but then when his headlights swept over a form huddled on their steps, he couldn't have gone back anyways. His brother's truck was nowhere in sight; the newlyweds often hit Hinkley's for dinner or went to the next town over's little steakhouse. He pulled in, put the truck in park and opened the door, sliding out. Lily lifted her head and her hand in greeting. As he got closer, he saw she was wrapped in a big cable-knit sweater with Tucker curled up at her side.

"Hey. I came to make sure you were okay." He crossed the space between them and squeezed himself onto the steps on the other side of Tucker. The pup groaned in complaint, shifted to try and get comfortable again, and then finally vacated to a lower step.

Lily straightened, then leaned back, stretching. "That's nice, but I'm fine."

He watched her for a second, sensing words she hadn't said. That was probably how she'd convinced Noah and Emma to leave. He knew she was way more shaken up than she let on. "You seemed pretty shaken up earlier."

"Yeah, that's just...I don't know. I do that sometimes."

She'd completely shut down, frozen in place, and then, after he'd moved her out of the way of Encore's furious feet, she'd doubled over against the fence, drawing huge, gasping breaths like she'd run a marathon unprepared. It scared the shit out of him, so he'd done the only thing he could think to do when someone looked like they were shattering to pieces—hold her together. He couldn't imagine experiencing that kind of reaction once, never mind with enough frequency that you recognized it as something that happened 'sometimes.'

He leaned over with his elbows on his knees and looked straight ahead into the failing daylight, clasping his hands together. He wasn't convinced he'd held her hard enough to put those pieces together again but this didn't feel like the right place, especially with Sunny's memory so close at hand, and his motivations still unclear even to himself. They had a business relationship. She clearly had some sort of issue, and he was too fragile himself. And she'd be gone after they worked through her horse's problems. Back to Denver, to her job, and her family.

The quiet stretched out between them, disturbed only by the sound of the quiet breaths she took, until he heard her move and felt her hip bump against his. A second later, he felt her head on his shoulder.

*

Lily was hard pressed to keep her eyelids from drooping closed, especially once Finn got close. Those little 'episodes' she experienced from time to time drained her both physically and emotionally, and his big, warm body right there was hard to resist. It drew her like a magnet.

He didn't say a lot, but that was alright—how she preferred it, in fact. The slew of questions and concern that usually followed when someone witnessed her meltdowns, as she called them, was almost as exhausting as the event itself. No, she didn't know why she'd sweat and stutter and have flashbacks. She didn't know if she was okay. She couldn't articulate what someone could do to help her, even if she knew what it was she needed.

What Finn had done *had* helped, though. Somehow telling her she was alright instead of asking if she was had been reassurance, and when he'd closed his arms around her, she'd never felt safer.

She felt him shift under her cheek, and she thought, based on his hot-cold behavior since she'd arrived, this might be when he put her out. Instead, he shifted back, sliding his arm around her shoulders and arranging their bodies to draw her closer. She was aware of every part of him, from the warmth of his skin seeping through the rough denim fabric under her fingers, to the hard muscle of a man who worked long days, down to the faint smell of leather and horse that clung to him. It soothed her.

"Can you tell me what happened, Lily?"

For the first time since the round pen, she drew in a breath that felt like it filled her lungs, and let it out slowly. Her story came with it.

"We were prepping for a 50 mile race, but it had been so wet, all my woods trails were swamped, so we used the road." She felt his grip tighten around her. She could stop, if she wanted; that was the message she got. But she kept on—she owed him the truth. What had happened today with Encore proved it—he needed all the details if he was going to stay safe while working through the horse's issues. Already raw and vulnerable, it wouldn't hurt that much more. "I always wear high vis clothes so I can be seen, but the driver was texting. We were almost home. I checked behind me when I heard her and she was drifting toward the shoulder. We had nowhere to go.

"She saw us and had time to brake but she still hit us. I told you it pushed Encore out from under me and I landed on the bumper. The next thing I remember, I came to and they were strapping me to a stretcher."

She paused. When she stopped, Finn's hand made a slow trek up and down her bicep, soothing. She'd never gotten this far through the story; it usually stopped here, and picked up again at the hospital, where she could rehash the details with the same sorts of clinical terms the doctors had used. Finn's gentle touch was all the encouragement she needed. And he deserved to know why she'd insisted on staying, why she couldn't just give leave Encore and hope he came back a changed horse.

"There was blood all over the place, and he was in the ditch and couldn't get up. I wouldn't let them put me in the ambulance until Nate showed up with the vet, and I made him promise they would save my horse. I owe him everything for that."

The pain and fear were as close as they had been in the round pen, as close as they'd been on the day of the accident, but with his arm around her, they couldn't touch her.

"They cut the rigging on my saddle to get him out of the ditch. It was tangled in some alders—" She stopped, and straightened, looking up at Finn as it dawned on her. "Do you suppose that's why he went nuts today? He hasn't even been saddled since then."

Finn considered, tipping his head toward her. His features were soft, and sad, like the way he'd looked when he'd caught her looking at the photo of his wife.

"It's possible..." He cut his words off when the headlights of Noah's pick up slid over them. She half expected him to push her away. He straightened and let his arm slide down her arm, until he was no longer holding her, despite how close they still sat. She heard him draw in a breath he held for two beats, and then let out in one long, slow release. Though he'd been completely at ease just seconds before, this was clearly uncomfortable for him. He'd supported her through her discomfort, so she could do the same. Lily lifted her head, straightening and putting a bit of space between them. So it didn't look quite like what it had been. So Finn wouldn't have to answer to Noah and Emma's prying looks and questions.

The truck pulled into park between Finn's pick up and Emma's car and the couple climbed out. Tucker got up off the step to greet them, his stubby tail-wiggling spreading to his whole body.

"Hey!" Emma called out. "I thought you'd be in bed by now."

"Yeah, we were just talking about Encore, and the new plan of attack for working with him," Lily told her. Normally, she *would* be tucked in on the couch. Emma and Noah usually went to bed early, too, for the sake of getting up and getting work done in the morning. She would have been there now, if she hadn't gotten caught up in the warm embrace of this delicious-smelling man. She felt safe, and comfortable, for the first time in longer than she could remember.

"You get something figured out?"

"We'll keep working until we get it figured out," Finn said with a note of determination, then rose to his feet. Lily felt the loss of his body heat deeper than just at skin level. She wrapped her arms around herself and leaned forward in much the same posture she'd been when Finn had found her. "I don't wanna keep you folks up; I'm going to head home."

He made no motion to leave, but stood at the bottom of the stairs.

"You guys go on, I'll be right in. Still settling my nerves." Lily offered Noah a reassuring smile, but his gaze had flickered between Finn and Lily a half dozen times. Emma might have missed it, but her husband had definitely seen Lily all tangled up in Finn when they pulled in.

"Have a good night," Noah said, looking hard again at his brother for a moment before he and Emma maneuvered past Lily on the stairs, then tapped his thigh for Tucker to follow them into the house.

She looked up at Finn when they were alone again. His tight jaw and furrowed brow were visible in the light from the windows of the cabin as Emma and Noah moved through it.

"You know my offer still stands."

She raised a brow, pressing her palms together between her knees until her fingers went numb. He tucked his hands in his pockets, and the quiet sank between them like a stone.

"I have a spare bedroom, and you have a need for it." He shrugged. "It's the least I can do after what I let happen to you."

-SIXTEEN-

FINN heard Noah's truck pull up in front of the cabin and took one last glance around the insides. He'd spent most of the night occupied with thoughts of what Lily might think of his home. For a long time, maybe too long, it had been his sanctuary, the place he could sit and think of his wife. Oh, he'd had company since Sunny's body had vacated—Noah, sleeping it off on the couch; Dane, during foaling season, so he didn't disturb Ren—but it wasn't quite the same. And while her *body* had vacated the home, he still shared it with every part of Sunny's spirit. She'd never been much for decorating, but there were a few things she'd put in place that he couldn't bring himself to move or get rid of. The rainbow colored decorative dish towels hanging over the handle of the oven door, for one. And that damn rooster tea kettle. He remembered the day she brought it home like it was yesterday. It was ugly, he'd protested, they'd settled it with a round of long, slow love-making in the middle of the kitchen floor.

By the time he pulled himself out of the memories and out the door onto the porch, Noah was shouldering a duffle bag and Lily was climbing down out of the truck with a laptop case and her camera bag. He wiped his palms—sweaty, like a teenager on his first date—on the thighs of his jeans and tried to strike a nonchalant pose against one of the supporting beams of the covered porch.

A sweet smile broke over Lily's features when their eyes met and Finn's doubts disappeared. She had resisted on this, hard, but he could tell she was relieved. Between the riding, which he'd promised himself they wouldn't try again until she was feeling better physically, and the episode with Encore the day before, she could use a little bit of relaxation. And his place was quiet, because that's how he liked it—lots of opportunity for her to edit photos, and sleep in without being woken by what she'd dubbed the 'Tucker Tongue Alarm.'

It was a stretch for him to invite another woman into his home. Especially one he cared even a little about—nix that, this was the first time he'd cared enough for it to hit his radar; even if he had no business caring about her. She'd come here for a business relationship. Sure, she'd been aggressive about having a cordial working relationship, but that didn't mean she was going to climb out of her bed and into his in the night.

That thought stopped him in his tracks. Maybe his mother had been right, maybe he should have started pursuing relationships before he'd been a widower for nearly half a decade. He cleared his throat, shifting as Lily and Noah made their way up the three steps onto the porch with him. He pushed the door open and held it for them.

"Come on in," he said, watching Lily's reaction. He'd never felt self-conscious about the little house before, but suddenly, he felt like he was under a microscope. Could she see how much sorrow he'd wallowed in here? Would she be able to tell it had only been eighteen months ago he'd started sleeping through the nights? "It's not fancy, but here it is."

"It's the Ritz compared to our place," Noah

insisted just as his phone ringer started to go off. He pulled a face and handed the duffle bag to Finn. "This is Mama, we've got an inventory shipment. You'll be alright?" He made eye contact and dipped his chin in Lily's direction and she nodded back. As quickly as he'd showed up, Noah left, the screen door falling shut behind him. And then they were alone. It was terrifying and thrilling all at once.

"I appreciate it, fancy or not," Lily said as she took in her surroundings. He tried to imagine what she was seeing, what she was thinking, as her eyes passed over the inside of the cabin.

It was a small spot; he'd always intended to expand on it when they had the time and money, but now he didn't have the need. The front part was open concept; living room to the left, with a love seat, a recliner, and the television. To the immediate right, the small eat-in kitchen with appliances lined up against the walls. The decor was sparse and rustic, exposed beam and barn board. The back half of the cabin housed the bedrooms, a short hall, and a small bathroom. A larger master bedroom that wasn't terribly spacious once you considered the queen bed and the dresser, and then the smaller room.

It had been intended as a nursery. It had been converted into an at-home hospice room when they'd told them there was nothing else they could do for Sunny but make her comfortable. She wasn't comfortable, and neither was he; sleeping in a separate room had been itchy and strange and he'd ended up sitting up in a chair beside her bed most nights. Sometimes in the bed with her. Eventually, she'd insisted he go back to the bedroom, but he slept light as a feather, waking every time he heard her shift or sigh in her sleep.

He crossed the main house with a few strides

and pushed open the guest room door for her. "This is the spare room."

After they'd removed the rented hospital bed, Ella and Caine had furnished it with a small double bed, a dresser, and a desk, erasing any notion of what it had been intended to be or what it had been in its lifetime, and that was exactly how it stood now.

"Oh, this is great," Lily said, brushing past him so close he could smell her shampoo when she went. She deposited her laptop and camera on the desk and turned back to him for the duffle bag.

"Make yourself at home," he said, even though she'd clearly already started to. "You want a coffee?"

*

"Sure," Lily said, tucking her hands in her back pockets as she let her eyes wander over the interior of the room. It wasn't decorated like anything; maybe it had been a guest room all along. She drew in a big breath and then let it go. She could hardly wait to sprawl out on her stomach on the bed, and she was grateful Finn had insisted. It had become so second nature to refuse help and try to do things on her own she'd forgotten what it felt like to let someone else care.

It took her all of five minutes to unpack her bag of clothes and shove them into the drawer, and Finn was just pouring coffee into a pair of mugs on the table when she poked her head out the door.

It didn't take her long to cross the cabin into the kitchen; the place was tiny, not unlike Emma and Noah's. Finn moved through the small space of the kitchen, ferrying a sugar bowl and a carton of coffee cream between the counter and the table.

She paused at the stove, her eyes immediately drawn to the brightly colored tea towels and a chipped enameled tea kettle. It was white with a bright red spray of molded feathers for a handle and the spout was the open mouthed head of a rooster, as if he was crowing. Reaching out, she ran her fingertips over it, a small smile manifesting as she thought about Finn using it.

She noticed first that he'd stopped moving, and when her eyes flicked from the rooster to the man, he was standing almost next to her, looking at her like she had two heads.

"I didn't peg you as the rooster tea kettle sort," she said, filling the loaded silence between them with an attempt at humor.

He cleared his throat, taking some time to draw his eyes away from her. "It was my wife's."

Self-conscious, she jerked her hand back and crossed it over her midsection. "Sorry."

"No reason to be sorry," Finn said, his tone unreadable as he nodded toward the table where the coffee was waiting. "Truth is, I don't know why I keep that old thing around. I never use it. And it's a lousy decoration."

"No, it's cute," she insisted, taking a seat at the table. She stirred a couple of spoonsful of sugar and a dollop of cream into her coffee, noting Finn took his black.

"Do I look like the kind of man who keeps stuff around because it's cute?"

She couldn't tell if he was teasing or not, but she still smiled. "Well, your niece and nephew are pretty darn cute and you keep *them* around. Aaaand you haven't given me walking papers yet, even though I thought you might at the beginning. So yes. Yes, Finn Baylor, you seem like the kind of guy who keeps stuff around 'because it's cute' and there's nothing wrong with that."

Though it looked like he tried to stop it, a slow

smile curled one corner of his lips. It made Lily's heart quicken and she tried to mask it by taking a sip of her coffee. He'd put a great deal of effort into the gruff exterior she'd seen, right up until they'd made peace. And even now, he tended to the tougher side. But the glimpses of his softness melted any hard feelings she might have harbored for the way he'd treated her earlier.

"Shit, you're right about those kids." His smile grew stronger. "And the last bit might be true, too."

Raising a brow at him, she buried her smile in her coffee. She'd just been teasing, and she hadn't come here expecting anything like this, but the flirtation was fun, and it took her mind off the fact that her horse had just about tried to knock her head off yesterday. She hadn't attended this morning's session; hadn't even asked about it, in fact. She'd spent the morning breaking the news to her friends that she intended to move out. When Noah had raised a dubious brow at her words, Emma had swatted him and told Lily it was a good idea.

She wasn't sure it was a good idea yet, but she couldn't say it was a bad one so far, that was for certain.

Finn shifted, pushing his chair back from the table rather abruptly, interrupting Lily's warm fuzzies. Draining his coffee cup, he stood, setting the empty mug down.

"Well, like I said; make yourself at home. I got a couple of colts to ride yet today, and I'm sure you've got some photo work to do."

She made a move to protest; they could enjoy the quiet moment between the two of them for another little bit, but he was already heading for the door.

-SEVENTEEN-

THE smell of cooking food hit Finn's nose at the door of his cabin. Despite himself, he stopped a moment before stepping inside. His afternoon rides had gone well; as well as they could with half his mind on the girl who not only was a pain in his side just being on the ranch, but had now taken up residence in his home. *You invited her in,* he reminded himself, and shook his head. It had been an act of kindness, a way to apologize for how he'd been cold to her when she first arrived, but now he felt like it was self-sabotage. She was sweet as homegrown honey and there was no way in hell he could treat her the way she deserved. After a sizable pep talk, he pushed open the door and stepped inside.

Lily was wiggling her hips to some country song with a jaunty beat on the radio while she tended a pot on the stove. At least she'd taken his advice to make herself at home.

He hung his hat and his coat inside the door, his nose leading him across the room to the stove where she was stirring something in a pot. Unable to resist, he leaned over her shoulder and took a whiff, his stomach grumbling in response. It might have been the spicy meat sauce she was stirring but it could have just as well been the delectable coconut smell that came off her; it *had* to be her shampoo. He'd find out soon enough, he imagined;

it was a womanly rite of passage to fill shower stalls with as many shampoos and body washes as possible.

"Ten minutes 'til it's ready, I think."

She turned her head and her face was right there, pretty as a picture and tempting as hell. He took a step back and shoved his hands in his pockets to stop himself.

"You don't have to cook. You're a guest."

She shrugged, turning her attention back to the meal she was preparing. "I cook. That's what I do."

"Among other things," he couldn't hide the smile in his voice. She was a woman of many talents, and most of them surprised him more than he cared to admit. "Did you cook at Emma and Noah's?" He leaned back against the table, crossing his arms, watching her. The view from behind wasn't too shabby at all. She hadn't been here long but already, she was changing him. A month ago, the thought of appreciating a shapely ass that didn't belong to his wife felt blasphemous. Today, it almost felt permissible.

"There was hardly enough room to turn around in there, let alone cook." She glanced over her shoulder at his dubious expression and laughed, a sound that pinged him right in the middle of his chest. "I mean, this place isn't that much bigger, but there *are* two less bodies."

"Two?"

"Tucker definitely counts as an extra body, with all his underfoot wiggling."

He chuckled. The dog tried hard to be good but there were things that only came to a dog with life experience, like common sense and the ability to go lie down. Dane's dog, Rex, had perfected those things long ago but he had a decade on the pup.

"He *tries* to be good."

AMITY LASSITER

"He does, but he's just got so much love to give," Lily said, laughing.

"He would have loved it if you cooked for him," Finn replied. She began to rummage in the cupboards and that was when he stepped in, rubbing shoulders with her as he opened the last cupboard on the left and pulled out two plates.

"Thanks."

"Think nothing of it. What do you want to drink? I've got beer...and water. Milk, maybe?"

"Beer is fine," she returned, heaping a pile of noodles and sauce on each plate.

The red sauce was thick and chunky, with tons of vegetables, and a healthy dose of ground beef. He hadn't realized how hungry he was until he found his eyes fixed on the steaming plates and his stomach growling loudly. He dragged his gaze away and dug a couple of bottles of domestic beer out of the fridge, turning back to the plates on the table and her bent over, retrieving a garlic loaf from the oven. He sure as hell knew he didn't have any loaves of French bread just hanging around.

"Did you go to town?" he asked, as she set the bread in the middle of the table.

"No, I made that."

"No shit?"

She grinned. "No shit. I mean, I had to borrow some...*most* of the ingredients from Ren."

"Did you get *any* of your photography work done this afternoon?"

With a shrug, she tugged the dishtowel she'd been wearing in her belt loop off her waist and dropped it onto the counter before taking her seat.

"Seriously, don't let your work fall behind because you're trying to play house." It should have been a tease, but it came out flat.

"That is *not* what this is," she said, lifting her

124

fork with a frown. "Don't flatter yourself. This is a thank you meal, not a daily thing. I wouldn't want you to get too spoiled."

Finn couldn't resist a second longer, and jabbed his fork into the mound of pasta on his plate, twisting it around until it was bigger than his mouth, and holding up the ends with a piece of garlic bread he'd broken off the loaf. He transported it to his mouth and had to work hard to keep his eyes from falling shut in pleasure at the taste. The food was incredible, savory and perfectly seasoned, rivaling Ren's own spaghetti. A man, especially one who had been living alone for five years, could get used to the idea of a hot meal at the end of the day, especially if it was served by someone like Lily.

"Too late."

"Damnit," Lily laughed, shaking her head as she tucked into her own food.

*

"God, is that the time already?" Lily frowned, peering at the clock on the oven as she stood on tiptoe to put the now-clean plates back where she'd seen Finn retrieve them. He'd insisted on doing the dishes, but she'd rock-paper-scissored her way into drying, at least. When she'd started putting the meal together for him earlier, she hadn't expected they'd find such companionable small talk over dinner, he'd appreciate her cooking the way he did, or that she'd actually find herself *enjoying* time spent with him without a horse between them.

"Sure is." Finn chuckled from the sink. "Time flies when you're having fun."

Yawning, she paused and stretched, before resuming her spot beside him with the dish towel. The three beers she'd consumed since dinner, while they still sat at the table talking even though they had no reason to, were hitting her harder than normal. Something about the fresh mountain air grew her appetite and lowered her tolerance for alcohol. She glanced up at Finn, who swiped a cloth over the pan she'd used to brown the beef, then rinsed it and handed it to her.

"Stick a fork in me, I'm done." She shook her head, lazily circling her cloth over the pan until it came dry. "I've never been the type to go to bed early but I can't help myself around here."

"Four am *does* come early."

"If you think I'm getting up at four am, you've got another thing coming."

"Didn't you know that was a condition of the invitation to stay here?" he asked, barely concealing a grin. Laughing, she flicked her damp dish towel at his behind.

"Oh girl, you don't want to start that war. You will *not* win."

The growl in his words pulled something in her insides. She raised a brow and flicked the towel at him again and before she knew what was going on, he was making a move to take it away from her. She jerked back three steps, then turned and made it halfway around the kitchen table before he caught up to her, wrapping his arms around her from behind as he tried to pry the towel from her hands. Shrieking with laughter, she tried to wriggle free, but he was considerably bigger and stronger and she didn't stand a chance. He'd circled his arms around her shoulders and held her back flush against his chest.

"This isn't fair; I have no strength when I'm laughing." Her words punctuated by her laughter, she flailed when he lifted her feet a few inches off the ground.

"Just give up." His words were close and quiet

in her ear and rumbly against her back and she stilled for a second, a wave of goosebumps rushing over her skin. He loosened his grip just enough that she could wriggle around, trapping her hands and the dish towel against his chest, and suddenly the playful mood had dissipated, as quickly as it had appeared. She expected him to let her go, push her away again, but he didn't, his grip still tight, but gentle, his dark eyes pinning her in place as effectively as his arms.

She swallowed hard when he lifted his hand, sliding it over her jaw, his fingers brushing the hairline behind her ear, inciting a fresh batch of goosebumps. His thumb made a slow trek across her cheek and she realized this wasn't like when he'd held her together outside of the round pen. This was something else entirely. Something that burned her up from the inside out. Something she wanted to give in to.

A quick breath rushed out of her two seconds before he lowered his head. Her fingers released the dish towel and curled into the front of his t-shirt as his lips covered hers, hot, and warm, and delicious. Gentle at first, but more demanding when she opened to him. He took, and she gave because there was nothing else she wanted to do. Her body boneless, she sagged against him, weak not from the laughter this time, but the pulsing rush of adrenaline going through her. When he lifted his head, she was breathless, clinging to him, and she could feel every beat of her heart through her entire body.

His grip loosened further; now she didn't want it to. Every part of her that touched him was on fire—in the best way possible. At this proximity, she breathed in the smell of a man who had put in a hard day's work; leather, sunshine, and the faint scent of sweat. His chest rose and fell as heavy breaths came out of him; suddenly, those dark, desire filled eyes looked stricken—like he'd just realized what he'd done and he was sorry for it.

He released her like a hot potato. "I'm sorry. That was... so uncalled for. Goodnight."

Completely dumbfounded, she watched as he backed away from her, around the table, and then went to his bedroom, closing the door behind himself.

-EIGHTEEN-

"WELL, if this doesn't work out, you can always sell him to the bronc string." Noah leaned over the edge of the round pen rail beside his brother as they watched Encore buck his way around the outer circle. When he passed by them, both brothers leaned back to avoid an accidental connection of flying hooves.

"Yeah," Finn said, frowning.

It was early, and Finn he'd decided to put Lily's theory to the test. With Noah's help, he'd managed to secure a breastplate to the saddle to stop it flying off over the gelding's haunches, and incrementally tightened the saddle. He'd send the horse around him with each advancement. The horse had barely even noticed until he'd secured the cinch, and then he'd spent the last few minutes doing his best to get rid of the equipment while the boys cleared the area.

He watched until the horse's body language indicated he was giving up—it wasn't his standard procedure to train this way, applying the 'scary' thing until the horse got over it, but the gelding had become dangerous quickly and he didn't get paid nearly enough to stand under 1200 pounds of furious feet—and then slipped between the rails of the pen, finding his spot in the middle.

"Easy, brother," he spoke quietly, his voice low and even. "You're alright."

When the gelding settled into a trot and then broke to a walk, Finn pushed him back into a trot for another circle, just to remind him the work was over when he said, not when the horse decided. And when the gelding dropped his head, one ear turned back to the man in the middle, indicating he was listening and waiting, Finn removed the pressure and allowed him to decelerate to a walk. Before long, Encore's mouth worked, a sign of submission, and Finn turned his back, allowing the horse to approach.

From the rail, Noah whistled low under his breath and shook his head. Finn shot his brother a look before he turned and stroked the gelding's forehead. Noah was a good trainer himself, but he didn't have the patience to wait out the difficult horses. Finn, on the other hand, had all the time in the world. For a very long time now, his success with the problem horses was one of the most important parts of his day.

"See, I told you you're alright," he murmured, gathering up the lead rope that had been dragging from the rope halter the horse wore. So it hadn't been a perfect session, but it was a step in the right direction, regardless. "I know that saddle scares the bejesus out of you, but you've faced scarier. You're gonna live."

He heard Noah's chuckle, and then Lily's soft voice at the rail behind him.

"How's he doing?"

She wasn't that close, but close enough his body paid attention. Even when he'd snuck out of the house this morning, he was acutely aware she was just behind the door across the hall, all soft and warm with sleep. He'd loved Sunny for a long time, but that had been a slow burn, a friendship that developed into more when they were still young.

He'd always wanted her, but never with the urgency he felt for Lily right now.

"You're up early," he said, and swallowed, taking a second to check himself before he turned around. "Did you sleep well?"

She frowned when he answered her question with a question, but it didn't last long; a smile replaced it soon enough, and he was happy to be the one that put it there.

"Oh my God, yes. It was like going from an economy car to a Rolls Royce." Noah shifted beside her and cleared his throat and she glanced at him. "No offense."

"Yeah, yeah," he teased, bumping her shoulder with his own. "Anyway. If you're done here, Finn, I've got some stuff that needs looking after. Later, Lily."

She nodded to Finn and turned back to Encore, who had lost interest in Finn and approached the fence.

He watched his brother's back as he disappeared into the horse barn, leaving him alone with Lily and the memory of the kiss they'd shared not twelve hours earlier. She'd been so soft, so willing, and tasted so damn good. It felt strange to want someone, for the first time, since Sunny. And wrong. A double-headed churning of guilt and desire rose up in the pit of his stomach.

Oh, but he wanted Lily. He swung his gaze back to her, all dark brown eyes and sun-streaked hair and curves poured into jeans that fit just right. He knew by day's end, they'd be a little dirty on the knees because if capturing the right shot meant lying on her belly in the grass, that's what she'd do. She slipped between the rails of the fence and Encore dropped his head, pressing his forehead against her chest. It was comical, the difference in size between the two of them. Stroking his jaw lightly, she dropped her lips to his poll for a second, then blushed when she realized how closely Finn was watching her.

"Hey, you kept a saddle on him today, that's a bonus."

"Yeah, you missed the bronc show." He glanced at the horse, quiet as a lamb now, his head cradled in her arms. The pair had an undeniable bond, but he had no idea how he was going to make that translate back into the saddle. If nothing else, it would be a much longer endeavor, involving work on both sides, individually, and then together, than he had originally planned. There would be snow on the ground well before they were finished. The idea of being cooped up in his cabin with her during a snowstorm terrified and thrilled him all at once.

"Good," she said, and he patted himself on the back for the decision to try and avoid her witnessing too many more of the coming sessions. Sooner or later, he was going to have to try to get into the saddle, and if he made it that far, it would be neither easy nor pretty; it would be tough for her to stomach.

"It's a start."

"Good," she repeated.

He watched her as she continued to dote on the horse, something stirring in him that had been gone for a long time. *I should tell her,* he thought. Spill his guts about the way he'd hardly been able to sleep last night, thinking about her soft curves under his hands, knowing she was just in the next room over. At the very least, he could tell her he didn't know what he could offer her, but he wanted to kiss her again. He lost his nerve when she twisted and smiled at him. Not the expectant, eager smile he might have expected, but something a little sadder, a little softer. Something he didn't deserve.

He'd hesitated so long, she shifted, filling the silence.

"Anyway, the reason I'm up so early is to head over to the Anderson ranch, and I'm looking to bum a ride."

"You happen to be in luck," he said, moving to undo the latigo on Encore's saddle. He kept hold of the rope just to avoid any potential reenactments of the first time she'd been present when a saddle was involved. "I'm heading into town and I can drop you off."

She brightened. "Would you? I know Emma's busy and I'd go by myself, but this is my first trip out."

"Sure," he replied, sliding the saddle off of the gelding, who stood stock still—a testament to nothing more than the unpredictability Finn knew was going to make the act of bringing the two together nothing short of impossible. "I'll be in town a couple hours and I can pick you up on the way back, if you want?"

"Sounds good. Let me go get my gear."

Finn nodded, hoisting the saddle onto the rail of the round pen. "Let me put mine away. Meet back at the pickup."

*

When Lily emerged from the cabin with her camera bag slung over her shoulder, Finn was waiting by the truck. Looking past him, she saw Encore happily munching away on a couple flakes of hay in the round pen, a fresh water bucket in place.

"I appreciate you doing this for me, Finn," she said, climbing into the passenger seat of the truck. She'd known from the outside that it was several years older than the trucks Dane and Noah drove, but she doubted it worked any less hard. It had just been well taken care of, and the interior proved that. It smelled of pine air freshener and the faint smell of tobacco, even though she had never seen him with a cigarette or a lip full of dip. It was a comforting, earthy smell.

"Oh don't be silly. You're part of the fabric of the ranch now, don't hesitate to ask for what you need."

I need you to kiss me again. The traitorous thought crossed her mind so quickly she didn't even see it coming. Out of the corner of her eye, she watched his big, rough hand settle on the floor shifter between them, just inches from her knee. The rough, tanned skin of his fingers drew her mind to the feel of them on her back, pressing her body against his. She clutched her camera bag on her lap with her heart pounding at the base of her throat, and chastised herself. *Get ahold of yourself, Jacobs.* He wasn't making a move, he was driving his goddamn truck.

After he'd shut himself in his bedroom, she'd lain in bed, awake, considering the enigma that was Finn Baylor. There was no doubt she was attracted to him, to those soft little bits he showed her when nobody was looking, even if he hadn't made them apparent from the beginning. And maybe she shouldn't have given him the time of day because he hadn't exactly been warm when they'd first met, but she suspected there was something worth working for underneath the layers of prickly self-preservation. And she was never one to back down from a challenge.

Finn turned the key in the ignition and the engine roared to life just as Dane emerged from the big house with Gage, whose bicycle was flipped upside down at the bottom of the porch steps. Finn idled up to the pair and rolled down his window.

"You're heading to town?" Dane asked as Gage stood on his tiptoes to see into the cab of the truck.

"Yep, what do you need?"

"Inner tube? We've got a flat."

"Can do," Finn replied, reaching out to ruffle his nephew's mop of curly hair. "We'll get you fixed up in no time."

"Thanks, Uncle Finn!"

"Anytime, buddy." Lily watched the interaction between the Baylor men quietly. The family was all in sync, she couldn't imagine the heated arguments and long grudges of her own family happening anywhere on the ranch.

Finn waited until the boy stepped back and then shifted into gear, pulling out of the driveway.

"It must be nice having your family here so close."

He pressed his lips together, hesitating just a beat as they bumped down the drive past Emma and Noah's house before he replied. "It is."

"You all get on really well. We'd be fighting like cats and dogs if the Jacobs' were all in one place like this."

"Oh, that happens too," Finn replied with a laugh, guiding the truck out onto the road. "Not that often, but it's happened. Mostly, it's good having them close when you really need them."

"Like when Noah was having problems?" Emma had told Lily the general gist of Noah's issues when their youngest brother, Gavin, had died. According to her, Finn had been a savior during that particularly dark time. She could see it. Maybe he liked to be left alone, maybe he liked the quiet of working with the horses, but it was obvious how much he cared about his family.

"Exactly. Having everyone close when that was

going on was really helpful. Emma, too," he replied. She watched his jaw tighten, his gaze directed ahead, obviously thinking of other times when he'd needed to call upon the closeness of his family for support. "The only downfall is when everyone is so close, not a lot slips past them. Secrets are hard to keep."

"Oh yeah? You're a private kinda guy, huh?"

He glanced over at her then, and she might have imagined it, but she could almost feel the tension of longing, difficult to swallow, in the space between them. From him, from her. She knew what he was saying—their kiss was a secret that would be difficult to keep, and he wasn't interested in it being anything *but* a secret. He didn't need to answer, because his eyes told her everything, so he didn't.

"But," he continued, shrugging, and suddenly the mood had lightened. "It's a lot like that through this whole town, honestly. *Somebody* knows you're wiping your ass before you've even thought about it. And sometimes the stories get screwed up."

"Sounds brutal."

"It can be. And hurtful, sometimes. Don't get me wrong. There's not too many people in this town who would intentionally hurt someone else. But there's not much to do but talk, and when the wrong story gets spreading like wildfire, you've got a whole mess of hurt on your hands."

"I guess that's one thing I can like about Denver. Your reputation usually stays intact when you make a mistake."

"Except," he chuckled. "If you're from here and something happens there, everybody here still knows what you did. The news makes it home before you ever do."

"Sounds awful." Lily glanced out her window as Finn signaled a right turn. A ranch, not unlike the one they'd just left, sat back from the road, though there were less outbuildings, and what there were seemed unused.

"It's an acceptable trade-off if you got nothing to hide. So, for about one percent of the population." Laughing, he guided the truck into the yard, where a tall blond man waved from the steps of an older house. Finn nodded toward the figure as he killed the ignition. "There's Cutter."

*

Finn pulled back into the Anderson's driveway a couple hours later to find the pair sitting side by side on the steps with lemonade in hand, laughing like they were the best of friends. He couldn't deny the pang of jealousy that tightened his gut when he saw it. Cutter was unaffected by the rumor mill he'd told Lily about earlier. Or, people would talk, but it wouldn't matter, because working at the town's only bar, Cutter would have the opportunity to squash talk, or shape it into the truth. Finn, on the other hand, would have no opportunity to test his ability to kindle his feelings without a huge speculative magnifying glass on him.

He turned his truck and pulled up to the steps, rolling down his window.

"How'd you make out?"

"Good!" Lily said, rising and handing her glass off to Cutter before dusting off the seat of her jeans. Finn caught Cutter's eyes drifting to her fingers and that green monster rose up again. "I think I got some great shots. Easy when the stock is good."

He'd all but forgotten, watching her around the ranch as she shot things that *weren't* livestock more often than not, that this was her bread and butter.

"The time flew by," Cutter said, rising slow from his seated position and approaching Finn's window as Lily crossed in front of the truck and climbed into the passenger seat. "Easy when you've got good company." He stuck his head in the window and passed a wink at Lily. When Finn glanced back at her, she'd blushed a little.

Cutter was a persuasive guy and Finn didn't doubt he'd spent a good part of their time together charming her. Growing up, he'd always been the most at ease with girls, and there had never been any shortage. He was slick but not disrespectful, and it could probably have been attributed to growing up with two sisters. These days, he was usually so focused on the batch of random jobs he held down, including tending bar at Danny's and the dance hall it seemed he didn't have time to juggle a half dozen completely enchanted girls like he had in his youth. Unless, of course, Finn delivered one right to his doorstep.

Lily leaned forward and smiled past Finn; that soft, sweet smile he'd thought to be for only him. "I'll bring you by a memory stick with all the photos once I'm done editing. A day, two, maybe, tops."

"Lookin' forward to it." Cutter tipped the hat he wasn't wearing.

Like he wasn't even there. Finn reached for the shifter, putting it in first and letting the engine whine while he let up on the clutch.

"Alright, alright," Cutter continued, tapping his palm against the door of the truck. "See ya later Finn. Lily."

She waved and Finn pulled out.

"I thought you two were friends," Lily said as he pulled out the end of the driveway.

"What makes you think we're not friends?"

"Your curmudgeon was showing." She grinned and leaned back in her seat, pushing her hips forward and letting her arm hang out the window, considerably more relaxed than she had been on the drive out. He was, too, after a stop at Hinkley's for pie and then a visit to the store his parents ran. He hadn't *actually* been intending to come into town, but sometimes he just needed to get off the ranch, and this happened to be one of those times.

He laughed. "I see Emma has been influencing your opinion of my personality."

"Never," she said, turning her face to hide her guilty smile.

"Curmudgeon is definitely her word."

"Maybe she's swayed my opinion a *little*." Their teasing had produced a pretty blush on her high cheekbones. "But you've done a pretty good job convincing me, yourself."

He *was* jealous; he had no right to be, and he'd never admit it out loud. Emma had said she needed some good in her life, and maybe Cutter Anderson would be just that good thing she needed. Simple, uncomplicated, easy. Something she could relax into, the goodness she deserved.

-NINETEEN-

LILY tried to swallow, but her mouth was full of blood. Her legs were pinned between something hot and heavy and the cold, wet ground. The squealing of a car engine right next to her ear drove her nearly to insanity. Shivering, she looked down at her legs, both of which were trapped under a big, black mass of horse. She wanted to call for help, but she couldn't make a sound. The engine knocked under the hood and the only thing she could think was the car would explode and they'd all be killed. Her breaths came quick and painful, then interrupted by sobs that hiccuped through her diaphragm.

"Lily."

Hearing her name, she struggled to lift her head but found she couldn't. The knocking of the engine grew more insistent, and she flinched away from the noise. And suddenly, there were hands, lifting her, drawing her out of the mud, sliding her legs out from under Encore's lifeless body, and against a warm, firm chest. Big hands held her close, stroking her hair, and the steady thud of a heart under her ear.

She couldn't have mistaken the fresh, clean male scent of Finn. Her fingers found purchase in the thin material of a t-shirt, and with some effort, she pried her eyes open. Slowly, she became aware of each part of her body, the quiet of the spare room she'd been staying in, and the implication of Finn

Baylor holding her.

"Shh, just breathe, love." The rumble of each word under her cheek unlaced the tension that had seized her, and instead of being embarrassed he'd caught her twice, now, in the middle of a full blown panic attack, she gave herself permission to relax.

He sat on the edge of her bed in his boxers and t-shirt, and had drawn her right out of it, into his lap, cradling her against his chest like a child. He shifted back, but still held her close to his chest.

"Close your eyes, I'm going to turn on the light," he murmured, and she followed his direction as he stretched toward the bedside lamp.

Slowly, she opened her eyes again, and lifted her head to look at Finn. They were closer than was comfortable considering their relationship, but he didn't let her go. His hair stuck out in every direction and his slate eyes looked tired, but were full of concern, and something else, lurking just behind the empathy. She'd never been more grateful for his closeness.

She saw her fingers on his stubbled jaw before she even realized she was lifting her hand. He froze, watching her, and then let out a pent-up breath when she slid her fingertips to cup his jaw, the rough hair scratching her palm.

"Lily..." His voice was tight, controlled.

And then he wasn't, and his mouth was covering hers, the hand that had been stroking her hair moving to the base of her neck to tip her head back. She was surprised at first, but then fell into the kiss like it was the most natural thing to do. The hand on her waist dropped to her hip, his fingers pressing into the soft flesh there and drawing her closer. She couldn't get close enough.

She'd discovered Finn to be a careful man 99 percent of the time; the things he did were calculated, thought out well in advance, and purposeful. It was the one percent, the moment she was experiencing right now, as she tasted the spearmint of his toothpaste and the rawness of his emotion, that she liked to see the most. It was the whoop of joy when Tessa accomplished something new in her riding lesson, the quiet burst of tenderness toward his nephew and his nieces, and the scorching kiss that had taken her by surprise the first night she'd stayed here. Those were the moments she relished, the moments where he hadn't exactly thought out what would happen next, carefully choreographing his path to choose what parts of his hand he would show. This was one of those moments.

Her fingers knotted into his shirt at his waist when he strayed from her mouth, drawing his lips across her jaw, slipping her earlobe between his teeth for a gentle tug. He stopped then, his face buried at her hairline just behind her ear, and he drew in a long breath.

"I'm sorry."

"Don't be sorry," she whispered, her heart aching. She didn't want him to be sorry for kissing her, because an apology meant he didn't want to. And if he didn't want to, that meant she shouldn't have enjoyed it as much as she did. His kiss was like a breath of air when she needed to fill her lungs.

Uncurling her fingers from his shirt, she slid her hands over his back, up to his shoulders, and held her body against his, absorbing the heat and the emotion the best she could. There was pain in his apology, and she didn't know how to soothe it. She felt his breath drain out of him, and the arm around her waist tightened.

*

Finn lifted his head and dropped his lips to the

top of Lily's hair.

The first sound of crying had jerked him awake like a shot. He'd become the lightest sleeper when Sunny was on hospice care in the spare room, and it had never gone away. Not often, but sometimes, she would cry out in her sleep and he'd be out of bed before he even knew what had woken him. Tonight had been exactly the same. Except this wasn't his wife. This was the woman who had infiltrated almost every aspect of his life in less than two weeks, whether she had intended to or not. And she was soft, and warm, and tasted like home.

And now she was holding him, the opposite of how it probably should have been. He drew back and traced his thumb over the tear tracks on her cheeks.

"You were crying."

The smile she put on didn't reach her eyes. "Bad dream."

"Does this happen a lot?"

She blew a breath out between tight lips, her expression locked down. She didn't want to talk, but if he was going to be losing sleep on a regular basis, she was going to have to.

"Sometimes."

"Just like whatever that was that happened to you the day we saddled Encore."

"Yes."

"Lily, have you ever talked to someone about this?"

Her lips pressed together and then the lower one snagged between her teeth, a little line forming between her eyebrows.

"It's not a big deal..."

"It's no way to live."

He was the last person to be giving advice on how to live, considering how he'd thrown himself

143

into the ranch work after Sunny's death. It had been too much to handle all at once, and he wasn't the type to pour his heart out while a medical professional tried to fit his grief into a box with a label. But that worked for some people, and if it took away nightmares and whatever it was that had happened outside the round pen when he'd had to physically hold her together, he wanted that for Lily.

She swallowed but didn't respond.

"What can I do for you right now?" he asked. Obviously, he could try to talk her into Dr. Fields' office, but that would require daylight hours. He winced when he glanced at the clock on the bedside stand. 3am. Morning would be here before long, and they both needed some sleep. He'd do whatever it took.

Her gaze searched his for an agonizing moment. And then she spoke, her voice barely above a whisper. "Stay."

He hadn't shared his bed with anyone since Sunny. But this wasn't *his* bed, either.

"Okay."

Finally loosening his grip, he guided her back into the bed, under the covers. She wore a pair of tiny shorts and a giant t-shirt that barely stayed on her shoulders. She shifted, turning her back to him, and he slid in behind her. Close but not touching. Glancing over her shoulder, she motioned for him to get closer.

Tucking himself in against her soft body, he slid his hand tentatively over her hip, his fingers grazing over a soft stretch of skin where her shirt had ridden up, just above the waistband of her shorts. She shivered, but pushed herself back into him, twisting her fingers into his and wrapping herself up in his arms like a blanket. Her silky hair tickled his face, her scent intoxicating him.

She let out a soft breath—a satisfied sigh, barely audible. She would sleep well, but he had no idea how he'd be able to turn off his adrenaline, or his desire.

-TWENTY-

"UM, good morning."

Lily let out a yelp from where she was crouched down beside Finn's kitchen table. She'd assumed he was gone for the day, like usual, but there he was, nearly giving her a heart attack, standing just inside the door in his work clothes. She'd just snuck out of the bedroom in her sleep clothes to turn on the coffee maker, but then she'd gotten distracted by a fat, yellow wedge of sunlight spread over one corner of his battered table. Before she knew it, she'd grabbed her camera and put a pretty handmade ceramic mug in the space, pants be damned.

He hadn't noticed her right away because he was halfway across the floor, frozen in place, his eyes fixed on her bare legs poking out from under the oversized t-shirt she wore. She could feel a blush rising up her neck. Finn had looked at her in a lot of different ways in the time she'd been here on the ranch—sardonically, flippantly, even *fearfully*, once—but this was totally different. She was torn between covering herself and letting him look as long as he liked. She could almost physically feel a flicker of that same fiery intensity from the night he'd kissed her on her skin as if it were his fingers themselves.

She couldn't even halfway explain why a man who had only shown her brief kindness elicited this kind of response from her body, but she'd woken alone this morning, warm, and happy, with a low simmer in her belly when she thought about the taste of him and the gentleness of his hands as he'd held her through the night. Apart from her photos and her horse, it was about the only thing she *could* think about, especially when she woke and knew he'd been there.

After what felt like forever, but really could only have been three heartbeats, he cleared his throat and diverted his eyes and the heat in the room dropped a few degrees.

"I'm so sorry," she said all at once. "I lost track of time and thought you were out for the day."

"No, I'm sorry. I..." he floundered, gesturing loosely with his hands.

"You don't have to apologize, Finn. I'm a guest. I shouldn't be wandering around half naked."

His gaze shot to hers for a moment, almost panicked by the word *naked*, and edged backward toward the door. She eased herself in the direction of the bedroom, with her hands raised, walking backward, like he was some kind of frightened animal.

"Don't leave, have a coffee," she insisted. "I was going to bring you one in the barn anyway."

She heard Finn sigh as she slipped into her bedroom, her face hot and red. How embarrassing, waltzing around like she belonged here. She shoved her legs into sweats and re-emerged to find Finn fixing himself a cup, like she'd instructed him.

"I'm sorry," she apologized again, twisting her hair into a messy bun high on her head. "I just...the light was perfect."

"Ah," he said gruffly, seating himself at the table. She retrieved her own mug from the corner and clasped it between her hands, standing for a moment, and then deciding to sit. "An artist who can't resist their medium."

"Three weeks ago, I would have walked past that and thought 'oh that's pretty', because I'd have bulls and broncs on my mind." She smiled across the top of her mug at him. "I'm doing way more artistic work here than I have in years, and I think it's just snowballing."

A slow, easy grin spread over Finn's lips as he finally seemed to relax. "As long as I don't come to the barn to find you taking pictures of a pile of manure..."

Lily laughed out loud, and shook her head. "I think I can respect that."

"On that note, you interested in some new models?"

She cocked her head, watching him carefully. "I'm listening."

"There's someone coming by the ranch this afternoon that could use a little dose of the feel-goods your photos seem to give."

"Who?"

"You'll know when you see them." He grinned, pushing his chair back. "Now I've got some work to do. I'll see you this afternoon."

He stood and moved toward the door, pausing to glance back at her with his coffee mug still in hand. She might have imagined it if she couldn't feel his gaze on her now-covered legs. "Thanks for the...coffee."

-TWENTY-ONE-

AFTERNOON sun filtered in through dusty windows as Lily bent over an intricately stamped, but incredibly dusty breastplate, frowning. The leather work was beautiful but she would never understand why, if someone wasn't going to clean their tack regularly, they kept something like this around. She'd already washed and oiled it, but still, there was dust in the corners of the tooling. She pressed her lips together and then set it aside. She'd photograph it. Surely it said something about ranch life. And then she'd go into town and buy a cheap toothbrush and clean it properly.

It took a little bit of effort to pull herself out of the deep folding camp chair Finn had put in the tack room but she managed, hanging her cleaned items back in place. Another half day and she'd be finished cleaning and organizing. Once she'd gotten into it, it was a bigger job than she'd anticipated. Now, it looked amazing, but she was sure it wouldn't stay that way for long. Emma and the boys were in and out of it multiple times a day, and she couldn't blame them, as busy as they were, for not taking the best care at putting things back where they belonged.

With her back to the door, she folded her arms over her chest and surveyed her work.

"Excuse me," a little voice said behind her, and she nearly jumped out of her skin. When she turned, she saw a tiny red-haired girl standing in the doorway. "Do you know where Finny is?"

Before Lily could formulate a response, a harried looking woman landed in the doorway. "Tessa, what have I told you about running into the barn?"

Tessa's gaze hit the floor quickly, chastised. "Sorry, Miranda."

"Oh sweets, it's okay. I just don't want you to get hurt." The woman's voice softened as she folded the little girl up under her arm and gave her a reassuring squeeze.

"Um, I think Finn went for feed, but he should be back anytime." Judging by their conversation this morning, she could guess that the little girl might be her new model.

As if they had scripted it, she heard Finn's truck pull up to the side door of the barn, closest to the feed room.

"That must be him." Lily gave the little girl a warm smile and moments later, Finn appeared and scooped Tessa up into his arms without a moment's hesitation and like she weighed nothing at all.

"Hey Bug! Sorry I'm late. I wanted to bring you something for your birthday but I had a hard time picking." Reaching into his back pocket, he produced a pink hoof pick and presented it to delighted squeals. "Did I do good?"

"Yes, yes! It's so pretty!" The girl's feet kicked excitedly. She couldn't have been older than five or six, younger than Gage, and clearly head over heels in love with Finn. Lily could understand why. The tender side of Finn that was beginning to show through was largely appealing. A second later, Tessa's eyes focused on Lily, both hands still clutching the hoof pick. "Who's that?"

"This is my friend, Lily," Finn explained.

Friend. She knew he was using the word for Tessa's benefit, for easier understanding, because she certainly couldn't call the warm feeling in the pit of her stomach when he was near *friendly*, per se, and she was reasonably sure Finn felt at least a fraction the same. "Lily, this is Tess, and her friend Miranda."

"Hi Lily," the girl said. "Do you wanna watch me ride?"

"Of course I do." Lily smiled. The little girl's friendly openness was refreshing. Finn running a riding lesson program was news to her, especially since he'd been so adamant he *didn't* give riding lessons when she'd arrived with Encore.

"And she's going to take a few pictures of you, too, if that's alright." The little girl nodded, and Finn glanced back at Miranda, who also nodded.

Finn turned and headed up the barn aisle with Tessa's tiny body still perched up in his arms. Quickly darting back into the tack room, Lily grabbed her camera and then followed the trio up the alleyway toward the horse stalls. They stopped in front of Buckshot's stall and Finn set her down, handing her a lead rope that had been looped up on a hook outside the horse's stall. He opened the door for her and she disappeared inside for a minute before emerging with Buckshot following her, his head down, like a giant puppy. The horse was clearly enamored with the little person and, if Lily wasn't mistaken, so was the man.

There were so many good photo ops here, Lily lifted the camera and started shooting, doing her best to focus on the little girl despite the fact that Finn's interactions with her warmed her heart more than she cared to admit. It was like he was a completely different man than the one who had 'welcomed' her to the ranch originally. He was full of surprises.

He snapped the horse into the cross ties for her, handed her a dandy brush, and then lifted her up onto the gelding's back before heading back past them to the tack room. One eyelid dropped closed in a cheeky wink that made Miranda chuckle as he passed the women. His countenance was so different from what she'd seen when he was working with Encore or interacting with her that Lily couldn't help but shake her head, watching his back as he disappeared into the room for a minute and re-emerged with Gage's small saddle, and a pair of short stirrups over his shoulder.

From her perch, Tessa busily brushed Buckshot's mane, his withers and shoulders as far as she could reach, and behind her, on the top of his rump.

"All done?" Finn asked her. When she nodded, he used his free arm to slide her down off the horse's back and set her on her feet, where she went to work brushing his legs and belly. Finn swung the saddle onto Buckshot's back, mindful of Tessa's location at all times, and went to work cinching up and checking the equipment. He hung the buddy stirrups off the saddle's horn—the existing stirrups and fenders, despite being short enough for Gage, would have still been miles too long for the girl's petite frame.

"Ready for his feet?" he asked, producing the hoof pick again from his back pocket. At her agreement, Finn moved around Buckshot, carefully lifting each of the horse's feet while Tessa used the hoof pick to clean any shavings and manure out of them.

When it was time for the bridle, Finn handed it to her, unsnapped Buckshot's cross ties and rested his hand gently on the horse's poll, between his ears, while Tessa held the bridle up as high as she could hold it. The horse obediently dropped his face into the waiting leather straps, opening his mouth for the bit. With Finn's assistance, she slid the crown piece over his ears, and then flashed a huge, proud smile to the two women watching. Miranda gave her a double thumbs up as Finn organized the reins for her, swinging one over the horse's neck and handing her the other. The five of them made their way out to the big arena, bypassing the round pen where Encore nickered a greeting to Buckshot, who completely ignored him, dedicated to the task at hand and his tiny handler.

Finn lifted Tessa into the saddle, helped her push her toes into the stirrups and knotted the ends of the reins so they wouldn't go anywhere if she dropped them, then handed them to her.

"You go get him warmed up," he said, patting her thigh, then giving Buckshot an encouraging pat on the rump.

Lily held her breath a moment, but then was taken aback by the little girl's skill and the horse's responsiveness. She couldn't have weighed anything, and her legs barely draped over his back, but the old gelding turned and moved as she directed, with little effort at all. Any of the difficulty Lily had with him the day before was absent. Finn watched with his hands on his hips, instructing Tessa to change direction, make smaller or larger circles, straight lines and 'zig zags'.

"She's very good," she said to Miranda, who stood beside her, watching with her arms folded over the top rail.

"*He's* so very good with them," the woman responded, never taking her eyes off the trio in the ring. "Tessa has been riding with him since she came to me. She was so painfully shy at first, but she's come such a long way."

Lily chewed her lip, glancing at the woman. The ranch itself had a selection of different family configurations—Kerri being Ren's sister and Gage Dane's nephew, both raised as though the adults were their parents—it made sense that this would be another unconventional relationship.

"Came to you?" she asked. "I'm sorry, I'm nosy," she hurriedly apologized.

"Oh don't be sorry," Miranda said, waving off the apology. "I do foster care. Tessa has been with me for about six months. I always bring my kids out to ride with Finn because it gives them something to look forward to. Something good. It builds their confidence and gives them some pride. Emma Pierce's mom, Myrna, made the connections—she's retired from social services, now, but she keeps in touch with me... she really helped me out in the beginning."

The young woman's tone was sincere, her smile warm, and Lily nodded, looking back out at Finn, who now had Tessa making a circle so close around him that he instructed her to reach out and touch the top of his cowboy hat. The little girl laughed hysterically as Finn let her succeed, then moved two feet to the right and made her work for it again. They were a couple of old friends, playing around. The deep timbre of Finn's infectious chuckle warmed Lily's insides.

"They could ride at any ranch, really, but *he's* the reason we do it here. The kids adore him, and he loves them like they're his own," Miranda said, without taking her eyes off them. Lily looked at her a second—it could easily be that the reason the woman came back over and over was because of her own interest in Finn, but Lily didn't think so. He'd practically ignored Miranda, focusing on Tessa

154

from the second he walked into the barn.

It doesn't matter, anyways, she reminded herself. She had no claim over Finn Baylor, even if she wanted one, which she hadn't been sure she did... until she saw him engaging with the girl. Now, he was holding Buckshot while she swung her legs around the saddle, sitting forward, then sideways, backward, then back to forward again. The whole time, Lily kept on shooting.

"Look at my 'round the world, Lily!" Tessa shouted triumphantly.

"That looks *great*." Lily remembered all too well her childhood growing up doing the same sorts of things. Around the worlds, red light, green light, and all sorts of other games to improve balance and control. She doubted she could maneuver her legs around the saddle that way now, no matter how hard she tried. "He *is* really good with them, isn't he?"

"He is. It's a real shame he never had any kids of his own. But I'm also thankful, because it means he has more time for the ones I have. He's made such a world of difference for so many kids who have come through here. He gives them something they've been missing—confidence, joy, a respectable masculine figure."

"Oh you're not married?" Lily could have kicked herself for asking, but the question was already out. "I'm so sorry, you don't have to answer that."

"Oh," Miranda chuckled. "That ship sailed and it's not ready to come back into harbor yet. And when you grow up in a town as small as Three Rivers, the dating pool is *painfully* small."

Regretting the words even as they formed, Lily nodded toward the ring, where Finn jogged alongside Tess and Buckshot as they trotted up the long side of the arena. "What about Finn?"

Again she laughed, and Lily could imagine herself being friends with the easygoing woman. She supposed spending so much time with children, she was used to inappropriate questioning. "Finn is a great guy, don't get me wrong, but I'm pretty sure he still holds a candle for his wife. He pays me as much mind as this post here." She tapped the top of the nearest post and shook her head. "Besides, I've got enough going on in my life. Look, I've told you my whole life story and I haven't even made a proper introduction."

Miranda stuck out her hand and Lily took it, giving it a firm shake. "I'm Lily Jacobs. I'm a friend of Emma and Noah's and I'm sticking around while Finn works with my horse."

"Miranda Walters. It's good to meet you."

-TWENTY-TWO-

LILY stood beside Finn while they waved at Tessa in the back seat of Miranda's little car.

"She's sure something else," Lily said, turning her head and smiling at Finn as the car rounded the bend in the driveway and disappeared.

"She sure is." Finn took his hat off and rubbed his hand over his hair. "That was nice of you. To take her picture. I get the feeling like nobody probably ever cared enough to take pictures of her doing things she enjoys."

Lily shrugged, a hint of a smile playing over her lips, that cute dimple showing itself for a second. It was a shot straight to his heart.

"Sometimes seeing yourself in a different light can change the way you feel about yourself."

Finn knew her words to be truth; he'd almost felt like he was looking at a whole other person in the photos she'd shown him of himself. "I really think what *you* do for her is the best thing, though."

Finn's shoulders lifted and he drew in a breath. "Sunny and Myrna cooked up the program. I just carry through."

He was lying. He wasn't *just* carrying through. He'd taken a couple of weeks off for mourning, but when things were going nuts with Noah and he was still struggling to find a foothold, the kids Miranda or Myrna brought by were the highlight of his week. Lily obviously wasn't buying his statement, because she was staring him down under one arched eyebrow and looked like she was waiting for an explanation.

"Okay, so... a couple of years ago, Myrna came to me and said she could move the program elsewhere, but I asked her to keep it. I like the kids. They're like a breath of fresh air."

"I think you're probably the same thing for them," she said quietly, then tucked her hands in her back pockets.

"Yeah, maybe. Some of them have the saddest stories. Abuse, neglect..." he trailed off, shaking his head. Miranda usually gave him the details so he could be better equipped for triggers and crises of confidence, and he'd heard stories so upsetting they'd made him want to get in his truck and go find the low-lives who thought it was okay to do those things to their children. The way this part of the world worked often didn't make sense to him—people who wanted children couldn't have them, or in his case, didn't have *time* to have them, and people had them who didn't want them and treated them badly.

"Not unlike the horses you work with." Her return was accompanied by a sly little smile. "Your sister-in-law says you're better with horses than people, but I don't think that's entirely true after today."

"It might not be." He shrugged, turning toward the barn, eager to change the subject. Being anti-social was as much protection as it was a part of his personality, but she didn't need to know that. "So what have you got on your docket for this afternoon?"

"Tack room is a couple hours away from being done. Then some editing, I guess."

"You've been doing good work, Lily." He'd

expected things to be difficult with her around, but she was quiet and smart enough to stay out of the way. The best part was when she was intuitive about little things that needed done and he'd come to finish the task and find it already completed. It made his life that much easier, but made him cross into the dangerous territory of wondering what it'd be like to have her around long term. "Why don't you take the afternoon off?"

"Oh, I don't need to." She looked up at him and offered him a smile. "I don't know what I'd do with myself, really."

"You could come for a drive with me." The idea had been forming since she'd stayed at the rail to watch Tessa's entire lesson, chatting with Miranda like she belonged here. The sun was starting to sink but it had been a beautiful, bright, warm day and you could still barely feel the crispness of the October day. As he expected, both brows raised in surprise at his proposition.

She waited a beat, and he thought she might decline. Asking her in the first place felt like going out on a limb.

"Alright. Where are we going?"

He let out a sigh of relief and nodded toward the truck. "I know you walk out the West pasture every morning, but I have a feeling you haven't made it to the best part yet."

When her eyes lit up, he knew he'd made the right decision, even though he'd waffled back and forth a half dozen times. She didn't have any reason to want to go anywhere with him, but her artistic instinct overrode common sense here, apparently.

"I haven't. I don't want to get so far out that I get too worn out to come back or do anything for the rest of the day," she said, as he led her toward the truck.

"Then I'll take you. Figured you must be running out of things to shoot when I caught you in the kitchen this morning."

*

Lily's laugh died in her throat at the heat that blossomed in her belly when she remembered the look in Finn's eyes as he'd stared at her bare skin that morning. He slid in next to her on the bench seat, turned the key, and the engine roared to life.

"There's really no shortage of stuff to shoot on this ranch, but I would love to see what else is up there."

Finn smiled and tipped his head at her, then focused on guiding the truck out of the yard, behind the heifer barn, and to the first gate. They idled along in silence up a set of worn wheel tracks once they got inside the first pasture gate. Silence between them wasn't new, but the general comfort in it was. They'd crossed into a much more amiable climate without her even realizing it, and she guessed it had a lot to do with the little girl who had visited them today.

It wasn't long before they passed the farthest point she'd dared to go and a whole new world opened up to her. Finn was the farthest thing from her mind as she took in the expanse of lush field. To the left, a giant live oak stood proud in the middle of the field. The path they'd been driving along stretched until it disappeared on the crest of the field as they climbed upward toward the sunset. She could see mountains past the horizon and when he finally pulled to a stop, she had to resist the urge to squeal with delight.

She was already climbing out of the truck before Finn had finished putting it in park ten feet from the fence line. Pulling her camera out of the bag as she went, she was already clicking away before he even got all the way out of the truck.

"Finn, this is amazing!" she shouted without turning back to him.

*

Leaning back against the hood of his truck, Finn appraised the view. Pretty incredible, and what she was shooting wasn't that bad, either.

It *was* the prettiest part of the ranch, especially this time of day. The Baylor property and the Pierce property ran side by side straight back toward the mountains, cresting at the top of a hill. Below, a lush forested valley stretched out, and not far out, snow covered mountain peaks broke the skyline. Even when he saw it on a regular basis, the view never failed to impress, especially with the sun sinking down into the Rockies like it was right now.

He watched her work for a while, lowering her camera occasionally to just stare out across the valley, appreciating with the eye what she would capture with her camera. Sometime later, she turned back to him with a wide smile and a high, bright flush staining her cheeks. He hadn't seen her this excited about something in all the time she'd been at the ranch and a tiny kernel of pride rooted itself in his heart that he could make her that happy—even though it wasn't the one big reason she'd come to the Baylor ranch.

"Thank you so much for bringing me up here." She shook her head, and glanced back over her shoulder. "I never would have gotten up here by myself."

"It's no big deal." He shrugged as she crossed the space between them and leaned her hips against the hood like he had, looking out over the landscape from a distance. She shifted, twisting her torso away from him to swing her camera bag up onto the truck and her ponytail swung toward him, flooding his senses with that warm sugared coconut scent that had infiltrated his mind after he'd kissed her that night. There was barely six inches between them, and he could feel a little frisson of energy in that space that made him want to make it disappear.

When she turned back around, she gave him a pointed look that told him it *was* a big deal to her, but she didn't say anything.

"Look, I'm not very good at this stuff anymore," he began. Her pointed look turned questioning. "Maybe I've never actually been very good at this."

When you married your high school sweetheart, you didn't need to develop much game. Her dark eyes clouded with confusion as she waited for him to continue. Shifting, he rubbed his hand on the back of his neck, wishing he hadn't started down this road.

"I haven't been very nice to you since you got here."

"Maybe not at first," she agreed, and Finn grimaced. "But you took me on as a client, even when you didn't want to. And you offered up your spare room to help a girl out." Her words came quick and almost apologetic, and it wasn't making any of this any easier.

"Minor blips in a mean streak you didn't deserve."

She looked like she wanted to make a return volley but she bit her lower lip instead and the same feelings that had welled up inside of him and burst out in their flurry of a heated kiss rose up again.

"I'd like to take you out, Lily. If you'd let me."

Her eyes widened in surprise, then understanding. "To apologize," she clarified.

"For the reasons people go on dates. And to get to know you better. And as a way of apology."

He'd done all of this wrong, and he wouldn't blame her if she told him to go to hell. He could feel his heart rate just like a stampede of wild horses thundering behind his sternum. She shouldn't say yes, but he hoped she would.

"Okay."

"Dinner tonight, then?" There, it was out there and he couldn't take it back. Anxious for her answer, he stuffed down the nerves already twinging at the idea of taking someone out to a non-platonic dinner for the first time in years.

She raised a brow at him, but a sly smile curled one corner of her lips. "So I don't have the opportunity to think about it and change my mind?"

He laughed out loud, her playful response easing the anxiety eating at his belly. "Exactly."

"Okay," she repeated, turning back to the edge of the pasture. "But you need to give me a little more time to catch this sunset."

-TWENTY-THREE-

"TEN minutes." Finn's voice came through Lily's closed bedroom door along with a knock.

She frowned and turned to the side to survey herself in the mirror over the dresser again. There had been no apparent need for 'date clothes' when she'd left Denver—she hadn't had a need for them in a long while—but now she wished she had something else. The compromise had been her newest pair of jeans with a belt, a white tank top and a blue plaid elbow-length button-down shirt over it. In Denver, this wouldn't have cut it, not by a long shot, but in Three Rivers, it would have to do.

Smoothing her hands over her soft midsection, she twisted her face. She'd never been a slender girl, and after the accident, and not riding, she'd gained a few more pounds she wasn't a hundred percent happy with.

Finn knocked again and she huffed. This was silly. They were living together; he'd seen her in yoga pants and oversized sweaters, and—just this morning—half naked. *Anything* was going to be an improvement from that. Rearranging her pout into a smile in the mirror, she shook out her hair once more and pulled the door open.

He had walked away, and judging by the direction he'd turned, he was pacing a tight circle, but when he heard the door open, he stopped and lifted his head. A burst of butterflies filled her chest when he was silent for a moment. Had she committed a major fashion faux pas?

Drawing a deep breath, she stepped out into the door frame to stop herself from chickening out and just closing the door, because he had the same look in his eyes she'd seen when he'd caught her photographing the kitchen table, and until Finn Baylor, it had been a long time since anyone had looked at her that way.

"Wow," he finally spoke, sounding like someone had just socked him in the stomach and pushed all the air out of him.

"Good wow, or bad wow?" She shifted, crossing her arms over her midsection as she attempted to defend herself with humor.

"Don't cover yourself up, Lily. You look great." He didn't return the teasing; instead, appreciation read loud and clear.

She felt a flattered blush rise up her cheeks when he paid her the compliment, and uncrossed her arms.

He didn't look half bad himself. It was a variation on his regular daily dress, but somehow didn't look 'regular' to her. Clean dark-wash jeans sat low on his hips, accenting his long, lean body. A navy long sleeved button up shirt was tucked into them with the top two buttons undone, and he held an almost pristine black Stetson by the brim.

This was a man who didn't feel the need for the bright patterns and flashy bling of the rodeo cowboys. And it appealed to her, propelling her two steps forward, out of the doorway and into the hall with him, putting them just about chest to chest. The cabin was small, and the hallway was smaller. She pulled the door shut behind her and stepped out toward the living room to put some breathing room between them.

"So where are we going?"

She might have been imagining it, but the smile he flashed her looked downright playful. "You're just gonna have to wait and see."

Fifteen minutes later found them in his truck, turning left toward the highway instead of right toward town. She'd expected Hinkley's, based on the fact that it was really the only dining establishment in the city. The day was just beginning to get dark, and while some anxiety flip-flopped around in her empty stomach, she wasn't sure if it was because of the highway driving or because of the man sitting a couple feet away, who kept glancing over at her to gauge her reaction to the unfamiliar route. He seemed to be watching for her reaction, relishing the opportunity to surprise her. *Cute.*

A couple of miles down the highway, he hit his blinker and turned off on a small, unlit exit.

"Finn Baylor, I know I've been a thorn in your side since I showed up, but are you taking me out to the middle of nowhere to get rid of me once and for all?"

The reward for her wit was a deep laugh as he hit his blinker again and they pulled into a dirt parking lot. There were no houses around, but a converted travel trailer sat at the back of the lot, lit up with outdoor Christmas lights, despite the early season. A couple of picnic tables sat near one end, and a large plastic menu was posted next to a takeout window. He put the truck in park and tossed one of those slow, easy smiles her way again.

Amused by his boyish enthusiasm, she followed his lead and jumped out of the truck. They met again in front of it.

"Best burgers in Colorado. I promise."

"Really?" When they got closer and she could

see the menu, she spotted a little note at the bottom of the corrugated plastic that said *'Proudly Serving Baylor Beef'*.

"But seriously, still the best burgers," he said, when he saw where her eyes had been drawn.

When she scanned the rest of the menu, she noted everything *started* as a normal hamburger, but could be dressed up in a variety of ways—all of them with cute little themed names.

"How am I supposed to just pick one of these?" She shook her head, taking note of something tasty-looking called the California Sunrise, rivaled by the New York New York burger. She glanced over to find Finn watching her, just barely containing laughter.

"I recommend The Rancher, but I might be a little biased."

Lily checked the description—a third-pound burger with barbecue sauce, bacon, crispy fried onions and pepper jack cheese.

"If I eat that, I will explode," she said with certainty.

"It delicious, and you won't explode. I promise I'll roll you home."

She waffled for a minute, and then nodded. "Okay."

Finn turned to the older woman waiting in the window. "Yvette, you're looking better than ever."

The woman batted her hand in the air to brush his compliment off. "Enough, Finn. What can I get for yas?"

"We'll have two Ranchers, and...two root beer floats?" He checked with Lily as he ordered the latter, who responded with a nod. When Yvette appeared back in the window with the drinks, he dug in his back pocket and peeled a couple bills out. "Keep the change."

He handed her one of the drinks and nodded toward one of the picnic tables. "It'll be a few minutes, but it's worth the wait."

"Thank you for inviting me out here, Finn," Lily said as she slid her legs into the picnic table opposite where he sat sideways on the bench seat. She guessed he was keeping one eye on the window for Yvette to signal him their food was ready.

"I used to come out here a lot more often...they close up once the weather gets too cold. 'Nother couple of weeks. And I haven't been all summer, so I thought I'd kill two birds with one stone." He smiled at her and she noticed how his eyes crinkled at the edges; a sign of someone who had once smiled a whole hell of a lot more than she saw him smiling now.

"So that's how you're friendly with Yvette?" She twisted her straw in her drink, moving some of the creamy foam into the soda base.

"Well...Baylor beef." He tipped his head down and she blushed.

"Oh, right. Duh."

"But also, in case you missed it, Three Rivers is tiny. We share resources with the other towns around us, and everybody knows everybody. So I knew Yvette before she opened up this little spot. She was my fifth grade teacher."

As if she'd been summoned, Yvette appeared in the window of the trailer and called Finn's name. He flashed Lily a quick smile before he got up, and returned not long after with two paper plates, each containing one of the largest hamburgers she'd ever seen and a mountain of crispy, hand cut French fries that made her mouth water. With a flourish, he set one down in front of her, and then took his seat opposite her again.

"You seriously *will* have to roll me home."

"Good thing it's on my way," he winked.

*

If he'd been a gambling man, Finn would never have bet his first date in a decade would have gone so well. He wouldn't have put money on her saying yes, either. He'd sent her a million mixed signals, but he hoped she could read this one loud and clear.

Lily seemed to be enjoying herself, and it surprised him a little bit how good a time he was having. He'd always loved Yvette's burgers, and enjoying one while sitting across from a girl who looked as good as Lily did was a hell of a lot better than eating it from a takeout tray at his kitchen table all alone. He and Sunny had frequented Yvette's a lot when they were first married, but he'd only just started coming back last year—always on his own, until now. It felt less itchy than he expected. Dangerously comfortable, even.

"So you've always lived in Three Rivers?" Lily asked, taking her first bite of the burger. Her eyes widened and then she tipped her head back and let out a groan of satisfaction. He couldn't stop his laughter; it was a common reaction. "Ohmigod. Finn. Oh *my God.*"

"Right? And yes, I've always lived here. We're the fourth generation to run the Baylor ranch, and besides the time Noah spent in Denver with Emma, we've all always been here." He picked up a few fries and washed them down with his drink.

Lily leaned forward over her plate, her elbows on the tabletop. "You never wanted to leave?"

He shrugged.

"Hard to want to leave when you have everything you need."

Even as he said the words, he knew they fell short. There had been a time, when Sunny and

Gavin were both still alive and the family was free of the grief that had burdened them all, when Finn believed Three Rivers had everything he needed and he'd never need to leave. But in the last couple of years, more than once he'd considered getting in his truck and going somewhere where nobody knew him to start over fresh. He'd never acted on it because of his sense of duty to his family.

"What about you?" he asked, eager to take the focus off of himself. "You've always lived in Denver?"

She shook her head.

"We actually settled in Denver after my dad bailed on us. My mom's family is from there, but we lived all over before that. So we've been in Denver, as a family..." she paused, tipping her head back, her mouth moving as she counted under her breath. "Ten years."

"And you never wanted to leave?"

She shrugged, polishing off the rest of her burger, and then pushed her plate, with half of her fries toward the middle of the table.

"I wouldn't say Denver had everything I needed, but it was comfortable. And I didn't want to leave my mom. She took the divorce pretty hard."

He nodded, but it was hard to imagine those feelings. He'd never considered himself privileged to have parents that had been married for decades, but now that he thought about it, it was obvious.

"What about photography school?"

Lily shook her head. "Self-taught. I'm pretty lucky to have gotten the contract with the Stock Show."

He thought of the focus in her eyes this morning when he'd found her tilting her head at that coffee cup on the table. She obviously had seen something there he'd never in a million years have seen. And the shots she'd taken at the beginning of him working with Encore. She found something in ordinary occurrences that made them special. It was something like 'feel' in horsemanship—you could take lessons your whole life and never develop the sensitivity and good timing required to be a truly excellent horseman—something you were born with, that couldn't be taught.

"All done?" He tipped his head toward her uneaten fries.

"I really could not eat another bite."

"Alright, I'll roll you out of here." He laughed and got up, taking her garbage and depositing it in a nearby trash bin. Waving at Yvette, he ushered Lily toward the truck, holding the passenger door open for her this time.

She paused in the triangle of space between the door and his body, and turned to look at him with a brow raised.

"Just in case you need a push." He winked, and she shook her head with a rueful look, then levered herself into the truck by the running board and the handle by the door frame, without his help.

"See? Didn't need you."

She didn't need him, but maybe she could want him.

.

-TWENTY-FOUR-

LILY wasn't surprised when they headed straight back to the ranch. He *had* said dinner, and she wasn't sure there was anything else worth doing in Three Rivers. She *was* surprised when he pulled on past his cabin and started up the same path he'd taken just this afternoon to take her to the end of the ranch property.

Night had fallen but the sky was clear and bright with a big, round, full moon lighting the path as well as the truck's headlights did. She suspected Finn could have driven this route with his eyes closed, anyways.

This time, when he reached the end of the pasture, he made a wide arc and backed his truck up almost to the fence line, so they were looking back down at the ranch. It was a long way off but she could see the warm yellow glow of lights in the big house. Glancing over at him, she smiled.

"This isn't the view I want you to see, just wait," he promised, and got out of the truck. She got out and mirrored his path on her side of the truck as he walked the length of the box and then lowered the tailgate. "Hang on."

He disappeared back to the cab, and she heard a new country song playing as he turned on the truck's radio. The landscape she'd photographed just hours earlier was transformed. The inky black of night spread out and on the horizon, the spectacular display of stars was interrupted by the jagged peaks of the Rockies. She crossed her arms over her middle to ward off the chill of the evening and took a deep breath, her heart constricted in her chest.

She'd been reasonably certain this afternoon when she'd stood in this same spot that it was the most beautiful thing Colorado had to offer, but he'd gone and proven her wrong. There was no way her camera could have captured the feeling rattling around in her rib cage; wonder and the reality of their smallness in this giant universe layered over how it felt to know Finn Baylor had arranged for this for her.

She heard Finn behind her, and when she turned, he had a plaid blanket folded over his arm and a thermos in his other hand.

"Now I *know* you've brought me up here to off me," she chuckled as he spread the blanket on the tailgate.

"Trust me, if I wanted to get rid of you, I would have done it long ago." The playful tone in his voice had taken some getting used to, but it was good. She settled onto the tailgate, her legs swinging in the open space beneath her, and he sat beside her, close enough their arms touched, and despite the layers of fabric between them, her blood heated.

She wouldn't have pegged Finn for this kind of organized, thoughtful man, but it occurred to her she didn't actually know much about him. He hadn't let her. These glimpses he was finally allowing her to see made her want so much more.

He twisted, and she felt the blanket come up around her shoulders, blocking out the cold his body heat hadn't absorbed. He opened the thermos. Rich, chocolaty smelling steam wafted from it, and she almost clapped her hands with delight when he poured it over into the cup.

"You're the best." She grinned when he handed her the cup. She wrapped her hands around it and held it up to her face, inhaling.

His low chuckle warmed her almost as much as the sip of hot chocolate she took, almost as much as the way his gaze felt on her. "I've been told."

"Maybe too much," she teased.

"Probably not enough," he laughed, shaking his head.

"So you said you asked me out to get to know me better."

"That's right, I did."

"A question for a question," she said, taking another sip of hot chocolate. She couldn't imagine being warmer or more comfortable.

"Alright. Tell me about Encore."

He could have asked her a million things and she'd have willingly answered; favorite food, color, country song. She would have even volunteered to tell him about her dating history, more about her parents' divorce, anything. But he'd cut straight to the core of her hopes and dreams by asking about the horse she'd pinned everything on to the point of obsession.

"My dad bought him for me." She shrugged.

"So that's why you were so insistent about his rehabilitation?" Finn tipped his head toward her, and Lily glanced up. She'd discovered a whole different side to him tonight; the one she'd just gotten a glimpse of when she told him about the accident. Even Emma didn't know much about her parents' divorce. When Finn Baylor let down his prickly armor, he was easy to talk to. The kind of person you knew would keep your secrets, and say the right things at the right times...or nothing at all if that was what the situation called for. "He's special to you because he's a gift from your father?"

She shook her head resolutely. "I was an angry teenager, and it was easier for him to try and buy me off than spend time trying to fix what had been broken. I guess a small part of me wanted to prove to him it's worth it to keep pushing, even when things get tough."

"He's lucky to have someone as stubborn as you pushing for him," Finn said, letting out a low chuckle. "Most of the horses that come in are at their last stop. If I can't help them, there isn't another option. I have a feeling this horse will be with you until he expires of natural causes, regardless of how things turn out here at the ranch."

She nodded. "You're right. He's stuck with me."

Finn's eyes crinkled at the corners when he smiled, bumping her shoulder lightly with his. "Sounds familiar."

Her eyes drifted down to her hands circling the empty cup and she bit her lip. "When Emma told me you specialize in this kind of horse, I knew you'd stick with it until the end—whatever that is. And I needed someone as determined as I am."

"You mean stubborn," he laughed.

Glancing up at him, she caught his gaze, warm and welcoming. "Well, I was trying to be nice."

She watched as Finn's hand moved from where it had been resting on his thigh, drifting across the short space between them, and covered her fingers, slipping between the plastic of the thermos cap and her palm. He turned her hand over, stroking the back of it with the pad of his thumb. His gentle touch made her breath catch in her throat. It was as close and intimate as the kiss they'd shared. Maybe more.

"I will stick with this until the end." His low

voice rumbled through her, warming her insides. "I won't lie—I don't know what that end will be. But I promise I'll see it through."

He reached across his lap and took the cup from her with his right hand, and because it felt like the most natural thing in the world, she leaned into his side.

*

They sat like that for a long time, fingers clasped together, his promise hanging in the air. He wanted to promise her other things, but the horse was the only thing he knew he could deliver on, whichever way it turned out. The enormous quietness of the night sky stretched out over them. Finn had seen it a hundred times, but it had never felt quite like this. He'd originally thought he was so out of practice this night would be a disaster, but he couldn't have asked for anything better.

After a time, he let go of her hand, only to draw her closer to his side, sliding an arm over her shoulders. He buried his face against her hair, inhaling, and let out a slow breath as she melted into him, one warm hand sliding across his abdomen. He tensed for a second, but then relaxed into her touch. It felt good, and letting himself feel good was a new, but a welcome thing.

He'd never considered his life unhappy. He'd experienced immense loss, sure, but that wasn't the same as being miserable. And that was why it surprised him how different this felt. Not like unhappy versus happy; more like heavy versus light—and *she* was the light.

And then she crushed the light feeling with seven words that felt like a punch to the gut.

"Can you tell me about your wife?"

His first instinct was to say no. Telling her would have been fair. She'd opened up not once, but twice, about difficult things in her past, and he'd barely given her a crumb to go on. He regained his footing and slipped his right hand out from under the blanket, using it to tilt her chin up. A flutter of a smile crossed her lips when she met his eyes, and he pressed his mouth to the corner where it tipped up. Her hand moved to his chest, and she pushed him back just enough to catch his eyes again.

"Just promise you're not going to run away after this and not give me a drive back to the ranch," she said, laughing. Despite the dark, he could see a playful glint in her eyes.

"Give me a chance to get this right this time."

He bent his head, pushing back against her hand on his chest, and drew at the curve of her neck. She tasted incredible, and oh-so-sweetly, she tipped her head to the side to give him access, one of her hands sliding up onto his shoulder as his lips swept up her jaw, to the feather-soft spot behind her ear. He heard her shuddering sigh move past his ear and smiled, cupping the base of her neck to tip her head back and take her parted lips.

All at once, he wished he hadn't wasted these past few days *not* kissing her.

Like she had in the kitchen, she softened into the kiss almost immediately, giving in to him in a way that made him only want more. The desire surprised him more than anything. It was a feeling a man could get used to.

*

Oh, he was getting it right, alright. She didn't know how long it took before she came up for air, but when she did, Lily was clinging to Finn like her life depended on it. And maybe it did. She could have easily lost herself completely in the gentle, easy way he kissed her. Not with the same urgency

177

as before, but slower, more thorough, until she was grateful she wasn't standing because she would have just pooled at his feet by the time he was finished with her. A damp chill had started to settle in the night air, but she barely felt it.

He caught her eyes, cradling her cheek in his hand, and then shifted, shuffling them back into the bed of the truck. By the time it was all said and done, he'd positioned her with her back against his chest, nestled in a v he made with his long legs, the blankets wrapped around them. He gathered her hair off her neck, pushing it over one shoulder, and she could feel his warm breath just at the knot of spine where her neck and shoulders intersected. His mouth followed, and a shiver ran up her spine. She pressed back against him, and he smiled against the crook of her neck.

When he finally spoke, his words rumbled through her. "I knew Sunny since we were kids. In high school, she started traveling to rodeo events with us and Emma. After that, it came easy. We married the fall after we graduated. We were just kids, really."

A lump settled in Lily's throat as she listened to him speak. He couldn't show her the vulnerability in his face, but she could feel it in every word he spoke. She found his hand resting on his thigh and twisted her fingers into his to give them a reassuring squeeze.

"But we grew up, together. A lot of trial and error." He stopped then, and Lily shifted, craning her neck to try and catch his eyes.

"You don't have to keep going."

But he did, anyway. A deep, shuddering breath moved through him, and then he continued.

"She was my best friend, and my biggest cheerleader. And she was so young when she got sick. You say 'in sickness and in health' at the altar, but you're so happy you can't imagine then what it looks like—a hospital bed in your spare bedroom and your wife lying in it, all skin and bones and beeping machines. And there's not a thing you can do. Not one goddamn thing. No amount of love can cure cancer."

Lily swallowed hard, trying to keep her own emotion at bay. Her heart ached for him, but she was grateful for the little window into Finn's motivations. She could understand his hesitance; the need to protect himself from that same helplessness that had probably overwhelmed him when his wife was sick. She knew a taste of that from her days lying flat on her back in a hospital bed, but she'd at least been granted the kindness of a kernel of hope.

"She got sicker and sicker and we all knew what was coming. My brother and his wife were still fresh in the ground and I knew she was going to join them. But she kept on as long as she could. In the early days, between treatments, she'd make me take her to rodeo. She even ran barrels for a while, so weak I had no idea how she stayed with the horse, and she'd climb down and I'd have to carry her away because she couldn't even walk. People had a lot to say about me 'letting' her do something like that. But the truth was, there was nothing she put her mind to that she couldn't do—except survive the cancer.

"I can see that in you; the things you've told me about your recovery, how damn stubborn you are about that horse. Sunny's been gone almost as long as we were married, at this point. I'd be lying if I said I don't still miss her every day. Or that I'm not scared as hell of you."

That brought a sad little smile over her lips, but

he couldn't see it. It took everything she had to muster her voice when all she wanted to do was cry for this man, for his loss, and his pain, and the powerlessness he'd felt. "I promise I won't bite."

He chuckled and tightened his arms around her, pressing his face against the back of her neck. Maybe for his own benefit, maybe to stop her from doing what she wanted the most—to turn around and take his face in her hands and kiss him until he didn't hurt. They sat in silence for a time, while she processed the idea that he was scared of her. It was almost impossible to imagine a man who made a living facing angry 1200lb animals with a murderous streak scared of anything.

"I don't want to hurt you." It was a quiet admission, one she barely heard. She couldn't help but marvel at the thought that he was worried about hurting her, when he'd just laid out his emotions. There was clearly a lot more to Finn Baylor than she'd imagined, and there had to be a tiny part that was afraid of being vulnerable again. She loosened herself from his grip, rising up on her knees and cupping his jaw.

"I can take whatever you can dish out, cowboy," she said as she touched her lips to his; gentle at first, and then more forcefully, as if she could take the hurt away from him. It took him a minute to respond, but when he did, the urgency and emotion in the kiss overwhelmed her. The taste of longing, regret and sadness all but erased the few sweet kisses they'd shared in comparison. His hands at her waist drew her to his body, and she bowed toward him, eager for the contact.

She would have given him anything he asked for, because she knew what that need felt like, to validate yourself after loss and pain. To feel like yourself again. Wasn't that the same thing she was chasing right now?

*

As abruptly as the kiss had begun, Finn pulled back. Distraction was one thing, loss of control was completely another, and if he didn't rein himself in soon, he wouldn't be able to stop.

Lily's chest heaved and their quick breaths hung in the chilled night air between them. Bathed in moonlight, she was pretty as a picture. Unable to stop himself, he reached up and touched her cheek lightly.

"I should get you back home. You're going to freeze to death up here."

Especially if his hands went where his mind had, underneath the thin shirt she wore, flaying open the buttons and unhooking her bra... Her cheek swelled under his palm as she smiled, tracing one finger over his own stubbled jawline.

"It's cold?"

He chuckled, and shook his head, shifting carefully. He had expected the pain and self-deprecation that always came hand in hand with thinking or talking about Sunny too much, even now. Instead, Lily had erased it all, and he didn't know what to do with that.

"Yes, it's cold. And if I let you get sick, Emma will have my hide."

Finally, Lily shuffled backwards out of the nest they'd made, straightening her shirt as she got to her feet in the bed of his truck. He breathed a sigh of relief as the distance opened up between them. It'd been a long time since he'd considered alternatives for his F150 that extended beyond hauling hay and towing trailers, but she made him feel like a horny teenager who couldn't get a check on his roaming hands.

He followed her to his feet, then jumped off the

tailgate, offering his hand to help her down.

"I'm doing this for your own good," she said as she slipped her fingers into his and hopped off the tailgate, stumbling forward and into his arms. It might have been on purpose, and he might have been praying for it to happen. He gave her a quick squeeze—all he dared—before he released her. "I know how shitty your odds are when you go head to head with Emma."

"And how do you know that?" He laughed as he led her around to the passenger side of the truck and opened the door for her.

The look she gave him almost made him laugh out loud.

"I'm still here, aren't I?"

-TWENTY-FIVE-

"ALRIGHT, brother, it's just you and me. And I'm not letting you add any new scuffs to my saddle, you hear?" Finn slid a hand down Encore's nose and the horse lowered his head. Since they'd discerned the saddle was the problem, he'd spent every morning slowly and carefully saddling the gelding and working him with it on. Finally, the gelding had stopped responding to the tightening of the girth and the sessions were starting to move more smoothly. So smoothly now, in fact, with his confidence and urgency bolstered by his date the night before, Finn was going to attempt something stupid.

He'd put first rides on new horses without a spotter before, but it had been a while, and it was usually a horse he could trust. He still hadn't reached that point with Encore. The point he *had* reached was the one where he couldn't stop thinking about how incredible it would be for Lily if he could actually make her dream of riding Encore again happen, for real. She'd listened patiently, quietly, while he'd talked about Sunny the night before. Something he hadn't truly been able to do for years. The gentleness and compassion in her touch—empathy, not pity, told him she knew all too well where he'd been. And so now he ached to be able to do this for her.

Reaching into his pocket, he produced a treat

that Encore happily snuffled up, crunching away merrily. He'd been outfitted in a rope halter and a long, soft lead rope; a bit and bridle didn't always match this occasion. He'd made up his mind to see what the horse would tolerate, pushing him to the edge of his comfort zone before he backed off. It was a sound theory with most horses, but with one as unpredictably explosive as Encore could be, it would be risky.

Laying a little groundwork, he flexed the gelding's head from one side to the other, then gathered the rope up in the hand he put on the horn, so the gelding's neck and body arced toward him, and then carefully slipped his toe into the stirrup. Encore overflexed, sniffing the toe of Finn's boot before he released, and carefully, the cowboy bore weight in the stirrup.

"Bad idea, Finnegan."

That was Emma, ambling by the round pen on her way to the big outdoor riding pen, a client horse trailing behind her. He glanced back and in the second it took him to refocus, Encore, who *had* been relaxed, rooted his head down and let out a grunt, driving his locked up front legs into the sand and his hindquarters into the air. Finn stumbled back, landing on his ass in the sand, but was up in a hot minute as the gelding worked his way around the outside of the ring. His ego bruised more than his hind end, Finn stepped out of the round pen, cursing under his breath as he brushed dust off the seat of his jeans. Emma stopped up at the outside rail, shaking her head.

"What the hell are you doing, anyway? You shoulda just asked and I would have helped you."

"He's getting better," Finn insisted, gesturing at Encore, who had quickly stopped bucking and geared down to a high-headed trot.

"Um..."

"Sort of."

"What's the big rush, anyways?" When he made his way around their side, she stuck her arm out over the rail and snagged the trailing lead rope "Easy, buddy."

"No rush," Finn lied, but knew Emma would see straight through it. She always did.

"Uh huh." As he expected, she tipped her head toward him, one brow arched sharply. "Did he knock you on the head when he knocked you over?"

"What?"

"I'm just sayin'... this isn't like you. Normally, you'd go back, retrace your steps, take all the time you need."

"I don't have all the time in the world, Champ." The urgency felt like a boulder on his chest. He knew this wasn't the right way to go about this. She was right. A horse like this could take some time and he would normally tell a client with a horse like this that it would take as long as it took, full stop. But Lily didn't have all the time in the world. She had a contract in Denver in the winter, and he knew she wouldn't stay even til Christmas. He had a lot of ground he had to make up between now and then if he was going to shape Encore back into the horse she wanted him to be.

Emma leveled with him, catching his eyes. "You have enough time, Finn."

"Lily doesn't have enough time."

Shaking her head, his sister-in-law turned to the horse that had been patiently waiting for her, and flipped her rein up over his neck. "She does. I know *she's* not putting this pressure on you. Take a breath, go backwards if you have to. It's not worth getting hurt."

But maybe it was.

-TWENTY-SIX-

"'MORNING."

Lily bit her lip to try to stop the eager smile that blossomed when she saw Finn at the bottom of the stairs of his cabin. She'd been a little grateful when she'd woken after he left the house this morning. It gave her a few extra minutes to process their date the night before. He'd left her at the door of her bedroom with a kiss that was so chaste she ached when she climbed into bed. And now, here he was, like he'd been watching for her to come out of the house to start her morning of shooting, looking like the cover of some working cowboy magazine, so ruggedly handsome it made her knees weak. And worse, now that she knew what he tasted like, and his gentle, easy touch, she wanted it more.

"Good morning. What's this?" she asked, gesturing to the pair of tacked up horses behind him. Buckshot and a big, rangy chestnut were practically dozing behind him.

"I just thought I'd join you for today's ride."

She narrowed her eyes at him for a moment, then took a tentative step off the porch toward him. "You know, for someone who insisted they didn't give riding lessons..."

"Yeah, yeah, I'm not going to live that down, am I?"

"Probably not."

"S'alright, I'll take my lumps. Leave the

camera."

It felt counter-intuitive to leave her camera bag on the big rustic-wood chair on his porch, but she did it, and laughing, she stepped forward and greeted first Buckshot, then the other horse.

"Who's this?" Despite the time she'd spent at the ranch, there were too many horses in and out for her to have kept track of everyone. She thought that, apart from Encore, she'd never seen Finn work with the same horse twice, but knew that couldn't be true.

"My ole reliable, Jet. Client horse fail." Finn glanced at the horse and she saw a softness in his eyes that said there was more to the story than he was volunteering. There was *always* more to the story when Finn Baylor was involved, but the last few days had proven it wasn't always bad.

"Hello, Jet," she said, stroking the gelding's nose, before turning her attention back to Finn. They were tucked in together in the little space between the horses and he hadn't stepped back. Being this close to him, knowing him differently since their date last night, and hoping beyond all hope that two horses meant what she thought it did sparked a flight of butterflies low in her belly. "So...we're going to practice steering around other horses in the ring?"

"Not *quite*."

Now it was *him* trying to hide a smile, and she knew what he was offering her. A ride on the trails, through the woods; a tiny taste of what had once been such an enormous, all-consuming part of her life.

"Let me get my helmet."

Jogging toward the barn, her mind went back over the handful of 'lessons' he'd given her on Buckshot. While she hadn't gained any strength in her left leg, she was definitely feeling more at ease than she had been, well rested thanks to the double bed, and her core muscles were starting to hold her better. She grabbed her helmet off the peg in the now-neatly-organized-and-dust-free tack room and scooted back to Finn, who had made it halfway across the yard with the horses.

She stuck the helmet on her head without buckling it and took Buckshot's reins from him, her heart practically skipping at the idea that he was going to make this possible for her. He must have sensed her pent-up excitement, because he chuckled and shook his head, moving to buckle her helmet under her chin, like he had the first time he'd helped her ride. This time, he sealed it with a gentle kiss, the only thing that could have possibly distracted her from her enthusiasm to head out onto the trails.

All too quickly, it was over, and she briefly considered vetoing the ride in favor of more kissing, but Finn was already herding her toward Buckshot, and, without warning, like always, hoisting her onto the horse's back. From astride, she looked down at the top of his head as he looped the loose rein over Buckshot's neck and helped her push her left toe into the stirrup. His hand closed around her ankle and he glanced up at her with a crooked smile.

"Later," he promised, crossing in front of Jet in a few long strides. He legged up onto the gelding so effortlessly it made Lily just a smidge jealous, though she couldn't say his help getting her into the saddle was nearly as humiliating now that their relationship had taken a turn a little more intimate.

He reined his horse left of the cattle barn, the opposite direction she normally headed with her camera, and she fell into stride beside him as they cut across a tractor path between a couple of hay fields on the far side of the property, heading away from Emma's folks' side of the ranch. She glanced over at Finn, sitting loose and comfortable in the saddle, his rein hand resting over his saddle horn, the other on his long jean-clad thigh. He felt her eyes and glanced over at her, back at the treeline they were approaching, then back at her.

"What?"

"Nothing," she said, chuckling a little as she shook her head. "Where are we going?"

"You'll see."

They crossed a few fields with sparse treelines before Lily found herself in a field with a dense forest of evergreens beyond it.

"How you feeling?"

If she could put into words how it felt to be free of the rails of the round pen, she would have almost waxed poetic. But instead, she smiled, a smile she felt all the way to her toes, and shook her head, and said "Great."

"Good, we're just getting started." Finn laughed, and tipped forward, putting heels to side and urging Jet into an easy lope. The excited butterflies that had been keeping a low simmer at the base of her stomach moved up to lodge in her throat, a mixture of excitement and fear and adrenaline washing through her. His intention was clear, and she watched the chestnut's hindquarters grow smaller as they moved away from her.

"Oh, what the hell," she muttered under her breath, and wrapped her free hand around the saddle horn for a bit of extra security as she made a kissing noise to Buckshot, signaling the lope. The horse moved into a big, easy, rocking horse canter she hadn't yet felt. They'd barely trotted in the ring.

Those butterflies burst into a flutter as she felt her body relax into the horse's stride, her smile so wide her cheeks hurt. Her heart soared as trees and stubbled field flew past her. And then laughter bubbled out of her as she Buckshot's long strides brought them back neck and neck with Jet and Finn. When he looked over to check on her, everything about the moment felt perfect. From the good horse, to the woods around her, to the handsome cowboy at her side.

For the first time in a long time, she didn't feel like a victim of an accident anymore. And she felt victorious to be riding Buckshot, not disappointed it wasn't Encore. For a brief moment, everything felt like it was as it should be, not some broken, wrong variation of what her reality was supposed to be.

When they reached the end of the field, Finn reined Jet back down to a walk, and without much prompting, Buckshot did the same.

"How was that?" Finn's casual tone betrayed the huge smile he wore. Clearly, the way she was feeling was infectious.

"Seriously?"

He nodded.

She was way more accustomed to expressing her emotions with images than words, but she tried to assemble something that at least vaguely honored the freedom of an easy lope on the trail, and found herself with another lump lodged firmly in her throat and tears pricking at her eyelids. *Silly.*

Finn reached across the space between them and squeezed her knee lightly. Like he knew. She couldn't have asked for more.

*

"All set to head back?" Finn glanced at Lily. They'd taken a break at the midway point, and she had squatted beside the creek Buckshot stood in, drinking, to bring some water to her own lips in her cupped hands. She'd removed her helmet and her hair was flat and sticking out all over the place, but he couldn't have found her sexier than in that moment. Truth was, the sooner he got her back to the ranch, the sooner they could pick up that kiss where it had left off. And, judging by the high flush of pleasure he'd seen on her cheeks, she just might let him.

"No. I could stay out here all day." She straightened, cast a smile his way that made his heart lighter just for witnessing it, and clucked to Buckshot, tugging on his rein to bring him up out of the creek. He scrambled up the bank and she checked her rigging—he'd noticed her loosen it when they'd stopped and dismounted. "But then I wouldn't be able to walk tomorrow. And probably neither would this guy."

He watched as she moved around Buckshot, sliding her hands down each leg, presumably to check for swelling or warmth. When she moved back to his head, she checked that his bridle and bit were still comfortable, and then felt his chest to see how warm he was. He hadn't given her much credit as a good horseman at the beginning, and the helmet and neon tack he'd seen her move into the tack room hadn't helped much, but he warmed as he watched her tend to the ranch's oldest equine's well-being like he was her own. There was an instinct and intuition in her that he hadn't credited her with originally.

Although he hadn't said anything, she straightened and glanced at him, moving into position at the horse's side with a long suffering sigh. She lifted her hands onto the horn and cantle of the saddle. "Alright, I'm ready."

Jet remained rooted in the short grass at the edge of the creek when Finn stepped away to help

Lily into the saddle. It was becoming old hat, the way he wrapped his fingers around her calf and rooted his shoulder under the curve of her ass and hoisted her into the saddle, but he was beginning to appreciate it more as an opportunity to sneak an extra touch instead of just a functional action to help her onto the horse. This time, while she settled in, he slid his hand over her thigh and paused at her jeans-clad knee again. It was hardly a touch, but now that he'd done it a few times, he found himself strategically arranging to do it again.

"You're doing a great job."

"I love this, Finn." She paused and he felt her fingers cover his, squeezing lightly.

"I do, too." And just like that, her touch was gone. He glanced up at her and smiled, then moved around Jet to climb into the saddle. "Honestly, we'd come out these trails a bit when we were kids on ponies but these days, I'm so full up on client horses and ranch work I don't take the time. I really should, though."

He glanced out over the water, where the trail picked up on the other bank and continued through the woods. Far enough and you came to the Anderson spread. He and his brothers and Nate and Banks had practically been a gang of hoodlums, roaming through the woods on their horses. They'd pick up Cutter and tether their mounts and splash around in the creek. And then they'd become teenagers, and girls and pickup trucks and rodeo were more important.

Finally, his gaze landed back on Lily. She wore the same thoughtful expression he was sure he did and it was clear she was reminiscing herself.

"Sometimes I just like to get inside my head. And being in the woods on a horse does a good job of that," she said, turning to look at him. She reached down and stroked a hand along Buckshot's neck. He wished he had been able to make this happen for her with Encore, and he had his doubts he could at all, but this was a good start for a girl who hadn't even ridden for a year.

He smiled, reining Jet toward home. "Sometimes, inside my head is the most dangerous place to be."

Lily pressed her lips together, her dark eyes fixed on his for a second longer than would have been a cursory glance. He broke the contact first. In a perfect world, he'd tell her what was eating at the edge of his mind, the corner of his heart. In a perfect world, he'd be able to articulate why he couldn't offer her anything more than the sweet kisses he stole from her, a ride into the woods now and then, and the work on her horse. This wasn't a perfect world. It was a world in which he'd lost his footing five years ago and hadn't been able to find a real toehold since.

Lily didn't press him and that made him wish even more than he could spill his guts to her.

He swallowed and put his heels to Jet's sides. The horse knew they were headed home and his pace was quick. Finn settled deeper into the saddle and tipped his legs forward a fraction of an inch and the gelding's legs slowed, maintaining the walk, but at a much more leisurely pace. Buckshot and Lily soon matched pace.

-TWENTY-SEVEN-

A FEW hours later found Lily on the love seat in Finn's living room, her legs crossed and her laptop balanced precariously on the diamond made between her knees. She'd headed back to the cabin to go through some of the shooting she'd done for the Andersons but she was still so high from her little trail ride she couldn't settle in to work and had, instead, been flipping through the photos and discarding the ones that were obviously not useful for sale photos.

The morning's ride barely compared to the distances she'd once done, but Finn had done her a tremendous service taking her out. Even if she still hadn't gained any strength in her left leg. Even if she was sore already and had spent ten minutes stretching it out of her system before a long, hot shower. The ride he'd taken her on had reminded her of why she'd started long distance in the first place. Nothing beat the way you communed with your horse and with the beautiful nature around you when you rode into the woods. Normally, she preferred to be alone, but she had appreciated Finn's quiet, steady presence at her side, pushing her when she didn't have faith in her body's abilities, and backing off when she needed it.

She heard him before she saw him, climbing the steps into the house, and then the door pushed open and there he was. Warmth rushed her chest when he smiled at her and shouldered out of his coat.

"How you feeling?"

She shook her head, pulling her laptop partially closed. "Amazing."

"I meant physically," he said, tipping his head down with a smile. He slid in beside her on the love seat and his weight on the cushions tipped her toward him. She squawked, grabbing hold of her tipping laptop. Taking advantage of their new, close position, Finn took the laptop from her and set it safely on the end table beside him, then slipped his arm over her shoulder and drew her closer to his side, his lips falling on her forehead in a kiss so sweet and chaste that her heart must have swelled at least two sizes.

"Fine," she said, smiling up at him. "Now quit worrying. I left Denver to get away from my worry-wart of a mother."

He laughed, tipping her head a little farther with his fingers under her chin and brushed his mouth over hers. "I'm not worried, I just want to make sure you're feeling good enough for this."

Lily sagged against his chest, giving herself up to the kiss. His fingers gathered the hair at the nape of her neck and tipped her face back to change the angle, and it went from sweet and sultry to electric in half a heartbeat. She curled her fingers in the lapels of his shirt, drawing him down, closer, and he responded, pushing her back against the arm of the couch and shifted his body over hers, the fingers of one hand teasing the bare skin her t-shirt rode up to expose.

With a sharp exhale, Lily arched up against the weight of Finn's body on hers, the sweet ache of longing spreading through her bloodstream. He was so close, but still so far away.

Today, every innocent touch, every brush of lips or prolonged glance felt like there was an extra layer of need—for her, anyway. Finn, on the other hand, seemed to exercise that modicum of self-control she hadn't quite mastered. Or he particularly enjoyed making her wait. When he pulled back, a sneaky grin tipping up one corner of his lips, she suspected it was the latter.

"You know my parents just rolled in."

"It's Saturday, isn't it?"

"Mhm," he hummed, dropping his lips against the curve of her neck and tickling her with his stubbly jaw. She squirmed, arching her body into his almost involuntarily before she pushed at his shoulders.

"Get up, we have to go be social." Truth was, she could have lived in this happy little bubble for another fifty years or so without blinking.

"Mhm."

"Finn." She felt his smile. "Come on."

He let an exaggerated groan out and shifted back on his knees, looking at her in such a way that she wasn't sure if he was going to flay open the buttons of her shirt or get up. But then he got up, and offered her his hand, and she was almost as relieved as she was disappointed.

Together, they left his cabin and headed for the big house, walking into the typical Saturday routine in full swing. Ren and Ella hovered over the stove, working on something that smelled delicious, as always. Caine sat at the table with Gracie on his knee, and Noah and Kerri sat side by side, watching barrel runs on her cell phone.

They hadn't exactly walked in holding hands but so much had changed since the last Saturday gathering, she wondered if his family could tell. If they could see it on her face that just minutes ago, she would have easily forgone their gathering—one of her favorite parts of her week, second only to Tessa's riding lesson—for something a little spicier.

The flurry of greetings they received betrayed no suspicion, so she shrugged out of her coat and headed for the counter to see what she could do to help.

*

Ella Baylor knew. Finn was sure of it. Lily might not have noticed it, but his mother's eyes had narrowed almost imperceptibly—like she could see the monumental shift between the pair of them, even though he'd worked hard to hide it once they'd climbed the steps to the big house. He just needed a little more time to process what all of this meant. In the meantime, he was enjoying becoming reacquainted with the feminine form.

And what a form it was. Despite himself, he glanced at Lily taking her place at the counter to help out with the meal. A few short weeks ago, that sight had incited an entirely different emotion in him, but today, all he could think was this was where she belonged.

"So," Emma began casually, from her position at the counter where she was peeling potatoes. "I noticed Jet and Buckshot missing this morning."

He glanced at Lily, with a smile so bright it was almost immediately blinding. He'd enjoyed their ride out but he knew it meant more to her than just a little jaunt into the woods.

"Finn took me out for a little trail ride," she started. She glanced back at him and what he read in her eyes made his heart race more than the feel of her soft, willing body under his earlier. If Ella hadn't known before, she would know now. And everyone else, too, probably. *To hell with it.*

"Oh yeah?" That was Caine, lifting his head

from the drawing station with the kids. Finn very specifically remembered a conversation early in his horse training career where he'd informed his father that trail rides for pleasure were useless and a waste of time when a horse could learn whatever they needed outside of the round pen on the acreage, working cattle. He wasn't the only one who recalled the conversation, apparently.

"Yeah, out to a stream and back. The back of the Montgomery property, right?" She glanced at him, and he nodded back at her.

"And how was that?" Emma asked, smiling. She might have been the only other person in the room who realized just how important that 'little' ride today had been to Lily.

"It was *amazing*," she said, her voice lifting and her eyes bright.

His family picked up their enthusiastic discussion of her distance riding and he was able to sit back and watch her in a completely different light than the last time he had observed her interacting with his family. Instead of being irritated by the way his mother looked at her like she might be new daughter-in-law material and being rubbed the wrong way by the easy way Lily played along with Caine's relentless teasing, he appreciated it

And when she slipped away to the washroom while everyone was cleaning up after dinner, he met her in the same hall he'd come upon her in on her first night there, and that was entirely different, too. With the memory of her warm body pressed underneath his still right at the edge of his mind, he tugged her to him, covering her mouth with his in the darkness of the hallway, spreading his fingers across her hair to cradle the back of her neck and bring her closer still.

She responded quickly, her body pressed tight to his, opening to him almost immediately even though he'd taken her by surprise. She was too sweet for words, and he wanted her—badly. It was the first time he could remember wanting something or someone like this in the last five years. Hyper aware when he heard movement from the end of the hall, he lifted his head and stepped back, ending the kiss as quickly as he had initiated it. Just because it was easy to stop didn't mean his body appreciated it.

"You go back first," he whispered, propelling her, still starry-eyed from the embrace, back toward the kitchen while he let out a long breath, running his hands over the front of his shirt. As he settled himself, his eyes cast over the picture he'd caught her looking at on that first night—he and Sunny the day they'd been married. Something twisted in his chest. He couldn't do this much longer, but he didn't want to stop.

-TWENTY-EIGHT-

"DAYLIGHT'S burning, Dane!" Finn admonished his older brother as he watched him cross the yard with two travel mugs in tow.

"Hey, do you want coffee or do you not want coffee?" Dane asked, balancing the mugs as he opened the passenger door of Finn's truck and climbed inside.

"What I wanted was to not have to load those colts by myself," Finn scowled, but took the mug his brother offered anyway.

"You still want a steady supply of Ren's coffee, you best quit grumping." Dane inclined his head toward Finn, and the younger brother conceded... for now. Little did Dane know that Finn had found coffee just a little bit sweeter right in his own home.

"Alright, alright."

He shifted the truck into gear and made a wide arc in the yard, driving slowly past his house just as Lily emerged onto the porch with her laptop in hand. Pulling in close, he rolled down his window.

"Hey Lily," Dane said, leaning ahead to speak past Finn.

"Sure you don't wanna come?" Finn asked, hanging his arm out the window and tapping the outside of the truck's door lightly. "Lots of room."

Her dimples appeared with the soft smile that spread over her features and hit him right in the heart. Harder than he expected. "I'd love to but I've got lots of editing to do. And Emma and I are gonna do a girls' night tonight. Don't wait up."

"Alright," he waved and pulled away, rolling up the window.

"You're sweet on that girl," Dane said, as they were pulling out of the driveway.

Finn's gaze cut briefly to his brother but then returned his focus to the road. He already had his mama on his case; she could sniff out a blooming relationship... or whatever this was, from a mile away, the last thing he needed was Dane following suit.

"Then she's sweet on you."

He didn't qualify that statement with a response either, guiding the truck onto Three Rivers' main drag and toward the highway.

"You know, it's gonna be a hell of a long drive if you don't talk to me," Dane continued.

"It's a hell of a long drive even if I do," he replied, leaning forward to turn on the radio. His favorite oldies country station filtered through the speakers of the truck and he settled back in his seat, ignoring the prying gaze of his brother as they cruised along past the commercial center of their small town.

"Well, if you don't wanna talk, you can listen."

"I don't know how listening is any better than talking, but I can't stop you." Finn shook his head, guiding the truck onto the highway. The drive to the Reicher Ranch was about an hour in each direction, and it was going to be a long trip if his brother harped about Lily the entire time.

"Wouldn't you rather get this off your chest now than when mama backs you into a corner?"

He *did* have a point there. Glancing back at Dane, Finn let out a resigned sigh.

"She's a nice girl, and I'm attracted to her. And

that's all there is to tell."

"Bullshit."

Finn shook his head. "No, really. That's it."

"Well, what are you waiting for?"

Again, Dane's question went unanswered as Finn's eyes cut across the space between them. He was relieved when his brother shut up and turned up the radio.

They drove in silence the rest of the way to Reicher's, and pulled in slowly. It was only mid-afternoon but these trips usually took a while. They'd deliver the colts they'd ridden and worked with and pick up a few to bring home to start in on. Because this was the last trip of the season, there was always a celebratory beer and reflection on how the year had been for them. Grant Reicher bred some top notch quarter horses, and the families had a standing contract that went back to his father's colt-breaking days. When the horses sold, Reicher gave them a cut. For anyone else, it might be risky, but without the solid minds and good training foundations the Baylors put on the horses, they would only be worth half as much and Caine Baylor's long standing friendship with the man meant he always treated the boys more than fair.

The old man himself lifted his hat off his head in greeting as he came from the barn. He was a tall, rugged, barrel chested man with a penchant for big belt buckles. Reicher spit a wad of tobacco off to the side while Finn turned the rig wide, backing slowly toward the barn, then waved his hat to guide him, signaling for him to back closer, closer, until he made the cut-off sign and Finn put the truck into park, killing the engine. He glanced at Dane, steeling himself. Their employer was a big personality with a lot to say.

"You ready?"

"As I'll ever be."

"Dane, Finn." The older man greeted them, reaching out to shake their hands one at a time. "How ya been, boys?"

"Oh finer than frog's hair," Dane stepped in.

"Your daddy tells me you got another one on the way." The white haired man grinned slyly at Dane. "You got plans for a baseball team over there, boy?"

Chuckling, Dane shook his head. Grant Reicher was one to talk, with five grown children of his own. "Well, ya know. Many hands make light work on a ranch."

"That's damn right. What about you, Finn? Anyone special?" The normally jolly man's tone got about as somber as it could get when he spoke to Finn. Reicher meant well. Every damn person he ran into *meant* well. It didn't stop the rub of being asked every time you saw someone.

"No, sir. Too busy with these horses of yours." He nodded toward the trailer, happy to derail the train of conversation. Reicher never missed an opportunity to talk up his horses, even to the Baylors, who *knew* how good they were.

"That's right, and I wish I could send a trailer full home with you tonight."

"Well, let's empty the trailer before we try to fill it up again," Finn teased. They took the winter off from the Reicher work, and snow wasn't quite ready to fly, but it would be before they finished winterizing the ranch. "Besides, we still have those two younger fillies to work with still at home."

Nodding, Grant stepped back while Finn and Dane opened the trailer. The four horse slant load afforded them the time to unload each horse and fill their owner in on the details while they led them into the barn and a waiting empty stall. On the third trip out, Finn caught sight of Chase, one of the oldest Reicher sons, on a little bay horse, coming in from their back forty. The short powerhouse of a horse looked familiar, and Finn paused by the edge of the barn while Dane unloaded the last colt.

"Hey, is that…"

"Tank?" Grant appeared beside him. "Sure is. Hell of a horse."

"I thought you sold him."

The older man winked knowingly. "Nobody offered me the right price for him. So he stayed. Super quiet, smart as a whip and reliable."

"Oh yeah, we had him in…what…three, four years ago?" Dane spoke behind them. "The year Gage broke his arm, I think. Actually, I think he was the horse I was working when it happened."

Chase rode over to the group of men, raising his hand in greeting. Though they'd known one another their whole lives, the hour's drive hadn't fostered much but a friendly acquaintance. "Hey boys."

"Chase," Finn said, nodding in greeting. "Tank looks good."

"He's a pussycat," Chase agreed, reaching down to pet the gelding's neck before he swung down off him easily. "Surefooted and smart, bonus points for being close to the ground in case you part ways."

"Kid broke, would you say?" Finn asked, catching the movement of Dane shaking his head in his peripheral vision. An idea had rooted in Finn's mind.

"I don't see why he couldn't be. Not many kids around here to ride him, but I'd expect he's got what it takes."

Finn glanced back at Grant. "So what's the right price?"

*

A couple beer and a couple hours later, when they were on the highway headed home, Dane finally asked.

"So are you gonna talk *now*?"

"I don't know what you're talking about." Finn shook his head.

"Well, I know he's not a graduation present for Kerri, she has Kit."

Finn nodded in agreement.

"And Gage isn't ready to move up from Buckshot yet."

Finn shook his head in return.

"And you have no plans to replace Jet anytime soon."

"Damn straight."

"And we're not really in the business of buying broke horses."

It had taken some intense negotiation that never really amounted to any firm figure, but Grant had conceded they could take Tank on a trial and they'd 'work it out' if it turned out he was what they'd need. Finn suspected the horse would be just about perfect for what he intended, but wasn't sure the gift would be received in the spirit it was offered.

"Nope. But I happen to know a girl who needs a broke horse."

"I *knew* you were sweet on Lily!"

"I'm just trying to help her out. She wants to ride and I don't know if that horse of hers will *ever* be suitable for her to ride with the condition her body's in. I just want to offer her an alternative."

"Shoot," Dane looked out the window for a second, like he was collecting his thoughts. "I've seen you tell clients to find new horses. I've seen you give a riding lesson or two in your life. I've never seen you move someone who's 'just a client' into your house, and buy her a horse. This shit's serious."

Finn felt his jaw tighten of its own volition. More than anything, he wanted out from under his brother's scrutiny, and he needed a few minutes to figure out how he was going to tell Lily he might not be able to help her horse before he landed with a replacement.

"Alright, alright. I figured those beers might loosen you up but I guess I was wrong."

A tight laugh was all that emerged from Finn.

"Okay, just listen for another minute. I think I recall somebody in this very truck telling me once that life was way too short not to grab onto happy when you find it. And I haven't seen you smile about *anybody* the way you did when we pulled out of the yard. I think Sunny would want you to grab onto *that* happy. Or explore it a little, at least. See if it's as good as it looks.

"Nobody just shows up at our ranch for no reason. And whether it was Emma and Nate plotting against you or divine intervention, you might pay attention to what's right in front of you. Nobody's saying you have to marry the girl, but you might open yourself up to having a little fun. Getting a little of the happy you deserve."

Finn could remember the conversation his brother referenced as if it were yesterday. At the time, they'd still been telling everyone Ren was just an employee, but he'd known something was brewing between the pair for at least a couple of weeks before he found them wrapped up in one another on the porch of the big house. She'd given him a big, heartfelt hug afterward that had cemented her place in the family as far as he was concerned.

"You might be right."

-TWENTY-NINE-

FINN let himself into his cabin and closed the door quietly behind him. All the lights were off, but the full moon spilled blue light across the wooden floors, lighting his way. Not that he needed it. He knew the layout of this place like the back of his hand.

Lily must have still been at Noah and Emma's—he'd spotted lights on in their kitchen when they'd driven by, and her bedroom door was closed. Doing his best to avoid the squeaky floorboard just in case, he skirted past her door and into the washroom to grab a quick shower to wash off the grime of the day of travel. He emerged with a towel wrapped around his waist and nearly jumped out of his skin when Lily's door opened.

"Hey," he said softly, even though the only two residents of the house were clearly awake. She smiled a little drowsy smile, brushing her loose hair away from her eyes. "I told you not to wait up."

She shrugged, leaning her shoulder against the door frame. She was wearing that oversized t-shirt that exposed one smooth, soft-looking shoulder, her bare thighs poking out from underneath. It was entirely too dangerous to stand this close to her with so little separating them, with his brother's words today ringing in his ears. He might not have been receptive earlier, but that was some top notch subliminal message planting Dane had performed.

"I wasn't sleeping yet."

"You should be. Aren't you going back to Cutter's in the morning?"

"Afternoon." She smiled and shrugged again, that bare, creamy shoulder lifting. It begged to be tasted. *Another dangerous thought.* And before he could convince himself to just go to bed, he closed the space between them and traced his fingertips along the curve of her soft skin, to her jaw, tilting her chin up. Her bow-shaped lips parted, releasing a quick breath at the same time that everything between his heart and his groin tightened.

Instead of taking that invitation, he crooked his arm around her shoulder, drawing her closer and gathering her hair in his fist at the base of her neck, tugging gently as he dropped his mouth onto the skin he'd just been wondering about. As he'd imagined, she tasted of sugar and vanilla and a raw femininity he'd gone without for far too long. She tipped her head to allow him easier access as he released her hair and let his hand drift down her spine until he reached the small of her back, pressing her body against his much like he had in the hall in the big house. Only this time, there was so much less between them. He heard her draw a sharp breath and then he shifted up, their mouths crashing together like that was all the oxygen they needed.

Lily led the kiss, and the pair of them, into her bedroom, backing until she hit the bed, then broke the kiss to fall onto the mattress. He hesitated a moment, then nearly choked when she sat up, slipping her fingers underneath the hastily knotted towel. He should have been doing a victory dance; she was getting dangerously close to a muscle that had practically atrophied from lack of use since his wife died, and it was responding appropriately, but all he could do was draw in a sharp breath when she made contact with bare skin. His head dropped back and his knees threatened to buckle.

"Shit, Lily." She squeezed lightly and he nearly came undone. Pushing her onto her back, his mouth and body shifted over hers, demanding. If she was going to offer, he would take. Because he hadn't let himself take, hadn't let himself *want* like this in so long.

His heart thundered in his chest as she spread her knees to make a space that cradled him perfectly, notching his hardness against the soft warmth of her center. Two layers of fabric was too many. He shifted back to push her tee up over her rib cage, following the path with his tongue, pausing at her navel before he moved upward, her shirt bunched in his fists as he revealed the creamy whiteness of her torso inch by inch. She tightened her knees around his hips; one side decidedly stronger than the other, just as she'd said when she'd been riding Buckshot, and lifted her arms, motioning for him to dispose of the shirt altogether.

Carefully, he divested her of the soft fabric, and then sank back on his knees to take her in. She was delightfully soft and rounded in all the places that mattered. Her creamy skin was marred by some scarring around her hips and he could see part of a tattoo at her bikini line. He didn't know where to start—at the dusky pink panties that barely covered anything, or her pert, rosy nipples, straining upward like they were vying for his attention. He felt like a man offered a buffet after five years of starvation.

She watched him with clear, bright eyes and color high in her cheeks. Excitement, desire...the things he felt mirrored in himself. He dropped down onto his hands and pressed his mouth to the spot where her last rib met her sternum and she drove her fingers into his hair, curling and tugging as her back arched up into his touch.

He shifted upward and closed his lips around her nipple, drawing her into his mouth, pulling a high pitched little whimper out of her.

"Finn!" His name rolled off her lips in a breathy plea. He wanted to touch everything, taste everything, but the way her hips pressed up into his when he drew hard nearly pushed him straight over the edge. He pinned her to the bed with his body, taking his time with one breast, then the other, sliding his hands under her shoulders and lifting her to his mouth to feast on her soft skin.

He hummed against her flesh when she tugged at his hair. "Say the word and I'll stop."

"Don't stop," she panted.

Shit. He stopped, despite her command, pressing his face against her rib cage and trying to temper his breathing. It didn't deter her; she struggled for a second, but managed to turn him onto his back, shifting herself to straddle him. She bumped the heat at the apex of her thighs against his arousal and his jaw tightened, barely able to resist the urge to shred the fabric between them and sink into her wetness.

"Lily...Lily...I don't have any condoms." He swallowed. He hated to kill the mood, but they'd already gone farther than he'd imagined and he'd be lost completely if he didn't at least tap the brakes. Sunny had always been on birth control and since he wasn't a roving Casanova, there was no need for him to keep them on hand. He slid his hands over her hips to still her. "I'm sorry."

She looked like she was considering her options for just a second before a smile shadowed over her features. "Quit apologizing. Nobody says we can't have a little fun anyways."

His questioning expression prompted her to shift off of him, angling her body on her knees beside him with her head pointing toward his feet, and took hold of the towel with both hands. He breathed a prayer for control.

"What are you doing?" he ground out.

"I'm going to make you feel good."

Lord have mercy. He dropped his head back against the pillow as she loosened the knot in the towel, the generous globes of her breasts brushing against his erection as she did so. Ultra-sensitive, he jerked a little every time she made contact, and when she drew him in, he thought he might stroke out. Tipping his head up, he watched as he disappeared into her mouth and let out a shuddering moan. He was sure as hell out of practice with a partner. Touching himself out of necessity was an entirely different thing than watching her pretty little mouth slide over his erection.

His fingers formed into fists as a new wave of pleasure washed over him, desperate to hold on longer than a 15 year old boy his first time, when his vision widened enough to catch sight of her hips wiggling temptingly beside him. Before he knew what he was doing, he slid his fingers up the inside of her creamy thigh, tapping twice. His message was clear, because she shifted her knees wider, opening to him. The heady combination of this view and the feel of her mouth on him felt almost surreal. He moved his fingers up, tickling them over the crotch of the panties before he snagged the waistband, tugging it down to expose her. Her own invitation was obvious when she pushed her hips back, and he brushed his fingertips over her twice before he slipped them into her. She jerked forward for just a second, her rumbling moan vibrating through him when she didn't pull her mouth away, and then pressed back again.

*

Lily tried her best to focus, but the way Finn cupped her between her legs and the slow, steady movement of his fingers made her rhythm disjointed. She shifted again, widening her legs and bracing her elbows against the bed, draping herself over him as she swirled her tongue over his head. Pressure built inside of her as she slid her hand over his hardness, trying to focus, but she could hardly keep her train of thought straight, never mind her brain giving her body the correct signals to continue with her task.

It had been too long since anyone had bothered to take this kind of time to bring her along for the ride, and she pressed on, out of appreciation, using her hand and her mouth to mimic the way he played her body. Too soon, she felt his abs tighten under her forearm and a curse came out of him at the same time he drove his fingers deep, pushing her forward, off of him, her hand gliding down as she felt a hot splash against her chest.

Pleasure washed over her as she fell forward, her cheek against the soft skin of his thigh while he mercilessly pushed her toward the peak of her own orgasm. And quickly, she came, hard, her breath hiccupping through her, his name tumbling off her lips. He pushed her high further, stroking her inside and out as he drew out the crashing ecstasy until her body bucked and jerked, begging to come down. She was sure they could hear her keening cries in the big house, and she turned her face against his skin, hoping to muffle her noise. Her whole body vibrated with the intensity of the sensation washing through her until finally, gently, he let her down, sliding his palm over her exposed rear and giving it a playful tap. She slumped forward, sucking in great, heaving breaths.

After he'd drawn her back up to the head of the bed, Finn slipped out of the room and came back with a washcloth moments later to clean them up, then slid in beside her and held her against his chest, still rising and falling with his ragged breaths. He pressed a kiss to her forehead, then her eyelids, and then found her mouth, his fingers tracing a light pattern over her bare arm. Shifting, he drew the blanket up over them and squeezed her tight against his chest, like he intended to stay.

"Mmm," she murmured, pressing her cheek against his chest. She could hear his heart still beating wildly and it made her smile because hers raced to match. "Are you staying?"

"Like hell I'm getting up again," Finn replied, a laugh rumbling through his chest. "As if I could."

Her own jello-like legs could appreciate his inability to get out of the bed and she laughed, shaking her head.

"You are one incredible woman, Lily Jacobs."

She smiled, savoring the moment a bit longer before she replied, in her best attempt at flippancy. "Oh don't get down on your knees and say something you regret just because I got down on mine."

The truth was, when he showed her everything he had to offer; his kindness, humor, and attentiveness; his good heart and his sense of family, she wanted more than to just blur the line between business and pleasure. She straight up wanted this man.

-THIRTY-

IT was the sun that woke Lily this time, and she stretched and yawned like a cat in the beam filtering in through her window. It took her a moment to open her eyes and realize the other side of the bed was empty, and to process that she didn't know how to feel about it. Or the night before.

She could have blamed it on the alcohol she'd consumed with Emma the night before, giggling and gossiping like they were teenagers again. But it was more than that. It was taking something she wanted, something she'd been thinking about for days now, something she was relatively sure he wanted, too. She'd never had a partner who accepted her desire to take the lead, never mind encouraged her like Finn had the night before, attending to her needs as thoroughly as he had.

Embarrassment washed over her, chasing out any leftover traces of pleasure that had been floating around her bloodstream. She'd been brazen, bolder than she had ever been. And now she had to share this tiny space with a man she barely knew, but also knew quite intimately.

The longer she thought about it, the worse it was going to get, so she dragged herself into a sitting position and found her discarded t-shirt, tugging it on over her head and pulling her hair off her neck and into a halfhearted low ponytail.

Steeling herself with a deep breath, she turned

the doorknob as quietly as she could, poking her head into the hall to check if the coast was clear. Finn stood at the stove with his back to her...*whistling*. Like every guy-who-just-got-some cliché. She pressed her lips together and took the quietest step she could into the hall; only to find the only damn squeaky floorboard in the whole cabin. Finn whipped around, spatula still in hand. *Damnit.*

There was no place to hide. Wasn't he supposed to be riding horses today or something, like every other day?

To her relief, he smiled that slow twist of a half-smile that hit her right in her heart every single time, and while she still had a whole herd of butterflies beating around in her chest, she let out a slow breath. Maybe this wouldn't be so bad after all.

"'Morning," he said, giving her a quick once-over; but not quick enough she didn't notice. Her cheeks burned, but so did the memory of his hands making that same journey.

"I'm just...shower." She gestured loosely behind her.

"Right. Quick though. French toast in about fifteen minutes. And bacon."

"Okay." Had the world turned upside down? Shaking her head, she closed herself in the bathroom gratefully. Exactly thirteen minutes later, she emerged wrapped in a towel and managed to slip into the bedroom again without being detected and dressed quickly, because what he was cooking up smelled amazing and her stomach was growling. She still wasn't sure what time it was, but she'd definitely slept longer and better than she had in some time.

When she emerged, wrapping her big messy cardigan sweater around herself, he was setting the table. Like they were playing house. Exactly what he'd insisted they *weren't* doing at the beginning. He set a steaming mug of coffee on the table and gestured. It was the same handmade ceramic mug she'd been photographing when he'd caught her wearing barely a thing; the place where this had all started, really. The humor wasn't lost on her. She sat, smiling up at him.

"Thanks. What time is it?"

Finn leaned back, glancing behind him to check the clock on the stove. "Nine."

"Shouldn't you be up to your eyeballs in horses right now?"

He chuckled, setting two plates in the middle of the table. One was loaded with a half a loaf of bread's worth of French toast, and the other held what had to be a full pound of bacon. Okay, so she'd worked up an appetite, but...

"The advantage of having everyone living on the same property is when one guy needs a little time off, the other guys can pick up the slack."

"Right," she murmured, forking a couple of pieces each of the French toast and bacon onto her plate. Finn heaped his high and smothered the whole thing in syrup. Watching him eat, she'd never imagine how he kept as trim a figure as he had; except she also saw how many hours he put in on the ranch on a typical day. She worked damn hard to avoid her round hips getting any rounder, but he didn't seem to care at all as he cut off big chunks of bread with the side of his fork and shoved them in his mouth.

"Hey, how'd your girls' night with Emma go, anyway?"

"Good. We grabbed dinner at Hinkley's and then came back and watched movies til Noah came home."

"Did you talk about me?"

She was pretty sure, judging by the twinkle in his eye that he was only half serious. The truth was simple; they hadn't. Emma wasn't the type of girl who just let unfinished business lie, even when it wasn't her business to finish; thus Lily's quick turnover from Denver to Three Rivers. And this definitely wasn't Emma's business to finish. Lily barely believed it was hers.

But she could let him squirm a bit. Because as Emma's brother-in-law, she had no doubt he knew that truth about her, too. She smiled, tipping her head as she lazily took another sip of coffee, then shrugged innocently. "Maybe. But I'll never tell."

-THIRTY-ONE-

"YOU need anything in town?" Finn asked, gathering up their plates when Lily finished. He dropped them in the sink; he'd come back to them later.

He'd drug his feet long enough, he'd never hear the end of it from Noah if he didn't soon hit the ground. The half dozen times he'd needed his brothers to cover for him on the ranch, he still usually got moving by 7 or 8, but it was pushing 10 now. He just couldn't talk himself into leaving her.

Last night had exceeded any expectations he could have ever had, and exposed a whole new layer of Lily to him—physically *and* emotionally. Afterward, he'd slept better than he had in years. With her warm body wrapped around him and pleasure still thrumming through his veins, he hadn't moved all night and neither had she. He figured it was about the closest thing to peace he'd had since she arrived.

"Nope."

She pushed her chair out and got up, stretching her arms over her head enough that she exposed a little slice of skin at the top of her jeans, immediately bringing to mind that little tattoo he'd caught a glimpse of the night before, and what her body tasted like under his tongue. *God help me.* If he didn't get moving soon, he'd be sunk for the day.

He was almost relieved when he heard steps on

the porch—if anything could talk him out of kissing her breathless, it was Noah's presence.

Sure enough, his brother pulled the door open, Emma hot on his heels.

"I was about to call search and rescue," Noah boomed. Emma shook her head and rolled her eyes, heading for the coffee maker. His brother stopped up, raising a brow at the syrup and utensils still on the table. His gaze shifted to Finn, questioning. Clearing his throat, he looked away—the only safe person being Emma. Maybe. Who the hell knew what she and Lily had talked about the night before.

Noah had turned his gaze to Lily, who busied herself filling the sink with hot water and dish soap to clean up after breakfast and wasn't giving him any answers.

"You wanna get going?"

"Yeah...daylight's wasting."

"Yeah, yeah. This is one morning off in like, what? A thousand? *You* didn't want to make the drive to Reicher's."

Noah rolled his eyes in response, crossing the floor to hook his arm around his wife's waist and tug her to him for a quick kiss. She squealed, nearly sloshing coffee all over Finn's floor, and then laughed. It was hard not to be a little envious of the free, casual affection they showed one another. Finn knew he had to protect the little spark he was fostering with Lily, particularly based on her response when they'd talked about the rumor mill in Three Rivers. There were still a few people who, given the opportunity, would gladly shred on Finn's choices when Sunny had been sick, and he wasn't ready to turn their not-so-quiet disapproval on the new interest in his life, especially when he was still coming to grips with what it all meant.

Still, it would have been nice to cross the floor

and kiss Lily goodbye, but there wouldn't be an opportunity. Later, he told himself, willing her to turn from the sink and meet his gaze. She did, and a quick smile crinkled the corners of her eyes and tipped her lips up.

Noah shook him from his thoughts with a short whistle from the door. "Come *on*."

"Alright, keep your panties on," he frowned, following his brother out onto the porch.

*

"Where are they off to in such a hurry?" Lily asked, shaking her head as she wiped her hands on one of Finn's brightly colored dishtowels. She heard a truck engine roar to life and watched as Finn's pickup pulled away from the yard.

"Liquor store." Emma had been rummaging in the fridge, and she straightened, emerging with the cream Lily had just put away. "Annual celebratory bonfire when the last load of Reicher horses go home."

"Oh, I thought they still had a couple."

Emma nodded toward the table, crossing the floor with her cup of coffee. Lily could hardly sit still, but she sat with her friend, her half-full coffee still sitting on the tabletop. She could have used a few spare minutes to gather herself before she was forced to socialize, but she'd have to make do.

"They do have a couple fillies, but they need a bit more time to grow up, so they might work 'em, they might not." Emma shrugged. "Finn'll finish up his roster of clients, and so will we, and the winter will be pretty quiet. Then the crazy starts all over again in the spring. Calves, colts, crops."

Lily leaned back in her chair, cupping her mug between her hands, searching Emma's face. She counted as part of Finn's clientele, was she suggesting they'd be done with Encore soon? And then she'd move along. Her heart was near to bursting with feelings and thoughts she couldn't piece together or make sense of. She hadn't come here expecting to fall for this surprisingly soft-hearted man, but here she'd gone and bared her soul, pinning her heart to her sleeve.

She'd slept sound and free of nightmares with his warm arms around her, his warm breath tickling her neck, his calloused fingertips resting oh-so-lightly on the sensitive skin of her belly. Casual, and comfortable, like they belonged there. A warm throb of desire washed through her at the thought of what they'd done the night before. She made a mental note to hit the pharmacy at her earliest convenience, then turned to her friend, considering her next words.

"Can I ask you something, Em?"

"Hmm?" Emma glanced up from her coffee.

"This doesn't leave this room."

"Of course." Clearly interested, Emma set her mug down and leaned forward.

"Do you think Finn is ready to date?"

Emma's eyebrows raised and her mouth formed an o as she sat back in her seat, busying her hands with her mug. It was unusual for her brash, animated friend to be silent, especially when it came to the Baylor brothers.

"I mean, *has* he dated since his wife died?" Lily pressed. She'd ripped the band aid clear off the wound, so digging around wasn't as painful as she'd expected. He'd given her no reason not to believe he was ready to date—*he'd* been the one to initiate it, after all

Emma released a long breath. "Well, yes. I think the last one was a couple years ago. He took a couple girls to dinner a couple times but I think that's about all that ever transpired. Are you thinking about...?"

"I really mean it, Em, nothing leaves here. Not even to Noah."

"Scout's honor." Lifting two fingers, her friend nodded, but a playful spark of trouble was evident in her eyes.

Lily narrowed her gaze across the table. Emma might never tell her secrets, but that didn't mean she wouldn't intervene where she thought she might be helpful. "Forget it."

"No, really." Emma laughed. "I promise, I do. Remember, Finn's like a brother to me, it's just weird to think of someone *wanting* him like that."

"You told me *Noah* was like a brother to you, once."

"Guilty as charged. Now let's stop talking about me and talk about *you*."

She turned her mug around on the table top, watching the liquid inside remain stationary, not unlike the way she felt like she'd been standing still while her whole world carried on without her. Spending time with Finn made her feel like she was actively living her life again and not just reflected in the progress she made with Encore. It broadened her world up more than she had in the whole last year.

"We went on a date." She could feel her not-on-purpose smile warming her, and it spread to Emma quickly.

"That's...good. That's *good*, Lily."

"For him or for me?"

"For both of you."

Chewing her bottom lip, she frowned. Of course things had escalated way more quickly than they would have under normal circumstances, and she couldn't help but wonder if the reason it was suddenly coming so easy to Finn was convenience.

Here she was, in his home, available, and following after him like a lost puppy.

"But do you think he's really ready for this?"

"I think you should ask Finn about that, honestly."

"I just..."

"I get it," Emma said. "You want to find out the scoop before you lay everything out. But I want to tell you the truth, and the truth is I *don't know*. By my estimation, I think he should be, but Finn's always been a funny kinda guy. He'd be the only one who could tell you the truth."

Her friend rose, sliding her cell phone out of her pocket. "I just wanted to make sure you weren't going to hole up editing tonight. But if I intend to get anything done before this evening, I've got a couple horses that need rode."

"Gosh, yeah, I'm not going to get anything done if I don't get a move on," Lily said breezily, pushing her mug away. Unpacking her feelings would have to wait til later.

-THIRTY-TWO-

WALKING into the one and only pharmacy in Three Rivers wasn't the problem. It was the aisle Finn found himself in. *Family planning*. Made it sound so innocent. Made it sound like picking up a box and walking to the counter wouldn't ignite the rumor mill faster than you could blink. This was the sort of town where married folk didn't *plan* families—more heads made more hands on the family spread—but there was the rub. He was still getting used to the idea of not actually being married. Too many years later. And maybe this was why he'd been putting it off, sparing himself the embarrassment that made him feel like a teenager all over again.

He flipped the narrow box of condoms off the shelf and into his palm, turning the obvious logo against his thigh as he made his way to the counter. Vanessa Turner stood behind the register, her eyes glued to the screen of her cell phone. She was Kerri's age and he'd seen her around the ranch a couple of times. If the owner, Mr. Thorne, caught her like this he'd have a sharp word or two for her, but Finn was just as happy that her attention was diverted as he approached.

At the last second, he grabbed a pack of gum from the countertop display and set it on top of the box, sliding them both across the counter. She stashed her phone as if he hadn't just caught her texting.

"Hey Finn."

"Afternoon, Vanessa."

She scanned the gum, then picked up the box of condoms. Her mouth tightened into a line as she scanned the barcode and dropped both items into a bag.

"Twelve seventy six." One of her eyebrows lifted when she looked to him, but he'd already pulled out his wallet and was thumbing through it. He pulled a ten and a five out, tossed them down on the counter, and grabbed his bag.

"Keep the change. See you around, Vanessa." But he hoped he wouldn't. The last thing he needed was for her to land on the ranch, spilling his secrets all over creation.

The door couldn't close behind him quick enough as he legged it across the parking lot and to his truck. Fully aware it would do nothing to stem any rumors that might already be circulating based on the fact that he could already see Vanessa's fingers dancing across the keyboard of her phone through the big window of the pharmacy, he opened the driver's side door of his truck and slid the bag behind the seat. At least it would keep Noah's prying eyes out of things.

Speaking of...Finn checked his watch, then leaned his hips against the side of his truck, waiting for his younger brother. They'd already loaded the bed of the truck down with the laundry list of liquor they'd been sent with, and then he'd sent Noah off to check on Kerri, who was tending the family store so he could visit the pharmacy alone.

"Hey stranger." Cutter Anderson's voice sounded behind him, and Finn turned, resting his forearms over the edge of the truck bed. His friend mirrored his stance, glancing at the boxes on the back. Ever the bartender, Cutter took stock. "Looks like a good time."

"Should be. Say, I saw some fine looking stock in Lily's pictures. Things going good?"

Frowning, his friend rubbed the back of his neck, shaking his head. "The price of beef is up... way up... but not enough to make up for crop failure and a blown up combine."

Finn nodded. Farming was hard enough without added pressure. On top of that, Cutter's daddy had been sick. He worked a half dozen side jobs to try and pull them through but the lines on his friend's normally jovial face told him it wasn't enough.

"You know if there's anything we can do to help..."

Cutter shook his head. "I was just in to the bank. Think it's probably beyond help at this point. So we'll sell as much stock as we can and I'm hoping it'll tide us over 'til I can get something going in Denver."

"Denver?"

"Yeah, more work, maybe more hours. Something that pays better. Hell, I don't know."

"We'll be sad to see you go, Anderson." Finn clasped his hands in front of him. His family was lucky—they had enough side lines running to keep the place afloat if they ran into any kind of trouble like this, but it would still be tough. "Hopefully it won't be for too long, though."

"Well," Cutter said, straightening with a smile. "At least in Denver, I'd be that much closer to date Lily."

Cutter'd always had a habit of pulling at vulnerable threads, but that didn't stop Finn's blood from boiling just a little.

"Careful," he warned, before he realized he'd

put his foot right in it. Cutter was a cocky asshole, and he knew exactly what he was doing, no doubt. Struggling with the idea of just confessing to his friend, he was cut off.

"Thought so," Cutter laughed, tapping the edge of the truck bed with his palm. "'Bout freaking time, Baylor."

"Cutter." Finn's whole body tensed, and he worked to calm himself with a quiet breath.

"Oh don't worry, your secret's safe with me." He shook his head. "Lord knows you've kept enough for me."

It was true. Years of friendship—and hardships—meant that this wouldn't be the first time someone had kept something under wraps.

"Hey, just promise me you're gonna keep an eye out for Rosie. She's got enough on her plate now, but it'll be tough when I head out."

Finn nodded, a knot in his chest. Denver was only two hours away, but he couldn't imagine the strain of leaving your home behind, especially when it was in turmoil. His sister was a tough girl, but it was a lot for anyone to handle.

"Of course, buddy." He crossed behind the truck and held his hand out to Cutter, who clasped it and pulled their chests together in a half-hug.

"I knew I could count on you." Cutter smiled, releasing Finn, as Noah emerged from Baylor's General Store. He nodded. "Noah."

"Later, Anderson." The brothers raised their hands, seeing him off, then Noah turned to Finn.

"You ready to head home?"

"As I'll ever be."

-THIRTY-THREE-

"ALL set?" Finn spoke at the same time he dropped his knuckles against her door frame. It was a formality, really, but Lily appreciated that he thought of it.

"Are you sure it's okay for me to come with you? I know this is your annual thing with your brothers."

"What would you do? Stay here and edit?" he asked, and she glanced at her Macbook sitting open on the desk. She'd spent the whole afternoon catching up on the sessions she hadn't edited yet because she'd been busy kissing Finn. It would have been easy to brew a cup of tea and lose herself in more of the gorgeous Colorado foliage she'd shot today, but the handsome cowboy standing in front of her was more enticing. He was freshly showered and dressed in an easy smile and a blue plaid button-down with the sleeves rolled up, exposing his sinewy forearms and big, rough hands. Big, rough hands she couldn't stop thinking about. "Don't be silly. Emma and Ren will be there. I'm sick of being the fifth wheel."

"Alright, alright. If it helps your ego." She laughed, moving to squeeze past him in the door frame. Those hands she hadn't been able to take her mind off of just seconds before caught her at the hips, tugging her toward him. She let herself go with the movement, her heart banging around in her chest like it had been for days now, anytime he got close. It never got old.

"I dunno, it's taken a lot of damage," he murmured, drawing her closer, his fingers sliding into the back pockets of her jeans and pressing her closer. "I might need a little more than that."

"Oh yeah?" She chuckled as he bent his head, and then lifted up on her tiptoes when he got closer, brushing her lips across his as she murmured her next words. Her fingers curled into his shirt. "Anything I can do to help."

"Oh, don't tempt me, lovely. We might never actually make it to the fire."

The dark, promising undercurrent in his voice sent a punch of desire straight to her gut and Lily dropped back to the soles of her feet. He pressed his palms to her ass and tugged her closer when she tried to withdraw, overriding her playful kisses when he slanted his lips over hers. Her whole body sagged against his chest, that pressure in her belly blossoming into something warm and liquid and sinful when his tongue slid across her lips and into her mouth. One step and her back was against the door frame and she thought they might *not* actually make it to the fire. The weight of his body made her ache, and she pressed her thighs together, making a noise against his mouth.

And then as quickly as he'd initiated the scorching kiss, he lifted his head, and with that crooked, easy grin, wiped his calloused thumb across her lower lip. A shiver raced over her skin. The mischievous glint in his eyes told her he knew exactly what he'd done. She couldn't imagine how she'd sit through the evening as primed as she was.

"Alright, enough," she chuckled, slipping out from between him and the frame of the door, simply to stop herself from dragging him back to her bed and repeating the previous night's events. She headed for the door without looking behind her to see if he followed—she knew he would. He caught up to her and pulled a quilted red plaid jacket off the coat rack. Stopping her when she reached for her own, he shook his head.

"This one already smells like wood smoke," he said gently, helping her into the coat. It was a few sizes too big, hanging down to mid-thigh and well past her fingertips. When she gave him a plaintive look, he couldn't hide his smile. She didn't bother to try to hide hers. "What? It looks great."

His fingers went to the mother of pearl buttons, carefully closing her into the jacket. Shrugging her shoulders up, she inhaled. She loved the smell of wood smoke, but more than that, it smelled of him; a delicious, warm, and slightly spicy scent she wanted to climb inside of. He smelled like home.

Finn shrugged into a similar blue checkered jacket and held the door open for her.

The crisp night air stole her breath when they stepped out onto the porch. The chill meant fall was here, even if they still had those gorgeous Indian summer types of days. She was grateful for the coat, and she nestled into it as he stepped out beside her, reaching to loop his finger into hers. Not quite holding hands, but making contact. Happiness bubbled up from deep inside—so sneaky she almost didn't realize it—and bent a smile over her lips.

Between the two houses, about a hundred yards from one of the heifer barns, Lily could see Noah and Dane's figures moving around in the beams of headlights of one of the trucks, assembling a fire that looked considerably bigger than it needed to be. While she'd found the three brothers to be the type of humble, salt of the earth men she loved, they were still men. If the kids hadn't been assembled on a bench ten feet from the fire ring, she might have expected explosives of some sort.

When they got closer to the group, Finn released her fingers. She knew what he was doing—protecting this little bit of goodness they were fostering—but she couldn't say it didn't hurt a little that he wasn't ready to show his family, who were already highly suspicious. Or in Emma's case, aware. She brushed off her hurt feelings when Noah straightened, taking in her oversized jacket with a pained expression, and then laughed out loud.

"Nice wardrobe choice."

Sticking her tongue out, she took up a spot between Emma and Ren on the bench. Kerri had settled at the end with Gracie in her lap and Gage was wrestling with Tucker in the long grass behind them. Rex lay curled at the end of the row, watchful. Finn joined his brothers in assembling the wood, and Lily let out a long, relaxed breath. Day to day, she worried over Finn's progress with Encore, how her mother was doing in Denver without her, and a myriad of other things, but sitting here with the warmth of the Baylor family wrapping her up, she felt all her tension release. And when Finn went to the back of the truck and returned with a cold wine cooler, she smiled and accepted it.

Before long, the fire was high and crackling. Ren broke out marshmallows for the kids and Gage enlisted Emma's help with his stick. As the rest of them carefully assembled by the side of the pit, Finn slipped into the empty space beside her.

"You having fun?" His tone was casual, but she felt the warmth of his fingers through her jeans as he slid them across her knee, then up just a little. Already edgy, warmth spread through her at his touch, which *could* have been completely innocent, but she knew wasn't.

"Mhm." She pressed her knees together and shot a look at him; surely his family was going to see what he'd so carefully concealed. He was watching the rest of the gang gathered at the fire's edge, as if he wasn't playing on her previously aroused state. She might have thought he was just being oblivious to just how much his fingers playing over the inner seam of her jeans turned her on... if she hadn't watched the thoughtful, progressive way he approached just about everything else in his life. There was a reason behind every single thing the man did. When he felt her eyes on him, he tipped his gaze down and couldn't stop the grin that spread over his lips. She tucked her lower lip between her teeth to stop her own smile from running away with her but it was no good. His fingers tightened against the softness of her inner thigh, and then Dane started to turn toward them and like that, his hand was gone and she bit back a cursing protest.

"Finn show you your surprise yet?" the eldest brother asked, sidling over with Gracie on his hip, sticky-faced and drooping with sleepiness.

Beside her, Finn cleared his throat, and when she glanced up at him questioningly, he was shooting a glare at Dane. His brother's mouth formed an 'o' of recognition. He tipped his chin up and glanced at the child in his arms and turned back toward the fire, muttering something about helping Kerri get the kids settled in for the night.

*

This wasn't how he'd intended things to go. Finn's heart rate sped up, beyond reason. He knew a dozen women who would have been happy to discover someone had bought them a horse...but this was different. Offering Tank to Lily was a symbol of his failure, and she would recognize that right away. And she'd be pissed. He'd been suspicious Encore might not turn out to be rideable for anyone, least of all Lily, for a while now, but he hadn't shared that with her, and he was regretting it now.

She looked up at him now, the firelight flickering on her glossy blond hair, swimming in his spare work shirt, and he wanted to kiss her, to hold onto this moment just a little longer. Where she still believed he was a horse whisperer and could fix the things that were still wrong in her life. He wished he was the person she believed he was, and he was afraid to burst the blissful little bubble they'd been living in when she realized he wasn't.

Truth was, he didn't know what to do with himself if he couldn't fix her problems. He'd become so dependent on stubbornly ignoring his own personal issues in favor of righting the wrongs in the lives of others that when he was left alone with the truth of his own problems, the fears and insecurities nearly crushed him. If he disappointed her now, what did that mean about the future? And could he build a future with her while he was still terrified to walk away from loving Sunny?

Taking a big breath in, he straightened and offered her a smile, hoping she couldn't see in the dark that it didn't reach his eyes.

"Right, your surprise." He rose and held out his hand, squeezing her fingers lightly when she accepted his help, before he released them. Kerri was starting to wrangle up the kids, and he paused to kiss Gracie and give Gage a hug. He hoped Dane felt the daggers in his gaze as they passed by him, walking away from the fire. "We'll be back."

"You should give me a hint." Lily said, as they crossed the field behind the heifer barn en route to the horse barn. He reached out and found the ends of her fingers dangling out of the bunched up sleeves of his coat.

"You look cute as hell in that jacket." Safely away from the group at the fire, he threaded his fingers into her, then lifted their joined hands to press a kiss to the delicate skin on the back of hers.

"Don't change the subject." She laughed out, and the noise made his heart skip a beat. She'd been a cautious, closed woman when she came to the ranch—at least with him, and she'd really blossomed.

"We're almost there, don't be so impatient."

Maybe it would be alright, after all. They got to the closed barn door and he drew her to a stop, turning her toward him. She turned her face up, watching, expectant. Sliding his hand along her jaw and under her hair, he tipped her head back and pressed his lips to hers in a sweet, almost chaste kiss. And then he opened the barn door.

"You probably noticed this guy," he said, as they approached the stall where Tank's head hung out over the door. The gelding nickered to them, extending his muzzle in an invitation Lily took up, stroking between his eyes in that gentle, circular thing she did with Encore that seemed to calm him.

"I did. Client?"

"Not quite. He used to be, though. He was a Reicher colt that Dane put the work on. They've had him a few years, and he turned out to be a hell of a little horse."

She leaned ahead, peering into the stall, and noticed Tank's short stature. "You're not exaggerating. What is he? 14.1? Maybe 14.2?"

Finn smiled, remembering how awkward Dane had looked on the gelding, with his long legs hanging below the horse's belly. They measured horses in hands; four inches per, and to qualify as a horse, they had to be at least fourteen hands and two inches... "14.1."

Lily clued in immediately.

"He's just a pony!"

"Exactly. Heart of a horse three times his size, though—just not as far to fall. He'd carry you all day and never tire."

She glanced up at him, and he watched her brow furrow, and then slowly smooth as she worked out what he was getting at.

"*This* is my surprise?"

Her expression was hard to read now. He nodded, leaning against the stall door as she glanced back at the gelding. "He's for you."

"You got me a pony." Her tone was so flat he laughed out loud. Encore had at least eight, maybe ten inches on Tank. Despite *technically* being considered a pony, most of the ranch horses were short, stout little engines like him, but Finn could see how, comparing him to her other horse, she might struggle to get past the pony thing.

"He's sensitive but not quick. Level headed. And low to the ground." The things she needed. The things Encore wasn't.

"That's...Finn." She sucked in a breath, and so did he, and then the gelding nudged her to encourage her to pet him again. She slid her hand along the gelding's jaw, then scratched her way up behind his ear. Tank leaned into the scratches, his prehensile upper lip wiggling with pleasure as she reached the sweet spot. At least they'd hit it off. "He is a lovely horse, but this is too much."

Her voice had lowered to a trembling whisper. Maybe it *was* too much. But it was something he could do to try to make better the one thing he wasn't sure he could.

When she looked up, her eyes were filled with tears. He hadn't expected that. Anger, maybe, if not happiness, but not sadness.

"Hey," he said, reaching out to touch her hand, then her shoulder, then to cup her face lightly in his palm, brushing one escapee off her cheek. She closed her eyes, turning her cheek against his hand. "I didn't mean to make you cry."

And he would have done anything to fix it. He knew her dream was to ride her *own* horse again, but every day made him more sure it wouldn't happen the way she wanted it to—at least not here, because he didn't have the intestinal fortitude to watch her try after he'd seen the quick work the gelding had made of his saddle the first day they'd put it on.

He shuffled closer, brushing her hair back from her face with his other hand, and pressed a kiss to her lips. Her eyes were still closed when he pulled away.

Her voice broke. "Does this mean you're done with Encore?"

The pain in her voice made his heart ache. Using his fingers on the back of her neck, he tipped her head back and waited until she opened her eyes so she could see him shake his head. "No. I *told* you I'd see this through. But I want you to have options in the meantime."

She needed to understand he wasn't quitting, but the look on her face didn't give him much confidence.

"You love riding. And you're good at it. But I know how hard it can be to mentally overcome a wreck. So I'm just thinking maybe you need a partner with a clean slate for a bit. Just while you get your confidence back. Then we'll see what happens with Encore. It's only been a couple of weeks. We've got lots of time. Alright?"

She drew in breath, blinked slowly, and then nodded. "Alright."

Everything inside him that had tensed in anticipation for a much bigger struggle released. He hadn't intended to cross this bridge quite this way but he was glad it was out of the way now. Drawing her closer, he pressed a kiss to her forehead and she wound her arms around his waist, and then pushed up on her toes to catch his lips.

"Thank you," she murmured against his mouth.

He slid his hand over her hair, changing the angle of the kiss and took her mouth. The sweet cooler on her lips was nothing compared to the taste of her, and when she dragged her hands around his hips, slipping her cool fingers in underneath his coat and shirt, across his abdomen, he groaned. The heady combination of her touch, her taste, and her smell was drugging.

Taking two steps forward, he pressed her back to a stack of hay bales, and then slid his hands along her bottom, lifting her onto them to close the height difference a bit more comfortably. Lily let out a little yelp of surprise, then spread her knees and made a space for him, drawing him closer with her hands on his sides.

Deftly, he worked at the coat buttons he'd so carefully done up earlier, exposing her neck and collar bone, and moved on to the buttons on her shirt. Judging by the heat rolling off her skin and through his body, they needn't have worried about the cold in the first place. He slid his mouth over her jaw, to her neck, and she let out a tight breath in a hiss, tipping her head to allow him more access. Her knees tightened against his hips.

"Finn." He slid his tongue over the column of her throat, smiling and letting his breath cool the spots his mouth had dampened. And when she repeated his name, all full of ache and need—the exact way he felt—he bore his teeth down into her flesh lightly and her whole body jerked. Closer. Tighter. "You don't know what you're doing to me."

"Oh, I think I have an idea." He chuckled against her skin. She whimpered when he traced his fingers along the empty buttonholes of her shirt. Maybe it was because it had been so long since he tried, but he loved her enthusiastic response to the tiniest things. It made him feel like the man he'd known himself to be when Sunny had been alive, not the sad shell of a man he'd been masquerading as for the last few years. Capable of loving on and being loved by a woman.

"Then you're just being cruel," she panted as he slipped his hand into her shirt, cupping one breast and rolling her nipple lightly under his thumb before lifting her out of the cup of her bra and exposing it to the cool air. Her fingers tightened against his sides at the same time her nipple hardened, and then he dropped his mouth to press a wet-lipped kiss to the end of it.

She arched her back, offering herself more readily and he obliged, drawing her into his mouth and taking a not-so-gentle pull of her flesh. A strangled noise escaped her and when he moved to pull back, her hands moved from his sides, curling into fists in his hair.

-THIRTY-FOUR-

LILY wasn't one hundred percent sure how they got there between kisses and touches, or undetected, but she lifted her head when Finn pushed the door of the cabin open. He set her down just inside and stripped her of the coat in half the time it had taken him to help her into it, toeing off his boots and shrugging out of his own coat before he cupped her face in both hands, crushing his mouth to hers like he couldn't get enough. She could relate, and she pushed up on her toes to match him, kiss for kiss.

"Oh hell," he muttered then, anchoring his hands under her ass and sliding her body up against his. She broke away from him, letting out a little screech, but then got the idea when he slid his hand along the back of her jean-clad thigh, encouraging her to wind her legs around his waist. If she had had to support herself, she would have fallen, but he cradled her like it was nothing. She wasn't a small girl and she'd never really trusted anyone to hold her like this, but when she put her arms around his neck, felt his shoulders flex and tighten, she felt more secure than she had in a long time, in a lot of different ways. "Hang on."

Lily buried her mouth against Finn's throat as he crossed the small floor space of the cabin toward the bedrooms in the back. Instead of turning right, he turned left, and before she knew what was happening, he was laying her on her gently in the middle of his queen sized bed and pulling his shirt off over his head. She hadn't been in his bedroom before, and she barely had time to take in anything, including the broad expanse of his chest, before Finn followed her onto the bed, pressing hot kisses along her throat, then down to the spot where he'd stopped unbuttoning her shirt in the barn.

He made quick work of the rest of the buttons, nudging the shirt open to expose her bra and belly to the lamplight. There had been times before, other partners, where she would have asked to close the door, turn off the lights. But this was different. Even though he hadn't been around for the recovery period, Finn had already seen her body in various states of mutiny, and that somehow negated the vulnerability of being exposed to him.

She lifted her hips as he peeled her jeans down over them, her heart pounding in her throat. His eyes shifted to her bikini line, and she felt his finger trace along it before he hooked it in the waistband of her panties, tugging them down to expose the four tiny black horseshoes.

"What's this?" he asked, working her underwear the rest of the way down her legs and putting his mouth on the ink. She let out a frustrated moan and pushed her fingers into his hair. Between the hot kiss before they'd left the house earlier and the make out session in the barn, it would have taken no effort at all to send her soaring, but he took his time, circling his tongue over her skin again.

"Really?" she ground out, curving up from the pillow to watch him. He lifted his head and smiled at her, slipping his hands to grip her thighs from beneath and ease her legs apart. A hiss slid out of her.

"Really."

"I got it after I logged my first thousand miles."

"A thousand miles," he said, letting his warm breath flow over her exposed center. "Impressive."

She lifted her head again, shaking it with a rueful smile. "Finn Baylor, I will tell you about *every* one of those miles. *After*."

Laughing, he turned his head, despite her attempts to direct him elsewhere, and sank his teeth lightly into the soft flesh of her inner thigh. Her back arched up, her hips pressing into the bedspread as her thighs fell apart.

"After *what*?"

He didn't give her time to respond, because then he put his mouth on her and her head dropped back onto the bed, her eyes falling shut. Her heart did double-time, ricocheting around in her chest while she tried to figure out which way was up. She curled her fingers into the bedspread by her hips, hoping to ground herself, to hold on just a minute longer, but she was rushing too quickly toward an orgasm. And then his fingers found hers, twining their digits together, and she lifted her head, making eye contact with him. Closing her lower lip between her teeth, she let out short breaths through her nose, finding her footing as she watched him.

She shouldn't have been surprised by the easy, methodical way Finn's mouth worked, with just enough pressure to keep her on the edge but not enough to push her over. He read her body the same way he read the horses he worked with, watchful, until she was squirming, her fingernails digging into the back of his hand, her breaths coming quick and short.

Still, he waited. Until she was sure she was dying, deconstructing at a cellular level, pleasure simmering in her veins with no release in sight.

Desperate, she sighed his name, her eyes squeezed shut.

"Mmm?" The vibration at the apex of her thighs made jump.

"*Finn.*" It was what he was waiting for, because then he shifted, and finally, *finally*, she tipped off the other side of the mountain of pleasure he'd pushed her up. He didn't stop until she was completely spent, her legs like jelly, her chest heaving and the one hand that was still in his hair tugged, because she couldn't possibly handle a second more. He moved up her body, a slow smile crinkling the corners of his eyes as he cupped her face in one big palm and pressed their foreheads together. Everything inside her trembled with unspoken emotion.

"I need you."

*

He didn't have to be told twice, but still, anxiety pressed at the back of Finn's throat as he offered her a smile he hoped looked braver than it felt, and shifted off the bed. His fingers shook a little when he opened the box and pulled a condom out, making quick work of the foil wrapping.

Lily watched him from the bed, her lips tucked between her teeth, those bright cocoa-colored eyes tracking all of his movements. Her hair spread out on the dark bedding like a halo. He prayed for control, but should have known better. Because never, in five years, had he ever imagined himself in a position to make love to another woman besides Sunny—to *want* to make love to another woman. Not just another woman—Lily. There was something about her that had woken up parts of him he was sure had died with his wife, and no matter what happened, he'd always be grateful for that. And the way she looked at him—like he was all she wanted in this world... his chest constricted at the thought. She turned her palms over and reached one hand out toward him and he found his way back to the bed.

He felt her fingers at his neck, tracing down over his shoulder as he shifted, sliding his forearm under her to support her head, and his free hand along her hip, to her knee, making a space for himself. His mouth covered hers as he moved again, sinking into her warmth. She let the softest noise into his mouth, her body arching up into him.

A long breath blew out of him as he settled, landing kisses on her forehead, her eyelids, her lower lip. The sensation of her so close, so warm, her body so soft and willing, was almost more than he could bear, and he didn't move, just so he could hang onto that feeling for just a little longer. When he tipped his head back, she looked up at him and smiled in a way that loosened that tight fist on his heart. This woman was incredible.

The hand that had been on his neck slid down his shoulder blades, following his spine until she hit his lower back, pressing her fingers into his flesh at the same time she tipped her hips. He groaned, dropping his mouth against her collarbone. He couldn't put it off a second longer. Need, desire, and something a little deeper than that—something that tingled right at the base of his heart and pulled on his soul—overwhelmed him and he moved, finding a slow, easy pace within her.

The soft sighs and gentle noises of appreciation Lily made encouraged him, pushing him further. And too soon, she tightened around him, her voice rising as they found release together.

His heart thundering like a herd of wild horses, Finn slumped forward with his eyes closed, then rolled onto his side, bringing her with him, unwilling to break the contact just yet. For a time, the only noise in the room was their heavy breathing. Lily shifted her hand to cup his jaw much as she had on the night of their date. It seemed so long ago, now, that he'd made the conscious decision to want her, because now he couldn't imagine a different choice. Until she killed the silence with words that shattered him.

"I think I'm in love with you, Finn Baylor."

-THIRTY-FIVE-

"WHAT the hell is *that*?" Finn raised a brow as Lily led Tank out of the barn into the crisp fall morning. The horse was outfitted in the brightest orange tack he'd ever seen. Not poor quality, discolored leather, but *safety orange*. She looked back at the horse's bridle and breastplate, and then back at him with the most confused expression he'd ever seen.

"What?"

"It looks like a road pylon."

"What, my tack?" She looked back again at the offending items, and slid her hands over the reins.

"I don't know what the hell kind of leather..."

"Beta biothane," she interrupted.

"Well, that explains everything. Except why it's such an obnoxious color and how the hell anyone could have missed you in that." He saw her body tense for just a moment, and then a soft laugh bubbled out of her. It was a good sound, and it warmed his insides. Almost as much as waking her this morning with a soft kiss, their bodies entwined, with the sun streaming in on them. He couldn't have thought of a more peaceful way to wake.

It had taken him a few extra minutes after she'd dozed off, her soft, even breathing the only noise in the room, to loosen the stranglehold her last words had had on his chest. In the light of day, he could dismiss them as something she'd said in the heat of the moment. Her enthusiasm this morning about the gift he'd given her the night before erased almost all thought of it—except the little leap his heart did when Tank had buried his forehead against her chest and she'd smiled up at him like he was the best thing since sliced bread.

She led the horse across the ring to him and swung the reins over Tank's neck.

"I think it suits him," she said simply, a cheeky little grin highlighting the dimple near each corner of her mouth.

"You're damn lucky you're cute."

Lily winked over her shoulder at him, then moved to the saddle. He still drew the line at her silly little insecure treeless saddle—for now, anyway, while she was figuring out how to get herself onto the horse. Soon, she'd override his decision on that, too. Like she'd crossed every barrier and wall he'd put in place to protect the status quo. She couldn't help it, it seemed. She loved a challenge.

He watched her lips form a firm line as she focused on the stirrup, lifting her leg. Too soon, he moved in to help, but she brushed him off. "I gotta figure out how to do this myself eventually."

"Alright." He backed off a bit, giving her the opportunity to try on her own. It wasn't nearly as painful as her first attempt to get on Buckshot, mostly because Tank was so much closer to the ground. She managed to get her toe into the stirrup, bouncing on one foot a few times before she pushed off. About halfway into the saddle, her movement stalled. It made sense—it wasn't just range of motion that was problematic for her, but strength. He had confidence that with the right amount of work and practice, those long-discarded muscles would support her soon. She clung to the side of the gelding, her tongue poking out between her lips as she focused on trying to drag herself the rest of the way into the saddle. Tank stood still as a rock. He gave her about three seconds before he intervened, popping his shoulder under her ass so quick she couldn't think about it.

The smile she turned on him proved it was the right decision.

"You're almost there. But I think soon, you'll probably be able to get on him. And we'll teach him to sidle up to the fence in the meantime, that might help."

"You know, you're awfully patient for someone who 'doesn't give riding lessons'." Lily grinned, getting her feet positioned in the stirrups.

"I might make exceptions based on cuteness." He helped her with the stirrup on his side, sliding his hand up just above her knee to give her thigh a squeeze.

"Then I'm *really* lucky I'm cute."

"Sure." He chuckled, putting his hand on Tank's rump. "Alright, show me what you got."

*

Lily squeezed her legs and Tank moved off, easy as pie. She couldn't deny the horse was a good choice. She was a lot closer to being able to mount up alone than she had at any point prior to this. And the horse's smooth gait was an endurance rider's dream. He'd take a bit of fitting up to reach the point where he could pack in some of the longer distances, but she was a firm believer, and Encore was living proof, that *any* horse could do endurance.

The night before, she'd felt overwhelmed by the gift, believing it to be a sign of something else. If she was truthful, even if she *could* ride Encore again, she couldn't be sure if he would stand up to distance work, and here she'd been given a young, fit horse that might fit the bill. It felt wonderful to have options again. And she had Finn to thank for that.

He leaned against the fence rail, watching her as she put the gelding through his paces. When she passed him, he smiled a smile that made her heart swell. She'd said words last night that slipped out before she even realized they were coming, and afterwards, when he'd held her until his breathing evened out and he'd drifted off to sleep, she'd wondered if she hadn't said them just because she'd been caught up in the moment. And she'd definitely considered the fact that the feeling wasn't mutual. He'd kissed her and brushed the hair off her face and then just fallen asleep.

But this morning, he was the same Finn he'd been before she'd made her stupid confession, and so she could wait for any wild admissions of love. She could tell—in his touch, in his eyes, in his actions—this *horse*, for one. She sat back and pressed her legs lightly to the gelding's side and he shifted up into an easy rocking horse lope that barely moved her out of the saddle. Happy tears welled up in her eyes as laughter bubbled up out of her. She did three circles around Finn before she touched the reins and shifted her feet forward a tiny bit and Tank geared down to a walk.

Finn's chuckle in response warmed her insides, and she couldn't stop the huge smile that covered her face when she reined in beside him.

"You like to go fast, don't you?" he asked.

"Oh, don't act like you don't," she said, bending forward to pat the gelding's neck. "You're a man. 'Fast' is like, the genetically programmed speed."

His lips quirked as he watched her, his dark eyes intense.

"So are you happy, Lily?"

She drew a deep breath in, filling her lungs, and then turned to smile at him, nodding. "Yeah. Yeah, I really am. You know, I thought at first there wasn't anything that would make me happy the way riding Encore would. I mean...that was *so* perfect. We would get twenty miles into a fifty miler and I'd be in the zone. I wouldn't know where he ended and I began, and all I would have to do is *think* something, and he'd just know."

Her chest filled with so much emotion she wasn't sure what to do with it, so she kept talking.

"And then we had our accident and all I could think was I would never feel that way again. That we'd never be able to accomplish that again, and it was the only good thing that could happen to me. And Tank isn't the same...not at all. But it could be something good. Different, but as good as what I had with Encore."

"Mmm." Finn hummed as he stroked Tank's neck, his eyes averted.

Something didn't feel quite right, like maybe he wanted to disagree with her, but wouldn't say it out loud. She pressed her lips together, watching him.

"I feel like I got a second chance for a happy life. And you gave that to me."

"You deserve it."

"So do you."

His jaw worked a minute and then he looked up.

"Do you suppose people really get a chance to have happiness again? Real, *legitimate* happiness? Not just an imitation?"

She narrowed her eyes a little, considering all of the new information she'd gathered about him in the last weeks, and though she could probably pinpoint where his questions came from. That didn't stop them from deflating her a little. If she thought about it long and hard, the lines between what she knew to be true and what he was asking *could* be blurred. After you achieved true happiness, who was to say anything else wasn't just a desperate attempt to right yourself?

Instead of following the darkening path of her thoughts, she straightened, holding his gaze for a beat longer than might have been comfortable. If he was talking about his own situation, she was halfway insulted he might think their life together was just an imitation of happiness.

"Yes." The word hung strong in the air between them for a moment while their eyes remained locked, hers pressing her belief, his searching. Finally, he shifted, breathed, and touched her knee, his entire countenance changing, lightening the mood.

"Okay."

-THIRTY-SIX-

"DAMNIT!"

Though he'd landed on his ass—hard, Finn jumped to his feet quickly, keeping his eyes on Encore, who was bucking a blue streak around the outside of the round pen. Noah stood at the edge of the round pen but hadn't said anything or moved; which was the general policy—unless a man was down and not getting back up, don't interfere. He bent quickly and collected his hat from the dust and, not for the first time since he'd arrived there, considered the possibility he might not be able to help Encore the way Lily wanted him to. This was the first time it bugged him this much, though.

He considered himself a sticky rider—it took a lot to unseat him—but the gelding had done it twice in one session, now. He'd landed on his feet the first time, and tried to keep hold of the horse, who had jammed him into the fence. He would, no doubt, have bruises on his body to go with the ones on his ego.

Worse than the bruises on his ego were the thoughts of how badly this would devastate Lily. She had Tank, and that had been better for her than he'd expected—by her own admission, she could be happy with that horse. But Encore was what she really wanted. Tank would always been a facsimile of happiness for her...not the real thing.

Cussing under his breath, he stepped out of the

round pen, leaving the gelding to contend with his own demons. There was no calming him once he got going—that was a lesson Finn had learned *yesterday* when Encore had bucked him off. After a time, the horse stopped bucking, saddle still in place thanks to the breast collar, and let out two loud snorts, his head raised high, eyes wide.

Noah shook his head. "And Emma says there's nothing wrong with him physically?"

"*And* two vets and a chiropractor." Finn watched Encore finally settle, hands on his hips. That was a step in the right direction—at least he was comfortable with the saddle on, now. Just the rider was the problem. "Hell, I don't know. Maybe I'm just not good at this stuff anymore."

"Well I *do* think you'd be better off just training young colts for outside clients." Noah scuffed his boot on the sand under the fence rail. They'd had this conversation a hundred times in a dozen different ways. The money was better, and you were less likely to run into horses that were messed up by previous attempts, but Finn wasn't in it for the money. "But I don't think you've lost your touch. I think you've just met your match. Something maybe you can't fix."

His last words sunk a stone deep in the pit of Finn's stomach. This wasn't about just fixing the horse anymore. He was invested in this so deep now, this wasn't a 'client horse' anymore. Lily was counting on him to make this right. Because he'd made a promise and she'd fallen in love with that.

He'd known he was fighting an uphill battle from the beginning, but now he was too close, too distracted. He was a man of his word, and he'd promised he'd see this through to the end. This wasn't the ending he figured she'd imagined when she'd rolled into the ranch's yard with Nate promising her a horse whisperer.

Clearing his throat, he shifted, then bent and stepped inside the pen to slip the bridle off Encore's head and send him around the ring. He didn't get out of work just because he managed to get rid of his rider, but Finn was too stiff from yesterday's unplanned dismount to climb on again.

"You good? I gotta get that roan filly ready. Owen's coming out today to see how she's doing."

"Yeah, I'm good." Finn wiped his hand across his mouth and then tried to focus on the horse, driving him forward, as Noah walked away. Encore had given himself a good workout bucking, but that didn't mean he was off the hook. Finn shifted his body weight, pushing the horse into an easy canter, blocked him and made him change direction, shifting and changing things just when the horse got comfortable. He finished when he could see a bit of sweat darkening the gelding's chest and behind his ears, thankful Lily wasn't here. This was just the sort of thing that made clients uncomfortable—pushing horses just a little farther than their comfort zone. It was usually in that wide field Finn ended up making the most progress. The problem here was he wasn't sure there *was* any more progress to be made.

Finally, satisfied the horse was in tune, he finished on a good note, letting him downshift a couple of gaits and join up with him in the middle of the pen. As always, the horse lowered his head and chewed, which made it that much more frustrating. This wasn't a respect issue. This was one hundred percent fear and trauma and nothing else, and sometimes there was just nothing that could be done about that. Sometimes, you had to just work around the fear you couldn't work through, but that wasn't an option for Lily.

He rubbed the swirl in the middle of the gelding's forehead, and then moved to remove his saddle, undoing the fittings and slipping it off his back. Immediately, the horse walked away and rolled, satisfied the work was over.

He let himself out of the round pen and headed for the barn. The tack room was in immaculate shape thanks to Lily. She'd infiltrated parts of his life he hadn't expected. He couldn't stand the thought of disappointing her, of hurting her the same way vets and trainers and her own damn family had when they'd wanted her to give up on the horse. He needed a plan. And somehow, he needed to get out of this with his fragile heart still intact.

Because, at the end of the day, the warm, funny girl with the artistic inclination that never failed to surprise him had worked her way onto the ranch, into his home, into his bed...she'd rooted herself right into his heart in a way that would be agonizing when she pulled away. And she would, when she realized what she had here wasn't true happiness. It wasn't her heart's desire. And there wasn't a damn thing he could do about that now except hope he survived.

Sliding his saddle onto the empty rack waiting for it, he frowned, hitching his fists against his hips again before cussing under his breath and heading for the house.

-THIRTY-SEVEN-

"HOW'D things go today?" Lily glanced up from her spot at the kitchen table where she'd been editing photos from the Anderson ranch.

"Alright."

The grim expression on Finn's face betrayed his non-committal tone. She could see it in the lines in his face and the weight in his shoulders. She kept trying to convince herself the fact that Finn was actually climbing aboard her horse was a good sign, but yesterday he'd come off, and judging by his dusty jeans, it had happened again today. He'd also retracted the open invitation to watch their sessions, so she'd been busying herself with things like the Anderson's sale stock.

"You wanna talk about it?"

"No," he said, taking a seat at the end of the table, next to her. Normally, his quiet presence soothed her, but today it was agitating. She shifted back from the table, rising to her feet. She dropped her hand to his shoulder and gave a gentle squeeze when she passed by him. Her fingers met rock-solid tension.

"You want a coffee?"

"What are you doing?"

His rough tone surprised her and Lily pulled her hand back like he'd burnt her.

"Offering you coffee," she replied flatly. "Clearly, you're not interested."

With his back still to her, he laid his hands flat on top of the table and rose.

"I can get my own damn coffee."

"Finn..." It was that same little loose thread she'd sensed the other day when they'd talked about happiness. That niggling little snag in his paper wrapper that she knew would eventually get caught and tear the whole thing open, exposing his insides. She'd tricked herself into thinking she had him figured out, but she'd always known there was more to Finn than what he showed on the surface.

"*What*, Lily?"

He turned, now, and she could see what looked like a mixture of defeat and fear in his eyes. Like a bad storm coming on, and there was nowhere for her to take cover.

"I just thought..."

"You just thought I'd come in at the end of the day and you'd rub my shoulders and I'd tell you all about it? Playing the good little house wife?"

His voice was angrier than she'd heard it, even in her first days on the ranch. And more pained, too. The word 'wife' reverberated in the silence between them, filled with anguish and longing and every other feeling she was sure had accompanied his widowerhood in the last five years. She blinked twice and took a step back, anger bubbling up in her. *You're here for your horse,* she reminded herself. It was something she'd forgotten about all together. And that had been a foolish move. At the end of the day, she didn't even know this man, despite the lovely moments of intimacy and honesty they'd shared. But it was heartbreaking to think he suspected she had some ulterior motive.

"Excuse me? I'm not—" She tipped her jaw down, unable to finish, because the mere thought of it being true felt sacrilegious. That damn rooster tea kettle mocked her from atop the stove. The man still wore his wedding ring. They'd been carrying on something that was considerably more serious than a flirtation at this point and he still dropped her hand when anyone saw them, hell-bent on keeping it a secret. He'd bought her a *horse*. But she'd never tricked herself into thinking he could ever see her stepping into Sunny's shoes.

"Not trying to replace my wife? Because that's sure as hell what it feels like."

Lily's heartbeat echoed through her whole body, her chest constricting. She stepped around Finn, closing her laptop and collecting her mouse and phone off the table top. She cradled them against her chest because that was the only way she figured she'd be able to keep her heart from exploding out of it.

"That is on *you*, Finn Baylor. You invited me to stay, told me to make myself comfortable. We've developed... *something* here. And it takes two people to do that. So I'm not going to let you get nasty with me because you've started feeling *un*comfortable."

"I'm not uncomfortable."

"Like hell," she spit the words out, heading for her bedroom.

Fuming, she shut the door behind her, but realized her mistake too late. She'd shut herself into the cabin with him when all she wanted to do was leave. *What am I doing here?* She should have stayed in Denver, trusted the process, never gotten tangled up with this damaged man in the first place. Her eyes burning with unshed tears, she set her computer on the desk and flopped onto the bed. *Stupid.*

When she heard him crossing the floor, half of her hoped he'd come and knock on the door, come

in and apologize, let her work some of the knots out
of his shoulders, and settle the whole thing by
making love. Instead, she heard the squeaky
wooden screen door fall shut and the telltale sound
of his truck engine.

She'd thought they were on the same
wavelength. Based on his work with the horses, she
had assumed all along he shared the idea that you
didn't give up on something just because things
weren't easy. Maybe he wasn't the man she'd
thought he was all along.

-THIRTY-EIGHT-

"DON'T ask," Lily warned as she dropped her bags on Emma and Noah's couch. The line between her friend's eyebrows told her Noah had a lot he wanted to say—or at least ask. She flopped down beside her bags and Tucker immediately climbed into her lap, licking her face. The tears had dried but there were still salty marks on her cheeks. She loved everything about Noah and Emma and Tucker and even the little cabin, but she wasn't looking forward to more nights on the couch. *Maybe I should call Nate.*

After standing over her for a minute, with a concerned expression that was the equivalent of hand-wringing, Noah went to the kitchen. Frowning, Lily moved Tucker off her lap and followed.

"Seriously? You people drink coffee at all hours of the day."

When Noah turned away from the counter, he handed her a rock glass with an amber liquid in the bottom instead of a coffee mug.

"I won't say a thing, but if you want to say things, that's okay, too." Empathy softened Noah's voice. And it was nice to hear, after the rough coldness of Finn's. He poured himself a cup of coffee from the machine that always seemed to have a pot brewing, and gestured to the table. She'd spent almost as much time at kitchen tables with cups of coffee since she came to this ranch as she had with her camera actually in front of her face. It had been a wonderful way to get to know the family, Finn included, and she was grateful, but she would miss it.

"This is your family, Noah, I don't want to make any hard feelings between anyone."

"What did Finn do?"

She shot him a look and he shrugged innocently as he drew the coffee cup to his lips. "I've never been very good at following instruction."

"Where is your wife, anyway?"

"Don't answer a question with a question." Noah frowned and set his cup down. "She's at a rodeo team meeting at the school. She's going to coach this year."

"And Kerri made it?"

"Kerri made it. They train through the winter but most of the shows are in the spring."

"Maybe I'll have to make trips down to shoot her events."

"Maybe you'll still be here."

"What do you mean?" she asked, frowning.

"I just mean maybe you'll still be here."

"Better not be," she said, taking a swig of the whiskey he'd poured her. It burned its way down her throat and she grimaced, but then took another drink.

"Easy slugger, it's just to take the edge off."

She wanted to do a lot more than take the edge off, but getting drunk had never solved any of her problems growing up and she suspected it wouldn't do much now, either. In the morning, things would still be the same. A year ago, she'd have saddled up and ridden out instead. A few hours on horseback at least settled her, and sometimes even helped her work out the knots her brain and her heart were in.

And now she couldn't even do that. And based on Finn's response when he'd come in earlier, it was a hell of a long way away from happening.

"Were you there for Finn's ride on Encore today?"

The way Noah's jaw tightened when she asked told her everything she needed to know about *that*.

"So *that's* why I'll maybe still be here." She couldn't stop the sarcastic smile she shot across the table at him. None of this was Noah's fault. None of this was anybody's fault but her own, really. She wanted to care about how the ride had gone but she was still angry Finn had taken all her little budding feelings and screwed the heel of his boot right through her heart in two seconds flat. More than that, she was angry at him for *letting* those feelings grow if he wasn't going to be able to follow through. He was reliable, that was one of Emma's selling points. You could count on him to get the job done. When it came to the job of loving her, though, he'd failed.

"All I'm saying is that us Baylor boys are good at horses and ranching. Women, not so much."

He was toeing the line into an area she wasn't comfortable going so she drained her glass and pushed back from the table.

"None of us got it right the first time," he continued.

"Alright, Dr. Phil," she huffed, moving for her laptop bag. "I don't have time for a session right now, I have some editing to do, and then I'm gonna turn in early."

-THIRTY-NINE-

FINN rose early, before his alarm, before the sun, and dressed quickly and quietly. He pushed open his bedroom door and paused in the middle of the floor, glancing at Lily's closed bedroom door. The room was still empty.

He'd barely slept. He might have been mad he was having these sorts of thoughts and feelings, but he was reasonable enough to know Lily wasn't to fault for that. He couldn't punish her just because he couldn't get his head together. She was tough as nails, but he wouldn't make her need to be.

Rubbing a hand through his hair, he bypassed the kitchen and the coffee he was craving and grabbed his coat and cowboy hat off the hook before he stepped out onto the porch.

The whole ranch was wrapped the hazy, dim, pre-sunrise light, a chill clinging to the air. It felt appropriate. He slid into the driver's seat of his truck, and used the sleeve of his coat to wipe the damp condensation off the inside of the windshield. The engine purred to life when he turned the key in the ignition, and he pulled out.

There had been times when he'd made this trip more than once a day, but it had mostly petered out to his weekly visits. When she'd been alive, he'd carved out time every week for quiet one-on-one with Sunny over a milkshake at Hinkley's, so it seemed fitting that one day a week still belonged to her, even after his grief had died down to a dull roar. When he counted back, though, he hadn't been to the cemetery in *weeks*. Not since just after Lily had arrived. Maybe because he'd felt guilty from the beginning. Maybe because he'd been trying to trick himself into believing he could forget about Sunny and move on.

He idled slowly out past the big house and down the lane, turned left shortly after he passed Noah and Emma's little cabin, where a light already shone in the kitchen window. After a couple years' hiatus, Noah's keen work ethic had rebounded. Especially now that he had something to build on with his wife.

It wasn't a long drive to the cemetery. It wasn't a long drive to much of anything in Three Rivers, and he was thankful, because by the time he turned right into the grassy driveway of the tiny Three Rivers Cemetery, he was almost hyperventilating. *What the hell am I doing?*

He shifted the truck into park and stared at the cluster of headstones inside of the three-sided fence. There were a few floral arrangements, a couple of small statues, and by the marker for Joseph Leaman, Three Rivers' most recently returned veteran, a dozen tiny silk American flags outlining where the casket had been interred.

Finn could easily find a dozen headstones that said *Baylor* on them. Grandparents and great grandparents, back to the original family that had settled here. His little brother, Gage's laughing mother, and there, nestled beside Gavin, because Sunny had loved him so and Finn could think of no one better to keep her company in the afterlife, was his wife.

The plots where Gavin and June were buried hardly had time to sprout green before they'd put

Sunny there. He'd practically worn a path through the grass in the first couple of weeks after she'd died. It was like the ricochet after a punch that rattles your teeth; it almost hurt more than the initial strike, and he couldn't make sense of it. He wouldn't have said he'd found his peace, but it did get easier with time, as long as he didn't try to change anything. Having another woman living in his home, making him dinner, making him laugh, and awakening parts of him that had been long dormant was the kind of change he'd generally tried to avoid. But here, he'd invited it in with open arms. And then he'd punished *her* for the fact that *he* wasn't ready.

After some time sitting there, he finally opened the truck door and slipped out. As he took his time crossing the lawn and making his way through the headstones, he thought not of his wife but the softness of Lily's body against his side the night they'd sat on the front steps at his brother's. Of her halo of sleep-mussed hair and bare legs when he'd found her taking pictures of that mug. The easy way she deflected his father when he teased her, and her gentleness with Dane and Ren's brood. Frustrated, he shook his head, slipping between a couple of Montgomery headstones to the plots in the back corner where his family lay.

He smiled down at Sunny's marker. They'd transposed an image of her turning the third barrel in the middle of the granite piece. It was how he'd always remember her, fearlessly shooting down the homestretch, giving everything she had. It was an accurate portrayal of the way she had lived most of her life—wide open throttle, focused on her goals. He'd always aspired to be like that, but he'd gotten lost somewhere along the way. Or lost the desire for making the goals in the first place.

He tucked his hands in his pockets and examined the stone for a moment. The short distance between the years of birth and death always pinched his heart when he saw it. Life hadn't been fair. That was the funny thing about your wife dying. You didn't choose to be apart, but all of a sudden, you were missing the other half of your life. Her body was gone, but the relationship still existed—the past, and the uncertain future without them. He'd been hurt when she left, too, but he would have given up their life together if it meant she could have had more time to pursue the things she deserved in life.

Scuffing his boot against the grass, he shook his head, one corner of his lips turning up. In life, she would have smoothed her hands over his shoulders and insisted he tell her what was on his mind. He could almost feel it now, the way she would lean over him and her long, blond hair would follow, smelling of honeysuckle and citrus. He'd lived this way for so long, with her memories instead of her body, that waking with Lily in his bed felt foreign; not wrong, but different.

He swallowed hard and turned. This was supposed to make him feel better—surer, in one direction or the other, but it didn't. When he swung around, Noah's truck had pulled in next to his.

Finn let out a long breath and tucked his hands in his pockets as he started back toward the trucks. He knew there was no way in hell Lily had gone back to their place the night before and not told Noah or Emma or maybe both at least a *little* of what had gone on. And eventually, he'd have to face up to that. But not today. Not right now.

"What the hell are you doing here?"

"I saw you drive out."

Noah leaned on the hood of his truck, watching

him approach. And Finn walked right by, climbing into the driver's seat of his truck. Without missing a beat, Noah jumped into the passenger side and grabbed the keys from the ignition.

"Not so quick."

"Get out of my truck, Noah."

"What'd Sunny have to say?"

Finn's fingers tightened around the steering wheel, even though he hadn't turned the key. He blew a short breath out. "Look, Noah..."

"No, *you* look, Finn."

Finally, he swung his gaze to meet his brother's. He hadn't always seen eye to eye with Noah, but he'd always had his back. Years ago, a well-timed poke in the mouth was the most effective method of communication with the youngest living Baylor brother, and Finn wasn't opposed to it now if Noah didn't get the hell out of his truck. Every emotion he'd had over the last month was all wadded up in his chest with no place to go.

Noah closed the keys into his fist, tipping his chin up as if he was waiting for his payment for interference.

"What do you want?"

"I want you to make things right with Lily."

It would have helped had he actually known what making it right would be. He couldn't deny he wanted Lily, but the fear in the driver's seat right now was twofold. Opening himself up to the vulnerability of loving someone he could easily lose again was terrifying, and so was the possibility of not living up to her expectations—her one desire that had tipped off the entire whirlwind of attraction was the one thing he couldn't make happen for her.

"Noah, I respect that she's your friend, but this is none of your business."

"It might not be, but there have been times when you straightened things out that weren't any of your business, either. And I'm here to repay the favor." Noah turned his body in the seat to look at Finn head on. "And you're probably gonna cuss me for it, but you're going to listen."

Finn's jaw worked, and he drew in a slow breath through his nose, stopping just short of counting backwards to try to calm himself. He had messed up with Encore, he had messed up with Lily, and now he just wanted to be alone and lick his wounds in peace. The other downside of the family ranch.

"I know Dane's already had this conversation with you, but we had a chat and we're well aware of how thick-skulled you can be. And it's important, now. Because that girl is gonna go back to Denver and you're gonna go back to where you were before. And that's not good for anybody."

"Well it isn't *bad* for anybody, either."

"Isn't it?"

Finn couldn't look his brother in the eye.

"I got by."

"Barely."

He wouldn't give Noah the satisfaction of acknowledging how much more fulfilling his day-to-day had been since Lily had come to the ranch. Even in the beginning, when they'd been at odds. And especially later, when he found he preferred his house with someone in it at the end of the day that wasn't just his own shadow. But his brother didn't know what it was like to lose someone you loved permanently, irrevocably, like he had. He'd lost Emma for a couple years, but Finn couldn't just clean up his act and make things right with Sunny and have her back like Noah had been able to do with Emma.

"You might not have ever turned to the bottle

the way I did, but you sure as hell aren't living the best life you can. And we've let you slide along under the radar for a while because you've never looked as happy yet as you do when Lily's around.

"So we've come to the consensus that we're not going to let you just let this go. Because you deserve to be happy, just as much as anybody else in this town. And it's not right for you to deny yourself that."

"Who's *we*?"

"Dane... Emma... Ren..." Noah paused, tightening his lips and Finn knew what came next. "Mama."

"You told her?"

"Actually, *she* came sniffing around for details. You know not a single one of us can keep a secret from her. Not even you, holed up in that little cabin all by your lonesome."

He *did* have a point, there.

"So you have a couple of choices, I figure," Noah continued. "You either listen to what I have to say and work at it, or Mama is gonna come at you with both guns blazing and nobody wants that, either."

Finn's hands dropped off the steering wheel and he exhaled slowly as he sat back against the seat, staring ahead. A heavy fist of anxiety caged his chest, his heartbeats stuttering. He'd never said this out loud, or even articulated it in his head, and speaking the words made it feel true.

"I can't lose someone like that, again, Noah." His brother shifted, but Finn still didn't meet his eyes. "I'd die."

"You wouldn't die. You've picked yourself up before."

"You have *no idea* what it feels like to pin all of your hopes and dreams on a life with somebody and have that pulled out from under you, and be completely helpless. So don't try to tell me what's gonna happen here, because you don't know, Noah. You've never been through this. I have. Trust me on this one. No, if I had to do it again, I *couldn't* pick myself up."

"So you're going to give up before you even try?"

It sounded so much worse when it was phrased that way. But the overwhelming need for self-preservation made him nod.

"I guess that's what it is." Finally, he glanced at Noah. His brother still held his truck keys tight. There was no way out at this point, and he was tired. He swallowed.

"Bullshit. Complete and total bullshit." Noah shook his head. "An insult to the way we were raised, for one thing. And a piss poor tribute to your wife, for another."

Finn's lips tightened. If Noah had come here to rile him up, he was doing a good job, touching on what had been the cornerstones of his adult life.

"Hit me if it makes you feel better." The younger Baylor tipped his chin up, taunting him. "Hit me."

Though his hands were balled into fists on his thighs, Finn sighed. "I'm not going to hit you."

"If that's what it takes for you to get whatever's messing up your head out and get over yourself and make things right with Lily, I'm willing to take one for the team."

Wrinkling his brow, Finn took a moment to open his hands, resting them palm down on his thighs now; an effort to show his brother he wasn't going to take him up on his offer, no matter how badly he felt like it.

"That's ridiculous."

"So is this." Noah leaned across the truck, putting the key in the ignition, and opened his door.

"You can't just not live your life because you're afraid of what happens next. It's like saying you're not gonna keep riding horses because Encore bucked you off. Sure, you might eat dirt again. Might even hurt yourself. But what about all that good stuff that comes in between? That sure as hell makes the tough times easier to bear."

Finn watched Noah slide out of the truck. He hadn't shed a tear for Sunny in years but now he felt them in the back of his throat, suffocating his heartbeat. There *had* been so much good, but the end had been the hardest thing he'd ever had to deal with. Harder, even, than losing Gavin and June just six months before. Because it hadn't mattered what he'd promised her, he didn't get to pick how things ended.

Noah closed the door behind him and then leaned in the open window.

"You'll do the right thing."

-FORTY-

LILY sucked in a frustrated breath and leaned back against the fence, blinking hot tears away. Her vision still blurred. Tank turned his head, soft eyes watching his obviously frustrated would-be rider. He'd stood stock still the whole time she struggled to wrench herself into the saddle but it wasn't working the way she had envisioned it. Not by a long shot. Finn had flung her into the saddle that first ride, and she'd let him do it every other time after—it was just easier. Walking up from Noah and Emma's this morning, she had convinced herself her body was getting stronger from the regular riding sessions and she'd be able to do it on her own.

She'd hoped sleeping on things would make her feel better, but there hadn't been much actual 'sleeping' happening on the little couch in Emma's living room. A lot of tossing and turning, aching insides and unspent tears, but not a lot of sleep.

Now all she wanted was a long ride into the woods to clear her head, and she couldn't even accomplish that. When she thought things were about as bad as they got, she heard Finn's truck pull into the yard. A burst of adrenaline had her jamming her toe into the stirrup and making a valiant attempt to wedge herself in the saddle that only ended with her foot slipping, and her weight piling back into boards of the round pen with an intensity that knocked the air out of her lungs. Tank took two slow steps sideways as she crumpled to the ground.

And she stayed there, because it was the easiest thing to do, with her knees jammed up against her chest. She dropped her forehead and let one sob and a couple of tears squeeze out.

"Lily!" Finn's voice strained with worry, and she heard his boots on the gravel as he crossed the yard, leaving his truck engine still running. She lifted her head, sniffed, and brushed the tears off her cheeks. She'd done way too much crying in the last sixteen hours. More than she'd done in a year. She was soft, and vulnerable here, and the man who was now letting himself into the round pen while Tank snuffled near her feet, had, whether he knew it or not, poked a bruise, and barely showed her anything that wasn't tough and impermeable.

She was struggling to her feet by the time he reached her, and she shrugged off his help, brushing sand off the seat of her jeans. She collected her fallen reins and swung them over Tank's neck.

"Are you okay?"

He couldn't have asked a more loaded question. With tears still burning her eyelids, she couldn't bring herself to look at him.

"I was just trying to..." She gestured at the gelding.

She felt him beside her and then watched as he reached for Tank's reins and drew him nearer, telling him to 'whoa' and stand still.

"Get ready," he said quietly, and before she realized what was happening, he'd given her a boost into the saddle and she was gathering her reins. He didn't look back at her when he walked away and opened the pen's gate.

"Thank you," she said, pausing in the open space beside him.

"Go up the crop fields and follow the road. It's easy and there's no gates. I know it's not the same thing."

She pressed her lips together and squeezed her eyes shut to discourage the fresh flood of tears. He knew exactly what she needed. In a world where they could have gotten their shit together, he would have been the right man for her. Without having to be told, he knew what made her tick. And she could have loved him fiercely. If he'd let her. But he'd always want his wife. Or at least he'd be so busy tip toeing around the idea of his past married life they'd never be able to have a normal relationship.

She wanted to thank him but the words got stuck in her throat, so she clucked to the gelding and they headed out.

*

He had things to do, but Finn hung around the horse barn, busying himself with little stuff while he waited. His first instinct was to saddle up and go with Lily but judging by the way she recoiled under his touch when he first got to her, she wasn't interested. And he didn't blame her for a second.

The house had been way too quiet, his bed way too cold, and he'd had to brew his own coffee this morning. He'd barely slept a wink. He had nobody to blame but himself. He checked the time for what felt like the thousandth time, and then started topping up water buckets for the horses that'd be coming in for grain later on.

Tank will take care of her, he reminded himself. He knew he could trust the horse with children and beginners; many with less knowledge and physical ability than Lily herself, but he couldn't stop himself from worrying just a little.

273

Though she'd come a long way in the last month, she still expected more of her body than it would give and he knew that frustrated her.

Pausing outside of the stall Encore was temporarily occupying, he sighed, rubbing the horse's big jowl. "What are we gonna do, brother?"

It was becoming pretty obvious even if he could make Encore into a horse that could be ridden, the odds of him being a horse *Lily* could ride were pretty slim. If she wanted him to keep going, he would—until he and the horse were both old and gray—but he had a sinking feeling she probably didn't want to have anything to do with him now, regardless of how things worked out with the horse. And that was on him.

He stood by Encore's stall for a while, stroking his head and ears—he was a sweet horse, who wanted to please but clearly had too many demons to conquer. When he couldn't make any more work for himself waiting for Lily, he stepped out into the daylight. She was just dismounting, carefully lowering herself down Tank's side to land as softly as possible on her feet. She stroked the horse's neck, and when she turned, Finn was relieved to see she wasn't crying anymore.

Taking a step toward her, he held out his hand and offered to take the gelding, but she walked past him. Naturally, he followed. Because he couldn't imagine not. He'd let her go because he knew a long ride would clear her head, and maybe her heart, and then maybe she'd be open to his attempt to articulate what had been banging around inside of his head since he'd come home to find the door of her bedroom standing open the night before and all of her things gone.

"How was your ride?"

"Good." She clipped the gelding into the cross

ties and set to work divesting him of the saddle and bridle.

"Look, Lily..."

"I'm taking Encore back to Denver."

Her words were a bullet in the chest. His mouth moved to form words that just didn't happen. Now that he'd made up his mind, he'd assumed she'd be as open and receptive to it as she had been in the beginning. He hadn't planned for what would happen if she cut and ran before he had a chance to make this up to her.

"But..."

"I think I just need to accept this isn't going to work. And you probably should, too."

Finally, he found words. "You've come all this way just to give up like this?"

Her sad shrug vised his heart in a way he hadn't expected. "You don't get to win every time, I guess. Not every banged up thing can be made shiny again."

She turned back to Tank, checking his legs, feet, and chest, the way he'd seen her do with Buckshot. He watched her for a long moment. She was so thorough, so intent. Despite their differences when it came to things like treeless saddles and helmets, she was one hell of a horsewoman and it hardly seemed fair he couldn't give her the one thing she wanted. But he wasn't going to let her just give up and feel sorry for herself. If he didn't get to crawl in a hole and die after what he'd gone through, neither did she.

"Bullshit."

When she straightened, she looked as angry as he felt. He didn't deserve another chance, but damnit, that didn't mean she got to turn her back on her entire life philosophy.

"Excuse me?"

"I call bullshit on that. You just rode that horse, didn't you?"

"That's not the same thing."

"It's a win. They told you you'd be lucky to *walk* Lily, and you just spent an hour and a half on horseback."

Her spine stiffened and she lifted her chin, that stubborn will that brought her here was just as determined to take herself back to Denver. But when she spoke next, she turned her back, putting space between them as she unhooked the cross ties and guided Tank back to his stall.

"I hired you for my horse, Finn. And it seems like that isn't going anywhere, so we'll stop wasting your time."

He could see the pain etched on her face when she emerged from the stall.

"Lily, you're *not* wasting my time."

She was so close, he wanted to reach out and bring her into the circle of his arms, feel the way she melted against his chest like she had so many times. To comfort her the way he had when she was telling him about the accident, soothe her like the night she'd asked him to stay after her nightmare. But *he* was the problem this time, so instead of putting himself between her and her troubles, it would only make things worse.

"I brought you a horse you couldn't fix."

"You brought me a hell of a lot more than a horse, and if you can't see that..." he trailed off, shaking his head. They worked together so well physically; he was convinced if he could get close enough to hold her, she'd soften. But he couldn't even bring himself to do that. He wiped a hand over his face, and looked at the ceiling, letting out a breath and praying for strength. When he leveled his gaze again, she was watching him expectantly.

She was going to make him come out and say it. "Damnit."

Crossing her arms over her chest, she shifted her weight to one side, a slice of bare skin between the waist of her jeans and the hem of her shirt tempting him. He knew if he traveled an inch lower, he'd find a long, jagged scar, an inch lower than that, the tattoo of those four horse shoe imprints. Riding Encore was important to her, but *she* was important to *him*. And he'd have to figure out a way to make that clear to her.

"Lily, I'm not a perfect man. I'm a long ways from it. I've made my share of mistakes—*more* than my share with you. And I'm sorry for that."

"I accept your apology, Finn...but this changes nothing."

"Damnit, Lily, I've been trying to ignore it because it changes *everything*. I *need* you. Like I need a horse to ride and air to breathe."

*

Trying to draw a breath of her own, Lily found her chest too constricted. She hadn't expected that admission, not after he'd let her walk away from him like that. She was exhausted—emotionally and physically, and his words weighed on her shoulders. The smart thing to do was call Nate, go home, try to sort through her new normal. She'd fought for a lot of things that weren't smart, and she couldn't help but feel like she owed it to herself to just let this one thing go easy. Of course, it wouldn't be easy on her heart, but leaving Three Rivers meant she didn't have to continue to grapple with her feelings for Finn, and worse, with the way he felt about *her*—if she knew anything, it was that this was one struggle she couldn't shoulder. He could say anything between the two of them, but until he stopped hiding his feelings from *everyone else*, it didn't mean a thing. She'd had a taste of something more and now she'd rather have nothing than go back to the status quo.

"I'm sorry I accused you of trying to fill Sunny's shoes."

Lily's jaw tightened, but she didn't reply. He'd already apologized, it didn't change anything. If nothing else, she should have been thankful for the way he'd sideswiped her; she was dodging a bullet.

"I know that's not what you're trying to do. You're just doing your best to care about someone who's hard to care about."

He wasn't right. It was easy to care about him— that was the hardest part. The man had been through hell and back and she *wanted* to love him. But she knew it wasn't always that easy.

"I'm just a man trying to get his head on straight, and you're..."

"The bitch trying to make you forget your wife?" The words came out before she could stop them. Finn lifted his head abruptly, his dark gaze searing hers, making her heart clench to the point of pain.

"The woman who showed up and made me fall in love without even trying."

His words made her feel tiny. She was angry, but he was hurting. He had been for years.

"I'm scared as hell, Lily."

He wasn't the only one.

"I don't... Finn. I can't do this." He opened his mouth like he had something else to say and then closed it, but his pained expression told the whole story. She uncrossed her arms and reached out to touch his forearm lightly, but wasn't able to meet his eyes. Squeezing hers shut, she said the four words she'd been thinking since he'd helped her onto Tank two hours earlier. "Just let me go."

She'd gotten too close, and without realizing

what was happening, she found herself in his arms, her face pressed against his chest. His familiar scent filled her nostrils and his body heat seeped into her; she'd been cold for hours and suddenly, she felt comfortable again. He folded her tight into his embrace like it was the most natural thing, and dropped his lips to the crown of her head. His words rumbled through her. "I can't."

And that was when she realized she didn't want him to. Curling her fingers in the fabric of his shirt, she let him hold her and imagined what it might be like to just let this happen. When they were touching, everything made sense; her heart rate slowed and her body warmed. He'd never have accused her of trying to replace his wife if they'd just been wound up in one another's arms. Tears rose in her throat and her eyes and she did her best to swallow them back down.

No matter what happened, she couldn't guarantee the outcome of their relationship. She'd always wonder if he was comparing her role in his life to his wife's. It really *was* better for her to leave. She let out a breath through her nose and then lifted her head, straightening. His arms fell away so easily she ached.

Reaching up, she touched his jaw and smiled sadly.

"You can."

And then she walked away.

-FORTY-ONE-

LILY curled one arm around her knees, perched on the front stoop of Emma and Noah's place with her cell phone pressed to her ear. It rang four times before Nate's generic answering machine message picked up. She ended the call quickly because leaving a message felt final. In truth, she was just looking for someone to talk to.

With fall rodeo season in swing, Emma and Noah were busy coaching and working client horses, so she'd been on her own since she'd walked away from the horse barn, and it sucked. Despite her resolve not to drag her friends into this...whatever it was with Finn, she just needed an ear. Tucker wasn't much of a conversationalist and he'd long abandoned his post at her feet in favor of flushing frogs out of the long grass surrounding the property. She'd done everything she could to keep herself busy, including opening up her computer to edit, only to find even the frames he wasn't in reminded her of Finn.

Her heart ached thinking of the way he'd looked when she said she'd go back to Denver, of the way his body had trembled when he held her that last time in the barn. Maybe she should back up and let him try...but she had dealt with enough ups and downs in the last year; she was done. This was protecting herself. No matter how bad it hurt now. She was saving herself trouble in the long run, from a man who was too afraid of the rumor mill to even hold her hand in public, or to give himself the chance to love her.

Girl, you are in big trouble. Sighing, she scuffed her feet, and pulled out her phone again. By heart, she dialed a number and held it to her ear. Her mother picked up on the second ring.

"Lily! I've been missing you, sweetie."

"Hi Mama."

There was a brief pause on the other end of the line. "Are you okay, love? You sound blue."

"Oh, things just aren't going the way I imagined."

Another long pause. Lily braced herself for her mother's 'told ya so' speech, but then heard Julie exhale slowly.

"I'm sorry, honey. That's tough. Is Encore okay?"

"He's fine, mostly. Just not making the kind of progress we hoped he would."

"So you're not out riding seventeen miles a day to fit up, then?" Lily could hear the teasing in her mother's voice, and a little smile tipped the corner of her lips.

"No, and Finn's not getting him ridden, either. He crumbles under the pressure." Crumble was too nice a word for what Noah had eventually, after a great deal of bribery, described to her. She was grateful she hadn't been there to see it. "But I did ride out today, on one of the ranch horses."

"That's great, Lil. It sounds like you're doing alright."

Over the time she'd been in Three Rivers, the phone conversations had definitely gotten easier. Julie had stopped asking when she'd come home and started to have an interest in progress. It seemed to be something positive for her mother, so she couldn't tell her she'd been trying to get a hold of Nate all day to book a ride home.

"Yeah. I am," she lied, and because she couldn't stomach any more, she leaned back, letting out a breath. "Okay mama, I gotta go. I'll talk to you again in a couple of days." *Maybe over coffee.*

"Alright, sweetie, I love you."

"Love you too, Mom."

-FORTY-TWO-

LILY paced a tight circle. On her left sat a huge canvas of Encore, head up, ears perked. What the shot didn't show was the subject of Encore's attention—Finn Baylor with his back to her in the foreground. She remembered the uncropped image too well.

With her heart thundering in her chest, Lily paused in front of an easel with a close-up shot of Jonas Pierce, Emma's father. He'd been whispering words of encouragement to a new calf; born the wrong time of year, out of a first-time mother, the little bull calf had needed a little help to get going, and gentleness and compassion showed on Jonas' weathered face.

Not since the very beginning had she been nervous to show her photos to anyone, but this wasn't just 'anyone'. She hadn't spoken to Finn in days, and she didn't know if he'd show up tonight. Too many of the photos pinched her heart to see— images that either had Finn front and center, or had his energy in them somehow. She'd realized too late her heart was pinned securely on her sleeve, and she wasn't sure she was ready for him to see that, especially considering how close to his chest he played his hand.

Emma stepped up beside her, appraising the photo of her father. She'd seen all of the shots before Lily had traveled to Denver to have them printed, and then she'd helped assemble them in Three River's library tonight. It wasn't a fancy gallery collection, but it was the least she could do for the big hearts of this small town, who had welcomed her like she was one of their own.

"Would you stop?" Emma finally said.

"What?" Glancing up at her friend, Lily tried to swallow but found her throat too dry. Emma handed her a glass of punch, and Lily took it, grateful.

"You're nervous. Your hands are shaking," Emma nodded toward the tiny ripples in the surface of the punch. "You stare down furious sixteen hundred pound bulls for a living. *And* the stupid alpha asshole cowboys that ride them."

"Hey, I take offense to that," Nate said, laughing as he flanked Lily's other side and slid his arm over her shoulder. It was comforting to have him here—she'd spent the last couple of days in Denver getting her canvases and visiting with her mom and Nate had been a huge support during that. "The show looks great, Lilypad. The way they looked all wrapped up in the back of my truck, I had no idea what you were hiding."

Lily twisted and halfheartedly planted her fist in his side. Putting on a show, Nate yelped and jumped away, wandering toward a tall blonde standing just inside the door. Beside her, Emma laughed, then nodded after him. "Mom and Dad are here."

Letting out a slow breath, Lily turned and saw that not only Jonas and Myrna had arrived, but the Andersons, and Nan and Banks Montgomery, along with a few faces that were only vaguely familiar. She'd expected her friends to turn up, but as the small space began to fill with people—some she knew, and some she didn't at all—she felt a smile start at her toes. Before long, she was circulating through the room, proudly discussing the work she'd done in Three Rivers.

Even if she hadn't been able to fix Encore *or* Finn Baylor, she'd made friends here. She'd met amazing people, and had experiences she wouldn't have had in Denver. For the first time in a year, she'd decompressed, and allowed herself to breathe again, to appreciate some of the smaller joys in life. And she'd ridden again. She couldn't regret it, even if the unfinished business made her ache.

"Lily!"

She'd have known the little girl's voice anywhere. Tessa had become a regular part of Lily's week, and there was more than one shot of her—with Finn—on display. She crouched just as the girl barreled into her, nearly knocking them both ass over teakettle. This week's lesson had been the first one Lily had missed since her arrival at the Baylor ranch and she doubted Finn had been able to give her any more answers than Lily herself had about her whereabouts.

"Hey you! Did you see the pictures of you and Buckshot?" She straightened, lifting the slight girl into her arms.

"Finn showed me." With her heart throbbing right at the base of her throat, Lily did a quick survey of the room, finding Miranda near the punch bowl, and then the man himself coming straight at her. She'd wondered if he'd show up, but based on the crowd in the room, moving from image to image, and clustering around the table of finger foods Hinkley's had provided, she shouldn't have. Without exception, everybody in this town took any opportunity for a social gathering.

Even curmudgeons, apparently.

Lily put on her best attempt at a smile as Finn

got closer, ducking his head in greeting, his hands tucked in the pockets of his jeans. It was disappointing the way her heart quickened, but she supposed the wound was still open. With some time in Denver, it would heal, and then she'd move on. She just hadn't figured out that part yet.

*

If Lily had suffered as much as he had over the last few days, she didn't show it. Or she was good at hiding it, anyways. Or maybe he'd just missed the sight of her so bad she would have looked good with all her hair shaved off, wearing a paper bag. She'd have looked pretty as a picture either way, and his heartbeat thudded at the base of his throat.

Finn shifted, glancing at Tessa, then tipped his head toward Miranda at the refreshments table. "You gonna go get yourself some punch?"

She nodded, wriggling out of Lily's arms and to the floor, skipping off as if she didn't have a care in the world. The girl had been sorely disappointed when Lily hadn't been present for her last riding lesson, but he hadn't had the heart to tell her he wasn't sure any of them would ever see Lily again, even if her horse was left behind. When Noah had told him about the show at the library, he couldn't have stopped himself if he wanted to.

And now that he had her in front of him, he had no idea what to do with her, what to say. He wondered if she'd noticed he'd taken off his wedding band, if she could see in the extra worry lines in his face that he'd retired the rooster tea kettle and the silly colored dish towels. That he'd moved his bed across the room so he had a different view when he woke up. And that he'd discovered none of that stuff was *bad*, even if it was different.

She stepped up to bat, filling the silence like she always had.

"I trust Encore's not giving you any trouble? Dane said you guys put him out to pasture."

"For now." He nodded. "Just waiting to see how his owner wants to proceed."

She shifted, looking uncomfortable.

"I'm looking into retirement farms for him. Dane said it was okay to leave him until I found a place."

Well, *that* smarted more than he expected. As long as Encore was still at the Baylor ranch, he had a tie to her.

"He's fine with us as long as you wanna leave him. But you don't have to move him, Lily."

She cleared her throat, her lips pressed together in a thin line when she looked back up at him, her eyes filled with regret.

"I know you think you do, but you're a part of our family now and so is Encore, so he's welcome to stay as long as he needs." *And so are you.* "It's not like he's a bother or we don't have the space. And it gives you an excuse to come and visit Emma and Noah once in a while."

He shouldn't have kept going—he knew as well as anybody that here, in front of everybody, wasn't the place to have this conversation, but he couldn't help but feel like if he let her go without at least giving her an idea what he was feeling, he wouldn't get another chance. So maybe you got a second chance at a good life, but you didn't get third and fourth chances to make things right when you'd made a mess like the one he had.

From a spot near a huge picture of the Baylor children, Nan Montgomery called out to Lily, and she turned, her entire body slumping with what he could only assume was relief, as the older woman made her way toward the two of them. As she did with everyone, Nan had found her way to and made instant friends with Lily during her time with them.

"Lily, these photos are amazing!" Even Nan hadn't been neglected in the series—wedged in between a picture of Cutter on his front porch and Jonas and his calf was Nan, standing proudly next to the fall blooms in her garden. She wrapped Lily up in a hug and Finn wished he could do the same. "Aren't they amazing, Finn?"

"They sure are," he said quietly. It hadn't gone unnoticed that there were a good number of photos of him. Even if she wasn't saying it out loud, she'd intentionally chosen him—in the photos, at the very least. And that had to count for something. It was time he intentionally chose her.

*

"Can I have everyone's attention, please?" Noah's voice boomed over the crowd gathered in the library, and Lily turned from where she'd been showing Tina, the waitress from Hinkley's, a photo from her shoot at the Anderson ranch. "Lily, why don't you come up here?"

Blushing, with cheeks already sore from all the smiling she'd done, she crossed the floor. Noah raised a punch glass. "Here's to Lily Jacobs. She's made the whole lot of us look better than we ever have. And for that, we are grateful."

A chuckle rippled through the crowd as they raised their glasses and drank to her, and her heart warmed. Nate, and Caine Baylor, and a couple others stepped forward to raise their glasses in her honor, and then Finn cut through the crowd, his eyes locked on her, and she felt her stomach sink all the way to her toes.

"I have something to say," he said, stepping out into a clear space in the middle of the floor. "And it isn't a toast. But it's something."

His gaze focused on hers and Lily felt her

stomach rise into anxious butterflies. He let out a long breath and she felt, for a moment, like she should cross the floor and stop him from saying something that might embarrass them both, but instead she crossed an arm over her midsection and bit into her lower lip.

"I know there's probably been a bit of speculation around town about what's been going on with Lily Jacobs and me. And that's a bit juicier because I've been a bachelor since Sunny died." A wave of nervous energy moved through the crowd. Apparently, they weren't keen on being called on their rumor mill. "So I'm going to tell you the truth, so that it's out there. You all know how much I enjoy fixing people's horse problems. Lily brought me a horse to fix. He's not an easy guy, but she cares about him, and she's stuck by him through a lot. And I don't know if I can fix him. But I learned a couple of things while I was trying. One of those things is I have some problems that need fixing, too. And the other thing I learned is I can still love a woman."

Lily could feel her heart beating through her entire body, and her fingers dug into her arm. Her heart ached, and felt like bursting, all at once. As private a man as Finn Baylor was, to expose himself like this, in public, to put fuel directly onto the fire of the town's gossip line—well, that meant something. She could barely believe what was happening.

"And I love *this* woman. I love *you*, Lily Jacobs. And I'm not afraid for my family, or my friends, or the whole town to know that. I was scared before, and I messed up a good thing up. I didn't think you got to have a second chance when you'd already had a good life, but I was wrong. I'm not looking for a replacement for my wife, and it's a good thing because you're not her, and you'll never be her. But that doesn't mean I can't love you just as much. Maybe more. And that doesn't mean I can't have a good life—the *best* life—with you."

Another murmur rippled through the gathering, but Lily couldn't take her eyes off him. Finn Baylor was standing in front of God and the world and telling her he *loved* her. And she knew the truth was she felt the same. It was then she noticed his missing wedding ring—something she'd always subconsciously been mindful of. She swallowed, waiting for his next words, tears stinging her eyelids.

"I'm not an easy guy, either. I've made a mess before and I can guarantee I'll make at least a hundred more. I'm a little rough around the edges...a *curmudgeon*, I think, is what you and Emma call me. I don't deserve for you to stick with me like you stuck with that old horse. But I'm hoping you will. We don't have a decade of good times to fall back on, but I'd like to look forward to making that happen" One corner of his lips tipped up in that playful smile she loved so much. "So what I wanna know, Lily, is...will you stay on and give this a go, or am I gonna have to follow you to Denver and spend a few more months convincing you to stick with me?"

A laugh bubbled up in her as she crossed the floor in a few quick strides and stepped into his arms. Just like that, everything that had felt wrong for the last few days seemed to right itself as Finn cradled her close this chest, one hand sliding over her hair. She felt his warm breath close at her ear as he spoke words just for her.

"I love you. And I'll spend the rest of my life showing that to you if you'll let me."

"I love you too, Finn Baylor," her words barely

squeaked past the big ball of emotion in her throat. She relaxed into his embrace, feeling the most certainty and ease about the future that she had in a long time.

-EPILOGUE-

FINN shifted foot to foot, hands folded in front of him, his heart about to explode. Noah's hand landed on his shoulder, his fingers tightening, and Finn let out a long, grounding breath.

"You've got this," his brother reminded him.

If someone had told him even six months ago that he'd be standing in front of a group of his friends and family, waiting on a woman to walk down the aisle to become his wife, he'd have laughed them out. Now he was stone serious, flanked by his brothers, his eyes trained on the door of their cabin as he waited for Lily to emerge.

He held his breath when the door opened, but it was Emma, then Kerri, who came into view, not Lily. Half the time they'd spent planning this wedding, he'd worried Lily would get cold feet. He hadn't made things easy for her, afterall. But once he'd made the decision that he wanted to spend the rest of his life with her, it was simple for him—all of his stress and guilt and anxiety faded away, replaced with the certainty of loving the woman who'd essentially brought him back to life after losing Sunny.

Emma and Kerri reached the front and flanked him on his other side, and finally, the acoustic guitar music being played by Chase Reicher changed from a little twangy and fun to soft and solemn as the door opened for a third time and Lily emerged on her mother's arm.

Beside him, he heard Banks ask the assembled guests to rise for the bride, but he couldn't focus on a single thing except how amazing Lily looked as she made her way slowly toward him. She'd chosen a simple, lacy dress that hit her just below the knee and accented the curves he loved so much, but she could have been wearing a paper bag and still looked incredible. Every movement, and noise, and person around him faded away in favor of the huge smile on her face and, as she got closer, the tears welling up in her eyes.

They stopped halfway up the short aisle and Finn stepped forward, offering her his hand. She smiled up at him and slipped her fingers into his before they walked together the rest of the way to Banks, who motioned for the group to sit.

"Friends and family," Banks began, addressing the audience. "It's my great pleasure to welcome you here to witness the joining together of Finn Baylor and Lily Jacobs as husband and wife. I have been blessed to know Finn his entire life, and Lily...well, she's a dear friend of my brother, and that makes her family to me. Three times I've been privileged enough to officiate the marriages of the young men of the Baylor family, and I think I speak for everyone when I say that today is special.

"Many people only get one chance at great love, but this man right here has been deserving enough to be given a second chance."

Finn glanced at his friend briefly. These words hadn't been included in the initial run-through they'd done last night.

"And I can say that, because Lily told me to." Banks' eyes twinkled with mischief and Finn directed his gaze back to Lily, who was smiling through tears.

"Love is a pretty amazing thing," his friend continued. "It brings light to the darkest corners, forges the deepest connections, and heals even the most broken. I think it's safe to say love has done these things for Finn and Lily, and we couldn't be happier that she showed up on the ranch when she did."

It was only then that Finn could finally tear his eyes away from Lily and glance back at the group assembled around them. Behind him, Banks asked if anyone had any objections and the crowd was quiet. His mother sat in the front, tears visibly streaming down her cheeks. When he looked back to Lily, she was doing the same.

"Do you both come here of your own free will to be joined together as husband and wife, partners in the walk of life?"

"We do," they replied together.

"The couple have prepared promises for one another." Banks nodded to Finn.

He took a deep breath, his heart thundering in his chest. A decade ago, he'd repeated a set of generic vows after the sheriff, but the personal vows this time had been his idea. Words written by and repeated after someone else couldn't do justice to the love that filled him up now.

"A long time ago, I decided my lot in life was to be alone, but you changed my mind in half a heartbeat. I love your tenacity, your kindness, and your devotion—things that I might never have experienced if you had just let me run you off the ranch like I wanted to. You weren't about to give up on that old horse, and I'm thankful you didn't give up on me, either.

"I promise to never give up on *you*, Lily. To lift you up and support you in whatever way you need, walk beside you every day, and carry you when you need it. I won't ever try to snuff out that stubborn, spirited, creative streak you've got, because it pushes me out of my comfort zone and makes me a better person. That's the thing, Lily—everything you touch seems to come out better when you're done with it. You see things, in the beginning, through the lens of your camera, or just the frame of your heart, that nobody else can. Good things. Important things. Things that I had lost sight of. I don't know how I'll ever measure up, but I promise to always strive to be the husband you deserve, and to mirror the tenacity, kindness and devotion you've already shown me. I look forward to our next sixty years together."

She made a soft noise that sounded like a laugh and a sob, her eyes still streaming, and he found his vision was blurred by tears as well. With a smile, he pulled out the tiny, delicate handkerchief his mother had tucked into his pocket just before the boutonniere was secured, and, using the corner, gently dabbed at Lily's tears. She soon took it from him and returned the favor, while Banks looked on, giving them all the time they needed.

When she'd had a second to compose herself, Lily drew in a big breath and began.

"You aren't the man I thought you were when I first arrived in Three Rivers, Finn Baylor." She paused, and he held his breath, and then was rewarded with her broad smile. "You are so much more. You're patient, and kind, and *good*. You gave me time, even when you didn't want to. I've never felt more protected, or more cherished, than I do when I'm with you. You gave me back so much more than I knew I had lost when you let me into your home, and your heart. I love the support you give me for all the silly things I do, even if you don't understand them.

"I promise to be as patient, and kind, and good to you as you've been to me. I promise to push you when you need it and hold you when you need that, instead. To laugh, and love, and stand beside you every day. To be your partner, wherever this life takes us. And to never give up on you, or us."

He didn't have the words to express how grateful he was for *that*. He could be a stubborn man, but that was different than the gentle, insistent way Lily rallied for the things she loved, and the things she needed. He squeezed her fingers lightly, and Banks gave it a moment to be sure they were finished before he continued.

"Lily Jacobs, do you take Finn Baylor to be your husband, to love him and cherish him, and to carry him in your heart for the rest of your days?"

"I do." Emotion weighed heavy in her voice, and Banks turned then to Finn.

"Finn Baylor, do you take Lily Jacobs to be your wife to love her and cherish her, and to carry her in your heart for the rest of your days?"

Without hesitation, he replied "I do."

"Good enough," Banks said with a laugh, then motioned to Noah. "The rings, please."

Taking them from Noah, Banks held up the simple bands they'd chosen.

"A ring is a perfect, simple symbol—with no beginning, and no end. It reminds you of who you are, where you've been, and where you are going— together. A marriage is a journey, not a single destination. It has no beginning, and no end, just daily, moment-to-moment chances to love and be loved to the best of your ability."

With trembling hands, Finn slipped the ring onto Lily's finger, repeating line for line after Banks.

"Lily, with this ring, I bind my life to yours. It's

a symbol of my love, friendship, and the promise of all my tomorrows."

She smiled big, her tears had moved off in favor of a tiny little bounce. They were getting close to the big part—the part that made all of this real. What he saw in her was reflected in his heart as she slid the ring he'd chosen—tungsten carbide in place of the gold band he'd been wearing for the last decade—into place.

"Finn, with this ring, I bind my life to yours. It's a symbol of my love, friendship, and the promise of all my tomorrows."

"Folks, it brings me the greatest pleasure," Banks said, "to declare these two amazing people husband and wife. Finn, go on and kiss that girl already."

Lily stepped into his arms, the most natural thing, and he covered her mouth with his, dipping her back. And when they rose, he felt like every part of his heart was in the right spot for the first time in years.

*

As Nate took the mic to toast the newly minted Mr. and Mrs., Lily glanced for the hundredth time at the white gold band nested next to the simple channel set engagement ring Finn had given her just six months earlier. It seemed impossible that she could love someone this much, that she could tie her life to someone so unequivocally. And when she felt Finn's warm, gentle touch on her bare shoulders as Nate began, she knew it wasn't *impossible*.

While Nate regaled the gathering with the story of Finn mistaking her for his own girlfriend when she'd arrived, Lily took a moment to look out over the gathered group. So many of them new friends, so many of them lodged so deeply in her heart it didn't matter how long they'd been there.

Her mother sat at a big table with the Baylors. At another table, next to Nate's empty seat, sat Tessa, Miranda, and Cutter Anderson. The rest of the group were people she'd met taking photographs, or doing her shopping, or who had just swung by the ranch—all of them happy to see her, all of them willing to lend a hand to make this wedding happen. Family had always been a tough concept for her, but all of these people around her now *were* her family, and she couldn't have been happier.

"So you two," Nate finished, "you deserve all the happiness in the world. I couldn't think of two people who have passed over a rockier road and still come out on the other side as amazing as the two of you. Cheers."

The rest of the night passed in a blur, more incredible than she could imagine—from the quiet, intimate first dance as husband and wife, down to the warm hugs and best wishes from the residents of Three Rivers that had known Sunny and now welcomed Lily as a bright spot in Finn's life. Even her mother was enjoying herself—Julie had spent the last two weeks as a guest at the ranch, more relaxed and at peace than Lily had seen her in a long time, and it stood to reason. Lily, herself, was more relaxed and at peace than she'd been since well before the accident, and it seemed to soothe her mother.

Sometime after Lily's fourth or fifth partner on the dance floor, Finn elbowed his way back in for a slow song, beating out Cutter, who had been making a beeline straight for her.

"Hey," he said, with a smile, drawing her into his arms and brushing a stray hair off her forehead. "Wife."

"Hey, husband," she returned. Her cheeks hurt from all the smiling she'd done, and now that she was resting against his chest, the craziness of the day started to catch up with her.

"You look like you're ready to call it a night."

"This is more exhausting than an all-day photoshoot," she admitted, pressing her cheek to his chest. Even above the bass of the music, she could hear the steady thrum of his heart, and his warm fingers touched the nape of her neck lightly, both of them more comforting than words could say. "I can't believe you're my husband."

"I can't believe I'm that lucky," he murmured, lowering his mouth to her ear. "You know nobody would blame us for sneaking away early. It's been a long day."

She lifted her head to glance across the small dance floor. Some had left but those who remained were in full-blown party mode. He was right—nobody could blame them, and it was unlikely anyone would notice. Glancing up at him, she caught his smile.

"Besides, we've still gotta consummate this thing."

"Finn!" she squeaked, falling flat at her attempt to be shocked and offended. In reality, there wasn't much in this world she could have wanted more.

"They'll be asking about grandchildren before we know it. Might as well get a head start."

Her heart clenched. They'd had a couple of conversations about it, and she knew the regret he felt for the missed opportunity with Sunny. They'd left it undecided at that point, because this was something she couldn't push him into—a part of his former life that she wouldn't interfere with. Having him was reward enough; a family was more than she could ask for. Still, when he tabled the thought, she held her breath, anxious, glancing back up at him. Stone serious, he nodded back, and she released her breath.

"So what do you say?"

She nodded, and he released her, taking up her fingers. As they slipped away from the group, Finn nodded to Noah's questioning look. They could count on him to close down the party when the time was right.

He led her across the yard, away from the noise and lights, to the quiet darkness of the front porch of the cabin. He paused then, to cradle her face in his hands, his thumbs brushing over her jaw, and then press the sweetest of kisses to her lips before he released her. Suddenly, her feet were swept out from under her, and he'd gathered her up in his arms like it was nothing at all.

Squealing a little, she kicked her feet and swatted at his shoulder. "What are you doing?!"

"Carrying you over the threshold, lovely," he said, ignoring her protests as pushed the door open with his toe and backed them through it. He didn't stop in the kitchen like she expected, but carried her the rest of the way through the house to the newly renovated bedroom before he set her down. Turning her with gentle hands on her shoulders, he let out a quick, loud breath when he saw the row of delicate buttons that had taken both Emma and her mother a significant portion of time to fasten just this morning.

"Seriously?"

She pulled her hair over her shoulder, craning her neck to nod at him with a smile.

"Yep, you're gonna have to work for it, cowboy."

His warm breath tickled her neck as his mouth landed on the curve of her shoulder and his fingers started at the buttons.

"With pleasure."

—END—

-ABOUT AMITY LASSITER-

Amity Lassiter lives in Eastern Canada with her herding dog, her barn cat, two horses and her Mister. She has loved telling stories her entire life and even before she could write could be found in her grandmother's basement, reciting fiction into an ancient cassette recorder.

The most influential author in Amity's life would be Peter S. Beagle, the author of The Last Unicorn, who introduced her to her first achingly impossible love story and made her believe in magic. She met, and shared the most surreal small talk with Beagle in May 2014.

She loves critters, coffee, and cowboys—and she still believes in unicorns.

You can find more from Amity Lassiter online at www.amitylassiter.com